No Peace for a Soldier

Also by Walter C. Utt and Helen Godfrey Pyke

Any Sacrifice but Conscience [coming soon]

No Peace for a Soldier

A Historical Epic of Faith and Courage in the Face of Persecution

Walter C. Utt / Helen G. Pyke

Pacific Press® Publishing Association
Nampa, Idaho
Oshawa, Ontario, Canada
www.pacificpress.com

Cover Design by Gerald Monks
Cover art by John Steele
Inside Design by Steve Lanto

All Scripture quotations are from the King James Version.

Additional copies of this book may be obtained
by calling toll-free 1-800-765-6955
or online at http://www.adventistbookcenter.com

Library of Congress Cataloging-in-Publication Data

Utt, Walter C.
No peace for a soldier : a historical epic of faith and courage in the
face of persecution / Walter C. Utt and Helen Pyke.
p. cm.
ISBN-13: 978-0-8163-2172-8 (pbk.)
ISBN-10: 0-8163-2172-8
1. France—History—17th century—Narrative. I. Pyke, Helen Godfrey.
II. Title.
PS3571.T77N6 2007
813'.54—dc22

2007022184

07 08 09 10 11 · 5 4 3 2 1

Acknowledgments

In preparing Part II of this book, I had an early draft of work begun by Dr. Walter C. Utt in the 1970s and left unfinished at the time of his death. The typescript that I received represented his personal engagement with his lifetime of scholarship in the history of France and the Huguenots in particular. I was compelled to take up the unfinished work not just because I found it interesting but because Dr. Utt's first book, *The Wrath of the King,* so inspired me that immediately after reading it in 1966, I set about research that led to my book *A Wind in the Flames.* (The young hero in my book was named Walter!) Like Brian Strayer, who completed Dr. Utt's scholarly work in *The Bellicose Dove: Claude Brousson and Protestant Resistance to Louis XIV, 1647–1698,* my career has been deeply influenced by Dr. Utt's work.

I wish to further acknowledge my debt to

. . . the Walter C. Utt Endowment Committee and its dedication to sustain this great teacher's passion for history for yet another generation of readers, and especially to Bruce and Audrey Anderson for their encouragement and hospitality.

. . . Brian Strayer, whose scholarly books and articles have provided solid background data and whose practical personal interventions prevented many blunders.

. . . Martha Utt-Billington for extending her support and friendship.

. . . my colleague Ben McArthur, chair of the history department of Southern Adventist University, who suggested that this project might be a good fit for me.

. . . Southern Adventist University, for granting me a sabbatical semester in which to accomplish this project.

. . . Rachel Boyd, for transcribing the Utt typescript to an MSWord file.

. . . my husband, Ted, for taking over many of the homely tasks of our household to allow me *long* hours for concentrated work—and then insisting that I join him for *long* walks to restore blood flow to brain and body.

Helen Godfrey Pyke

Contents

Foreword

A generation of readers who enjoyed earlier books by Walter Utt—
The Wrath of the King (1966) and *Home to Our Valleys* (1977)—may
have wondered about the fate of their Huguenot hero, Armand de Gandon. The publication of this new volume, *No Peace for a Soldier,* and its
companion book, *Any Sacrifice but Conscience,* provides the "rest of the
story" and completes what might be called the "Huguenot Quartet."

These new volumes are the result of serendipity and hard work. It
was long known that at his death, Dr. Utt had left uncompleted an extensive manuscript that described the further story of Armand de Gandon. A careful reading of this manuscript led to the realization that it
contained the full story of the further adventures and struggles of conscience of the Huguenot soldier created by Dr. Utt. However, the manuscript was clearly a work in progress. The seamless and satisfying narrative you will find in *No Peace for a Soldier* and *Any Sacrifice but Conscience*
is the work of the outstanding Christian writer Helen Godfrey Pyke.
The story of Armand de Gandon unfolds clearly and seemingly effort-
lessly because of her creative gifts and her love for this story. In its present configuration, *No Peace for a Soldier* combines the earlier story *The
Wrath of the King* with extensive new material from Dr. Utt's unfinished manuscript. Likewise, *Any Sacrifice but Conscience* includes the
earlier work *Home to Our Valleys* with the rest of the previously unpub-
lished material to complete the full story.

Dr. Utt was himself a hero to generations of college students who appreciated not only his legendary and apparently limitless knowledge of the past but also his abhorrence of pomp and pretense and his love of students, who so often became his friends and correspondents. After Dr. Utt's death, a group of former students, friends, and colleagues determined not to allow the legacy of this great Christian teacher to be lost. In 1985, this group formed the Walter C. Utt Endowment at Pacific Union College, Angwin, California. Among the results of their work have been an endowed professorship at Pacific Union College in the name of Walter Utt and the completion, with Professor Brian Strayer, of the book *The Bellicose Dove: Claude Brousson and Protestant Resistance to Louis XIV, 1647–1698*. The story of this Huguenot pastor, Claude Brousson, was Dr. Utt's lifetime research interest.

The support of Pacific Union College and members of the Walter C. Utt Endowment Committee, plus the generosity of hundreds of former students and friends of Dr. Utt have made the achievements noted above possible. Dr. Richard Osborn, president of Pacific Union College, and former Pacific Union College president Malcolm Maxwell have unfailingly supported these efforts. The Walter C. Utt Endowment Committee has been a rock of support. Members of the committee have included Earl Aagaard, Victor Aagaard, Bruce Anderson, Eric Anderson, Charles Bell, Martha Utt-Billington, John Collins, Ileana Douglas, Arleen Downing, Lorne Glaim, Elizabeth Hamlin, Wayne Jacobsen, Grant Mitchell, David Westcott, and Elle Wheeler.

Thanks are due as well to the editors of Pacific Press for recognizing the importance of completing this story of a soldier and a Christian.

Bruce Anderson, Chair
Walter C. Utt Endowment Committee
April 2007

Introduction:
France's Brutal "Missionary" Campaign

Late-seventeenth-century France had become Europe's first truly national state, and nearly absolute power rested in the hands of its monarch, Louis XIV. He had given his country a sense of self almost unimaginable even two generations earlier. French art, literature, and music dominated European culture, and French citizens gloried in the admiration with which the whole world gazed upon them, imitating their language, their fashions, and their manners. All things wonderful happened in Paris. London and Milan had become backwaters. With a population of well over twenty million inhabiting a single compact landmass, France boasted manpower superior to all the rest of Europe combined, if one didn't count the weaker Holy Roman Empire. And treaty after treaty had brought piece after piece of Europe into the French nation as its awe-inspiring military machine won the territory on the field.

The Edict of Nantes* hadn't given French Protestants—the Huguenots—religious freedom, but for a while it gave them extensive protection. However, Louis XIV envisioned a French nation that, under his supreme control, enjoyed uniformity of religion as well as economy and politics. So, beginning in 1681, to hasten the conversion of those French

---

* The Edict of Nantes was promulgated in 1598, nearly a hundred years before our story, by Henry IV, the grandfather of Louis XIV.

11

Protestants who were slow to be convinced by bribes or inconvenience, Louis XIV sent brutal soldiers throughout France in a "missionary" campaign called the *dragonnades.* His soldiers were billeted in private houses, where they were free to do as they pleased with the goods and persons of their hosts until those unfortunate people abjured their "heretical" beliefs.

As a result of the dragonnades, two hundred thousand Huguenots fled the country, and far more abjured their religion. The missionaries of the various Catholic orders who accompanied the "booted apostles" admitted that hardly one in a hundred of the "new converts" brought in by looting, assault, and occasional murder was sincere. But the impressive tallies of new members for his church pleased Louis XIV, and bringing His Most Christian Majesty pleasure was the highest service priests, soldiers, and functionaries could render him. What remained of the rights and protections Huguenots were supposed to enjoy were wiped out by the stroke of a pen in October 1685, and from that time on, the kingdom was officially entirely Catholic.

The Edict of Revocation ordered all Protestant pastors out of the realm within fifteen days but forbade the laity to leave the country under penalty of the galleys for life for men and assignment to a convent for women for those caught trying to flee. Fleeing Huguenot members and pastors lost all their property. True, there was the suggestion that if they didn't practice their heretical religion publicly, they weren't to be disturbed until "it pleased God to enlighten them like the others." However, what this meant depended on the interpretation of the edict by local officials and missionary priests who they could make life unendurable for those who clung to the Pretended Reformed Religion (PRR)—Protestantism.

As the storm passed and something like normalcy returned to communities, many new converts repented their weakness in anguish and frustration. Some, to protect property, lived a double life, attending the services of their new church so that outward faithfulness would be counted to them as "righteousness." More simply ignored Mass and secretly resumed worship according to the Reformed faith as well as they could without ministers or churches. Many were so ashamed of their denial of the faith, even if momentary, that they became defiant and willing to risk great danger to attend secret assemblies of the faithful or to try to escape abroad, where they could be received again into the church and worship in peace.

The story of the Huguenots reads like a continuation of Hebrews chapter 11. These devout Protestants combined faith and works in heroic proportions. They were famed for both their religious zeal and their diligence in business. In the severe persecutions to which they were subjected, some abandoned their religion to save their lives and property, but thousands of others died or rotted in dungeons or galleys "that they might obtain a better resurrection." Many escaped to the Low Countries, England, and America, leaving their homeland the poorer for their exit.

The Huguenots loved the Scriptures and liberally sprinkled their daily conversations with biblical allusions. They studied the book of Revelation and knew themselves to be a people of prophecy. They referred, for example, to their beloved country in its apostate condition as "spiritual Egypt" (see Revelation 11:8). The state church they often called "the Scarlet Woman" (see Revelation 17:4). They denominated their rural environment in southern France the "wilderness" or "desert" to which the virtuous woman fled (see Revelation 12:14–17).

The issues the Huguenots faced are those that Christ's followers in other times and places have had to meet: Can Christians outwardly observe the commands of an absolute ruler while in mind and conscience they cling to their faith? When persecuted, should Christians defend themselves if they can, meeting violence with violence? When is it the part of wisdom to flee the persecutor and when is it cowardice?

Someday, we as individual Christians may have to answer the greatest question of all: Am I willing to surrender possessions or even life itself to obey God rather than men? May we be better enabled rightly to answer this great question after we more thoroughly acquaint ourselves with the inspiring epic of the Huguenots.

PART I

1685

Chapter 1

Dark Clouds Gather

The tall man in a discolored riding cloak drew his big bay horse to a sudden stop and dismounted. "Ah! A new and splendid victory for the dragoons," he remarked acidly.

A soldier wearing the red coat of the dragoons turned, a black scowl on his leathery, unshaven face. "Who asked you?" he said furiously. The dragoon was holding a boy firmly by the collar, and the boy was kicking industriously at his shins. But the boy was handicapped by the tall, heavy riding boots of the soldier and by the fact that the latter held him clear of the ground. Eventually, the dragoon dropped him to terra firma but kept a firm grip on his collar.

"I simply asked this whelp where the priest lived, and he insulted me . . . sir." He added the last reluctantly, as he suddenly recognized an infantry officer's gray uniform under the faded riding cloak.

The officer and the dragoon now faced each other. The tanned, handsome officer stood a head taller than the stocky soldier. The officer's firm jaw and general air of competence suggested to the observer that he was a career man and not one of those fops from the Versailles ballrooms.

"And where are your manners, boy?" asked the officer severely, for the youngster was well dressed.

A knot of spectators gathered in the littered, unpaved street of the southern French town of Saint Martin. A few feet away stood a saddled horse belonging to the dragoon and a coach covered with yellow road dust, its leather curtains drawn in spite of the warm spring weather. A coachman nodded on the box.

The boy answered boldly. "When he asked for the priest, I asked him if he wore his red coat because he was in the service of the Scarlet Woman." The boy's eyes were a trifle too close together for him to be considered good-looking and his teeth were prominent, but he fairly radiated keenness and energy.

"You see!" cried the dragoon. "The rascal is one of these pestilential heretics. In the coach yonder is the subdelegate of this province, who comes to this town to deal with these brazen folk. I'd say it's high time!"

"Well, young man," said the officer to the boy, "you see you do the people of the Reform no service pouring out your sauce in this fashion. Give this gentleman his directions and crave his pardon."

The boy obeyed quickly and apologized insincerely. As the soldier released him, the officer spoke with some sarcasm. "It appears a little strange that French soldiers have no better employment than to harass peaceable folk whose only offense is their religion."

The dragoon averted his gaze a little from the piercing black eyes. "As you know, sir," he said, "there isn't much doing on the frontiers these days. Playing nursemaid to these civilians," and he gestured toward the coach, "is better than sleeping in wet straw or stealing chickens. Besides, something has to be done about these Huguenots—two religions in a kingdom is as unreasonable as two kings." He straightened his drooping tasseled cap. "The intendant is very zealous of late against the heretics, and we are here to stir up the local people to make things interesting for those who won't change their religion."

A shadow crossed the officer's face, and he shrugged.

"The king has turned devout, you know," persisted the dragoon, "so maybe this is a good time to see what makes these heretics think they are better than other folk." He hesitated. "Well, it won't be the first time soldiers have played at missionary."

"Your zeal does you credit, but then I fancy a dragoon has sins enough to atone for."

The dragoon had no time to reply for a bewigged head thrust itself through the coach curtain. "Monsieur wishes to know what is the reason for the delay," the man said crossly.

"I was obtaining directions," the dragoon explained. "We are almost there." He turned to mount his horse. "No offense, sir, I hope," he said, pausing. "I am Dupin of the Dauphin's Regiment, and sixteen years in His Majesty's service." He saluted.

"Gandon, major in the Regiment of Maine," replied the officer courteously as he returned the salute.

The coach and dragoon moved on, and the idlers began to disperse. The officer turned to the boy, who had been gazing up at him in open-mouthed admiration.

"Without letting that tongue of yours get away again, young man, can you tell me where I might find Monsieur Cortot, who was a tax farmer, I believe, when I was here ten years ago?"

"He's my father," exclaimed the boy.

"Good! You can show me the way. Your father and mine were friends long ago."

"Yes, monsieur, but monsieur will not need to mention this affair of the dragoon? Thank you, monsieur! Just come this way."

* * * * *

Somewhat to his surprise, Armand de Gandon discovered that he was enjoying the long evening worship of the Cortot family. It had been years since he had been a part of such a gathering, and as Isaac Cortot launched into the third Scripture passage, Armand recalled some of the warmth and security he had felt as a boy by the glow of other evening fires, before his mother died and he and his father had gone away to the wars.

He marveled at the readiness with which Monsieur and Madame Cortot had welcomed him, as if he were a visiting angel passing through Saint Martin rather than a travel-stained infantry officer who had not seen them since he was a boy in his teens. He recalled with awe the dinner—the endless platters of boiled and roasted meats, the soups, the sweetmeats. It must have been the finest table in town. His father's old comrade must be a most substantial citizen, for the establishment combined Huguenot simplicity with elegance.

Digesting the meal comfortably in the chimney corner, Armand watched the firelight play about the features of his friends. Monsieur Cortot, in blue serge and silver buckles, looked the part of a retired civil servant to perfection. With his spectacles down his nose, he leaned into the light of the candelabra on the table as he read a chapter in Isaiah. He was ruddy and of average height but more than average girth. At the moment, he was wearing his hat, but Armand had noticed that his hair was sparse and grizzled.

A glance at Madame Cortot—garbed in a dark gown, white cap, and apron and sitting primly in a high-backed settle beside her husband—confirmed that she fitted perfectly in these surroundings. A representation of the Ten Commandments hung on the parlor wall behind her head, and a scriptural motto was incised over the huge fireplace: "Who builds not the house in the Lord builds in vain." Madame Cortot's calm eye and assured manner as she sat with her embroidery needles temporarily idle in her lap spoke of the competent manager—the plump and utterly respectable queen of a provincial domain.

Armand realized that his attention had wandered from the reading. His slightly guilty gaze swept quickly over the four children. They were dark, and except for the boy Alexandre, rather handsome. Louis and Louise, the shy and solemn twins, sat on stools one on each side of their mother. They might be seven or eight, he guessed. He sympathized with them in their bashfulness, and he recalled how he, too, as youngest at the table, had had to offer grace before company. He had probably not been any more audible than Louis had been this evening. The twins had begun to warm to him just a little during the dessert course. Like all Huguenot children, they had probably been warned against strangers ever since they could remember. The gleaming gold braid, gilt buttons, and bright red cuffs of his uniform must have been a new sight at this quiet table. He would have to make special efforts to win their confidence.

There was no problem getting acquainted with Alexandre, now sitting beside him in the chimney corner. The boy obviously had more energy than he knew what to do with anyway. He couldn't keep his eyes off the officer's uniform, and Armand felt certain that if it weren't for the strong opinion held by Huguenots that children should be modest in the presence of their elders, the boy would have asked to try on his hat and heft his sword. With his toe, Alexandre dug absently at the furry underside of a gray kitten sprawled on the flagstones—until the movement caught the attention of his little brother. That, in turn, brought a stern glance from his mother.

The soldier found his roving eye resting longest on the pretty, thoughtful face of Madeleine, the tall and graceful eldest daughter of the house. Her eyes fastened on her father and her hands folded quietly in her lap, she seemed unaware of his scrutiny. The candlelight glinted on her shoulder-length dark hair, and her white cap and *fichu** seemed whiter for the contrast. In this poor light he couldn't see her eyes, but at the dinner table he had noticed they were a striking shade of blue—in fact, more violet than blue—and set off by long lashes. For all her demure manner, Armand noticed there could be a blue spark in those eyes, as when at the table she had used a sisterly elbow to cut off her talkative twelve-year-old brother.

With a pang Armand realized that his years of hard work and the genteel poverty of a career officer had not given him much opportunity to think seriously along such lines. He had certainly never met anyone like this in any garrison town he knew! He wondered what bucolic notable had bespoken this latter-day Esther. She certainly must have been promised, for she must be sixteen or seventeen at least. *And where,* he asked himself, *did she get her graceful slimness?* Both her parents looked like heavily built folk.

In the shadows behind Madeleine sat three or four servants. Armand recalled vaguely that there had been at least two other children in the family at the time of his earlier visit. One must have been lost young, and, his memory becoming stronger, he remembered that there had been a boy his own age who had died for the king in the Low Countries. The portrait done in charcoal by some itinerant artist that stood on the mantel between the Nevers figurines must be his.

---

* An ornamental three-cornered cape.

The voice of his host seemed dim in the distance as the words of the prophet Isaiah rolled over Armand. He was in a trance, far from the dangerous world outside, where greed, ambition, and hatred played unchecked. Here was an island of peace and trust. Armand felt lifted out of time and reality. This was the very anteroom of heaven.

* * * * *

Father Chabert, priest in Saint Martin, settled himself at his polished ebony table, interlaced his fingers over his round stomach, and beamed in high good humor at his guest, a hawk-faced young man in a rust-colored suit, with Venetian lace at throat and cuffs and a long, glossy black wig. The priest's chubby face was shining with sweat and anticipation. Dust specks glittered and danced in the shaft of sunlight pouring in through the open windows of the pastoral parlor. From the garden rose the hum of insects and the desultory conversation of birds. "The local Huguenots cling tenaciously to the abominable blasphemies of Calvin," the priest was saying. "They pretend a meekness of spirit that is belied by the obstinacy with which they resist the conviction of the True Faith and the entreaties of His Gracious Majesty."

The visitor stifled a yawn. It promised to be a difficult afternoon. Charles Marie Joseph de Beausejour, subdelegate to the intendant of the province, had come at last in answer to repeated calls to take stock of the situation at Saint Martin. Though one must pretend a certain respect for the cloth, the official found it difficult to conceal his antipathy for this balding little priest who perched so eagerly in his big carved chair. The reflected glare from the table top hurt his eyes, and there was the racket of those insects and birds. He felt a dull resentment at being trapped here in this overheated rural desert.

The priest droned on. "While I would not in any way criticize the work of my predecessor in this parish—God rest his soul—yet the laxity here must have passed belief. 'Tis even said that Father Forbin thought it blasphemy to compel an unconvinced person to assist at mass!" He paused expectantly, but the bored official made no effort to answer.

"It has been well nigh a quarter of a century since His Gracious Majesty has heeded the appeals of the clergy and has begun to deal stringently with the menace of the Pretended Reformed Religion." The priest clenched his fist. "I have, of course, done what I could to see that the laws are obeyed, but my humble efforts have been without fruit— yes, virtually without fruit. There are only a few hundred of these PRR openly practicing here, but much of the town was once so; even the mayor and the city council are mostly New Catholics. They make endless difficulties for me—quibbles, arrant nonsense." Father Chabert then sketched in a few thousand well-chosen words a history of the religious troubles of the preceding 150 years.

What a wearisome fellow, thought the subdelegate. *He never stops even to draw breath!*

"The hydra of heresy must be crushed, my lord. Its heads multiply when there is paltering with error. Its venom has infected the blood of our land, and we see the dreaded consequences on every side. We soldiers of the First Estate, defenders of the True Faith in the very forefront of the battle, as it were, never cease our prayers for the enlightenment of His Majesty. We count ourselves favored—imperfect vessels though we are—that he so vigorously prosecutes the cause of the Faith throughout the realm—"

De Beausejour interrupted in sudden desperation. "I pray you, my good father, have done with this sermon and let us get on with the business!"

Suddenly aware of the sour look on his auditor's face, the curé halted the speech in mid flight.

"The intendant has your letter," said the official, hastily exploiting his advantage, "and he has authorized me to take whatever steps may be necessary to raze the Huguenot temple. However, he is anxious that all the legal formalities be observed and has instructed me to examine all the evidence carefully. He would be *most* annoyed if ill-considered action gave the Pretended Reformed an opportunity to complain at court through their representative."

"Oh, most assuredly, most assuredly!"

De Beausejour shifted in his chair and raised a languid, white hand. "What are your proofs that the PRR have violated the law?" Too late he realized he had restored the initiative to the priest, whose explanations, he feared, might well start back of Noah.

But this time the curé got to the point. "Surely I do not need to refresh monsieur's memory as to the edict of 1679, which provides that if the heretics allow a new convert to attend their services, their building is to be destroyed and the pastor is liable to public penance—the *amende honorable**—as well as a fine and banishment if His Majesty pleases."

He dropped his eyes modestly. "To carry it out, I found a former lackey, somewhat decayed in his estate and willing to accept the customary payment to abjure the Calvinistic delusion." His little eyes sparkled, and he grinned slyly, pausing so that the deadly simplicity of his scheme might be fully appreciated.

"You have witnesses to this happy 'coincidence'—the backsliding of this lackey?"

Father Chabert thumbed through a sheaf of papers. "We have here his abjuration under date of June 15, 1683," he presently announced, "and here are the sworn statements—all notarized, all dated the first of last month—of my witnesses who saw him at the Huguenot services."

The subdelegate accepted the papers and glanced at them listlessly.

"I'll authorize your mayor then," he said, "to proceed with the closing of the temple. Doubtless he can arrange for the labor if the heretics don't wish to demolish it themselves." His chair squealed as he pushed it back. "My secretary can draw up the papers. I'll call on the PRR minister this afternoon."

The curate's face fell. He had hoped for this pleasure himself. "Well," he resumed a little grumpily, "there are also other ways in which the pride of the heretics should be humbled. There is the cross in honor of our Savior and Redeemer Jesus Christ that should be raised on the site of their temple. And may I call to your attention the edict of 1681, which provides that the children of the PRR above the age of seven who are converted or who evince a desire for conversion may be placed for instruction in the Houses for New Catholics. His Majesty's efforts in

---

* A humiliating confession of guilt with public apology.

behalf of these unfortunate children are now four years old and nothing has been done yet in this city.

"I have here," he continued, rummaging in his papers, "a list of the Pretended Reform Religion families of the town. I could send it to the bishop, but it might save time in such an important matter if you would examine it in the room of the intendant, so to speak. Now that we will soon have a House for New Catholics on the outskirts of town, I would earnestly bespeak the cooperation of the civil authorities to fill it."

"You have the authority already, do you not?"

"Assuredly we could fill the house and the one for boys down country also, yes, several times over. But it's a matter of funds, monsieur." He eyed his adversary expectantly. "Voluntary contributions are but a trickle, sir, and the mayor and the council are stingy in the extreme—they elevate cheeseparing to an art. You know how these merchants behave when there is a new religious house coming to their town! The work of conversion must, I fear, rest largely on the royal bounty."

"You churchmen are always putting the cart before the horse," de Beausejour said with a yawn. "The law provides for the upkeep of such inmates by their parents according to their means. Confine your recruiting to those able to pay their own way. The intendant has a thousand parishes plaguing him with ten thousand silly requests and squabbles, all of them expensive. Public revenues can't be called on for everything, you know."

"But, monsieur," the priest cried, his chins shaking indignantly, "is there *any* work of greater importance than to wrest these children from the very jaws of hell? The old are almost beyond redemption, but the young may still be persuaded. The Houses for New Catholics make devoted subjects for His Majesty from the children of his enemies. From bad trees, good fruit! It would seem that for this divine work of pacification, this plucking of brands from the burning as it were, that funds might be spared—"

"The houses should support themselves," interrupted de Beausejour stubbornly. He noted the disappointment on the priest's face and hurried on—best not to antagonize these zealots too far. "The work of conversion is dear to all our hearts, but taxes come hard this year, and we must go slowly. Now, if no further requests are made on the treasury, I'm sure the intendant will be happy to assist you to take as many children as the houses can accommodate." He rubbed his chin thoughtfully. "But stay within the law in this matter also. You are able to get all these children to ask for instruction?"

The priest brightened somewhat.

"That's no trouble. Well, not much, anyway. These children are often discreet beyond their years, but sometimes the younger ones will say 'Hail Mary' for a sweet or a gewgaw. Or, as the law is interpreted nowadays, if it is reported that an older child has admired the magnificence of an altar or a procession, we are able to construe such a favorable remark as a request for instruction. We must use care, for these people are to the last degree opinionated and may flee the country if they suspect we are after their children. But there will be no disturbance, my lord.

"Now this is my list as of last month. I have arranged the PRR families by streets, with the name and age of each child. It was much work, I can tell you," he added complacently. "Some we wouldn't want, it's true. Too young or sickly for good instruction, for example."

The official studied the sheets, crackling the papers as he looked through them. "Well," he said at length, "let's check the ones who can be supported by their parents. Perhaps some other likely ones may also be taken if the charges on the wealthy are placed high enough."

The priest beamed. "And might there not also be royal pensions for the poor at a later date, perhaps?" He moved closer so he could follow the list.

"I'm not paid to foretell the future," said de Beausejour sourly. "Let us do it my way for now."

"Certainly, monsieur, certainly," agreed Father Chabert quickly.

The subdelegate leaned back as the priest began to read the list. The secretary silently dipped a quill in the inkwell and made notations in the margin of his copy as dictated by his master.

"On the Rue de Montauban," began the priest, "we have the following: 'Isaac Cortot, bourgeois. Four children: Madeleine, sixteen; Alexandre, twelve; Louis and Louise, seven.' He is the richest heretic in town and owns land besides. He was in the controller's office until the Huguenot tax officials were dismissed. The children are all sturdy, and he can certainly support them."

"Take them all," dictated the subdelegate with his eyes closed. The secretary's pen scratched briefly.

"On the same street: 'Emile Robert, ironmonger. Three children: Denise, ten; Emile, seven; Rebekah, three.' "

"Eh, that's too young. Take Denise and Emile."

"On the same street, 'Jean Delzers, former bookseller. Five children: Samuel, fifteen; Jean, fourteen; Georges, twelve; Hannah, ten; Gaspard, nine. He is poor, the law not permitting him to follow his trade of late, but the children are healthy."

"They would be public charges," commented the official. "Write, 'Do not take unless later vacancies.' "

Father Chabert looked pained but continued to read. " 'Gabriel Piel, weaver, on the Street of the Three Lions—' " He broke off and said, "This family is reported to have gone into foreign parts. It is hard to keep such a list up to date," he added apologetically. "They fly from here in such stealth."

The secretary noted in the margin: "Disappeared."

"Also in the same street, 'Jules Pinet, tanner. Two children: Olivier, nine; Henri, eight.' Olivier is sickly. The father is reputed to do a good business."

"Leave Olivier—"

* * * * *

Monsieur Cortot had finished his chapter and had launched into the final prayer of the evening when there came a heavy rapping at the front door. The worshipers stirred uneasily on their knees, but the petitioner did not falter or shorten his prayer. When he had finished, one of the maids slipped away to unbar the door. While the group waited in some apprehension, the kitten rose, stretched, and lay down out of Alexandre's reach.

The maid ushered three solemn men into the room. Everyone rose, the men removing their hats and the women curtsying.

"Good evening, pastor," said Cortot heartily as he bowed over the hand of the first of the newcomers. "What brings you out at this time of day?"

"Nothing good, you may be sure," replied Pastor Merson with a thin smile. He bowed again to the rest of the company. "I would not lightly interrupt the devotions of my chief elder. I crave your pardon until I may make explanations."

Madame Cortot made polite deprecatory noises, and the host proceeded with introductions. "Brethren," he began, "I have the honor to present to you Henri Armand, the Sieur de Gandon, the son of my late friend and brother in the Religion Michel de Gandon. The elder Gandon and I served together—back in the fifties it was—under the illustrious Schomberg when our Protestant marshal was but a general."

Then, turning to Armand, Monsieur Cortot continued, "And these gentlemen are our good pastor, Jean Merson, and his nephew, Mathieu Bertrand, our schoolteacher and catechist here in Saint Martin. And this is our head deacon, Brother Etienne Lenotre."

The pastor offered Armand his hand with a kindly smile. "We are honored, brother, that you have come among us."

Armand bowed in his turn, taking in the whole group and then dropping his eyes as was mannerly when conversing with strangers. He was uncomfortably conscious of the contrast between his uniform and the sober hues worn by the visitors. The pastor was a slight man in his early forties in a black clerical mantle, wide-brimmed beaver hat, spotless white collar, and a short black wig. He had a thin, intelligent face with a spark of humor in his dark eyes. The soldier warmed to the atmosphere of genuine kindliness surrounding him. *Now here is a friend,* he told himself.

It was the more startling, therefore, when, as he took the hand of Merson's tall, blond nephew, he was subjected to an intense, hostile stare. Armand's breeding rescued him, and he didn't return rudeness for rudeness. Perhaps, he speculated, he resembled someone this Mathieu disliked.

Still murmuring pleasantries, the gentlemen replaced their hats, and everyone was seated. Now and again the black-clad nephew stole glances at Armand. His mouth was tight and censorious as he catalogued each gilt button and red ribbon on the soldier's uniform. Armand noted that the schoolmaster was of a size with himself, with a boldly handsome profile and a much lighter complexion. *Probably a Norman father or mother,* thought Armand. *That long blond hair is his own, I'll wager, and he's not a little proud of it.*

It was not until Armand saw that Mathieu was also covertly observing Madeleine Cortot that he began to understand. As Madeleine did not notice—or affected not to—that the newcomer was fishing for her eyes, Mathieu's expression became increasingly glum.

Aha! thought Armand, now a little amused. *So that's why he scowls. He suspects me as a serpent in his little Eden!*

"Yes," Cortot was continuing, "Monsieur Gandon's father remained with the army after I left the service to go into the controller's office, back in the days when Colbert protected us of the Religion. But as I was saying, the last time the Gandons came through here was on their way to the Catalonian campaign. Now let's see, that would have been in 1674. They were attached to Marshal Schomberg's staff. You are named for the Marshal, are you not?" He looked expectantly at Armand.

"Yes, I am," replied the soldier. "My father was wounded before Belleville and died the next year. The Marshal was kind enough to arrange a lieutenancy for me for the love he bore my father. I have been with the Regiment of Maine ever since."

"Ah, but Armand is no mere lieutenant these days!" Cortot seemed as pleased as if he were boasting of his own son. "In an action in the Palatinate, he saved his regiment—single-handed, mark you—with guns and standards when they were ambushed, and he was mentioned in dispatches. He is now a major and stops with us tonight on his way from his estate in Languedoc to the Court at Versailles!"

The pastor maintained his equanimity, but the deacon and Mathieu looked shocked. Versailles was the nation's focal point of sin and extravagance as well as the fount of Romish persecutions. To a provincial Huguenot of good morals and conventional viewpoint, Monsieur Cortot's statement of Armand's destination was like his announcing the soldier's intention of wallowing in a pigpen.

The young officer came as near blushing as was possible for one of his weathered complexion. He fairly stammered his disclaimers. "Monsieur Cortot is too kind, I protest! I've been so fortunate as to enjoy the interest of the Duc de Lauzières, who is colonel of my regiment. It's at his request that I am to visit him on my way north."

Mathieu Bertrand's expression was wonderful to behold. First distress flitted across his face, to be replaced by something approaching relief, for no proper girl would be interested in such an obvious backslider. But Papa Cortot was beaming and insensitive, and Madeleine's own expression was of pleased politeness. Mathieu's face darkened again. Was not the heart of woman notoriously frail where fripperies were concerned? And here were a gold-rimmed hat, a red tassel, and much more.

More aware than Cortot of some of these reactions, Armand wished the subject might be changed. *If I had just requisitioned the fellow's horse, that fellow's sour looks would be more understandable,* he thought to himself. *I must ignore him.* Mademoiselle Cortot was more pleasant to look at anyway, so he addressed himself to that agreeable duty.

So agreeable, in fact, that he lost track of the conversation. A cry of consternation jerked him back.

"What are you saying, pastor?" cried Cortot, half rising from his chair. His hat fell off, and his bald dome glowed pinkly in the firelight. He retrieved his hat with a shaking hand.

"You anticipate me, Brother Cortot," said the minister sadly. "Yes, the subdelegate has waited upon me within this hour and told me our temple is to be torn down within three days, and at our expense."

Madame Cortot screamed faintly and dropped her embroidery. The twins shrank closer to her, and Louise buried her face in her mother's skirt. Madeleine stared with slightly parted lips, and for once, Alexandre looked solemn. A long moment of silence followed. The fire sputtered fitfully. The room seemed suddenly darker and colder.

The pastor spoke again, quietly and slowly. "We cannot say this visitation is unexpected. The Lord has been most gracious to His people in this place and has stayed the hand of the persecutor, unworthy though we be to claim such mercies. Now He would try us also."

"But what's their pretext?" asked Cortot.

"They say we allowed a relapsed new convert to attend the last Communion service. You recall the lackey Petitjean? The one who lost his situation when the law was passed forbidding Huguenot servants in Catholic houses?"

Cortot nodded. "Yes. I was sent by the consistory to reason with him when he became discouraged and made scandal of the Religion by his disorderly living. I'd like to know how he came by the *mereau*.* He had to have one of the tokens to gain admission to the service."

"I heard a year ago that he'd abjured and gotten his money from the conversion fund," said the deacon.

"His name was on the list of new converts sent us by the bishop," admitted the pastor.

"Well, what if it was?" snorted Madame Cortot. Her needles flashed furiously. "There must have been four or five thousand people at the last Communion."

"Certainly it is not surprising the elders did not spy the fellow," said the pastor with a sigh, "if he was even there. Of course, there are 'witnesses,' but you know what that amounts to. We have no way to dispute them, so we can only hope if he was there that he was in agony of soul for his apostasy, and truly contrite."

"But at what cost!" burst out his nephew. "For six *livres*†—the price of a pig—he sells himself, and now we lose the last church for leagues around!"

Cortot growled. "Seeking comfort for his soul? The promise of a couple of bottles did it!"

Madame Cortot was not interested in quibbles. "What do we do now?"

"Private worship in our homes is all that is left to us, my dear sister. The law is explicit. No public worship in any building save a temple." The pastor paused sadly. "It would be well if we scattered the church records and the funds among the elders and deacons, I think. They are

---

* Receipt given to prove attendance at church.

† Old French monetary unit equal to twenty *sols*.

at my home but may be confiscated at any moment. The funds let us distribute to our own poor at once. The sack of *mereaux* must be hidden, too. We may never use the tokens again, but it would not do to let them fall into the wrong hands."

"One more blow," said Cortot heavily. He smote his fist in his palm. "If anyone had told me twenty years ago how we'd have to live in 1685—"

"It is amazing what one can become accustomed to," agreed the pastor. " 'Patient as a Huguenot' did not become a proverb for nothing."

The fire burned low, but no one seemed to notice. Eventually, Pastor Merson spoke. "I doubt the Edict of Nantes will last long now—what's left of it."

"Why, they wouldn't *dare!*" stormed Madame Cortot. "The king's own grandfather made it for us."

The pastor shook his head. "You give your enemies too little credit, madame. The edict is a poor tatter, violated in spirit and in letter."

"Well, what would you expect—" Mathieu's tone was bitter—"with cardinals for chief ministers?"

"We had too many ambitious nobles in the old days, I'd say," Cortot asserted. "If it hadn't been for their fools' games against the king, I doubt he'd have paid much heed to the clamor of the clergy. Cardinal Richelieu was no fanatic. He said there should be 'no discrimination among Frenchmen except in matters of loyalty.' And who, I'd like to know, have been more loyal to the crown these past fifty years than have the Huguenots? True, the cardinal took away our political rights, but when I was young that didn't seem a great matter. We stayed out of politics, and we prospered."

"I agree with you, brother," replied the pastor. "Neither Richelieu nor Mazarin was a very devoted churchman; they were first of all statesmen anxious to strengthen the crown. So they ignored the fury of the clergy and protected us. Mazarin himself said, you recall, 'I have no complaint to make of the little flock, for if it feeds in bad pasture, at least it does not go astray.' "

"This loyalty—nay, servility is a better word—what has it gotten us?" Mathieu Bertrand snorted. "Two years ago they closed forty of our churches, and last year a hundred. We encourage this persecution. But there are some who do right well by licking the boots that kick them." He looked carefully at a spot in the darkness about three feet above Armand's head. The latter tightened his jaw and said nothing.

"Well, at least they have not yet dared to revoke the edict entirely," said Pastor Merson. "But with every scrape we are forced into, the Romanists always gain something. Most professions and the Crown offices are closed to us now, and our seminaries are all shut down. Mathieu here must teach school, for there is no way for him to be ordained in France, and he is forbidden to study abroad. Then we are allowed but one primary school for each congregation no matter how many thousands of children there may be to educate. We haven't been permitted a provincial synod for two years or a general meeting of the church for twenty-six.

"Our churches are destroyed under any pettifogging pretext. Faulty titles are found for a building that has stood for a century undisturbed, or it may be within a hundred feet of a Roman church and the singing of hymns disturbs the priest at mass. We can hold funerals only at sunrise and sunset, and there must be no more than ten mourners in any funeral procession. We must not sing our psalms on the highway or at work. If we don't uncover when the Host passes, we may be fined, beaten, or jailed. No royal insignia may be displayed in our churches, and we must allow the Roman clergy to have special benches in our temples from which they may interrupt the sermons and cause commotion in the house of the Lord.

"Unless I wish to go to prison, I must not mention in my sermons 'Egyptian bondage' or 'tyranny' or even 'troublous times.' In all documents we must call ourselves the 'Pretended Reformed Religion,' the PRR. We can't proselytize—not even among Jews or Muslims. Such a great matter as letting Catholic visitors kneel during our prayers got our church in Orleans closed up. And the latest rule is that our pastors may not stay longer than three years in a place, so it appears I shall be leaving you this summer."

Isaac Cortot spoke again, addressing his remarks to Armand. "Perhaps as a soldier you haven't been aware of all that goes on, but if a

Huguenot businessman apostatizes, he's excused debts and taxes for two years. So when you try to buy stock, you can't get credit. They're afraid you'll become 'converted' and repudiate your debts. And lawsuits are hopeless. All your opponent has to do is cry, 'I plead against a heretic. I have to do with a man and religion odious to the king!' " Cortot drew his finger across his throat expressively. "But I suppose we could take this and the doubling and trebling of our taxes. The worst is the billeting. It's never a pleasure to have soldiers quartered in a decent house, but since four years ago, the Reformed have had to bear most of it, knowing that if they would but abjure, it would stop."

Madame Cortot disagreed. "No, the worst is the lowering of the age of accountability of our children from twelve to seven, so the authorities may steal them from us and raise them Catholics!"

"It is a melancholy list," sighed the pastor, "and no human help in sight."

Mathieu Bertrand had continued to eye the almost invisible figure in the chimney corner. "Our fathers fought for *their* liberties with sword in hand," he blurted. "Now if we fight at all, we fight *for* our oppressors it seems. Are we too timid to stand for what we believe?"

It was now quite dark, for the candles had gone out unnoticed, and the fire was low. Armand promised himself that he would not let this fellow provoke him to an altercation. Instead, he stared fixedly at a large black chest near him that was carved with scenes from the tribulations of the children of Israel.

The pastor broke the ringing silence. "There may be more heroism in not resisting evil, Mathieu," he said quietly. "But even if we wished to resist, would it be possible?" He, too, looked toward the officer. "What think you, Monsieur Gandon?"

Armand noticed the use of *monsieur* in place of *brother*, but he couldn't be certain that it was intentional. He picked his words carefully and spoke directly to the minister. "I've been in the king's army for ten years now. Louvois is the minister of war, and Vauban is the greatest master of siegecraft in the world. The army has scores of regiments of infantry and cavalry ready at a moment's notice. Then there are all the new guns—and everything controlled from Versailles. Gallantry counts for little today."

Cortot rose to stir the fire. As the flames leaped up, the tense faces of the group were brought into sharp relief.

"I agree with you, Armand," said Cortot. "I was a soldier once, and even in my day we could see it coming. The power of the Crown is established now. I think when the nobility saw that the king was supreme and it was hopeless to resist, they lost their interest in religion. I don't say all of them were this way, you understand, but far too many. The gentry were always lax—careless of their deportment and in Sabbath observance. And even the great Turenne left us. Now all we have left is this threadbare edict."

"Perhaps this is God's way to make us more aware of our dependence on Him," the minister said gently. "Certainly, we have no other refuge. As for those who have left us, be it Marshal Turenne or this poor Petitjean, we cannot know the heart. We should pray for their repentance and soon return."

Resuming his seat, Monsieur Cortot said, "Maybe we should have listened to Claude Brousson two years ago when the brethren in Toulouse wanted us to fast and pray publicly on an appointed day, law or no law, temple or no temple—in all meekness, of course. He wanted the king to see how many we are and pause before he went too far."

"Nay, brother," replied the pastor solemnly. "You know I opposed that scheme. Resistance simply plays into the hands of our persecutors. The clergy wish for nothing better than to convince His Majesty that we are disloyal and will make party with his enemies.

"God enjoins obedience to earthly sovereigns," he continued, "for they were ordained by Him. On this the Scriptures are very clear. All we have is at the disposal of Caesar, save for our consciences."

Madame Cortot shook a long needle at the pastor. "But surely we can't allow the king's men to carry off all that we have worked for, the inheritance of our children, yes, even the children themselves! Are we to flee to alien lands and bring up our children among strangers—to beg their bread perhaps?"

"We are told in Matthew chapter ten, verse twenty-three, 'But when they persecute you in this city, flee ye into another,' " the pastor said reprovingly. "But while we should count it no loss to leave all for the Lord's sake, it is also true that there are times when it is better to abide in one's place and faithfully live the truth.

"*We* have changed, not the Lord," he added. "We are waxen fat and increased with goods. All hate the Huguenot. He is wealthy, for he works harder and longer than his Catholic neighbor—fifty extra days a year because he does not keep saints' days. His sober living is a rebuke. He presumes to think differently in the realm of a king who wishes his subjects to conform in all things."

"Our enemies have been crying woe for ninety years," interjected his nephew. "So why do we have so much trouble now?"

"It may be a change in the king himself," said the pastor slowly. "He has in the past laid a heavy hand on the pope and may need now to prove his orthodoxy. He has also eschewed his immoral way of life and may need to show his piety by harshness toward heretics. I am sure his confessor whispers in his ear, and there's our ancient enemy, Chancellor Le Tellier, the father of Louvois, and there is much talk of this woman at court who, it is said, has secretly become his wife. She used to be the nurse of his children, and 'tis said she has great influence over him. And to think she was born a Protestant!" He paused. "In any case, the English philosopher Bacon spoke truth when he said 'no man doth a wrong, for the wrong's sake; but thereby to purchase himself profit, or pleasure, or honor.' "

The fire had almost died. It flickered unevenly and sent irregular shadows chasing each other vainly about the walls. Louise had gone to sleep on her mother's knee, and Louis sat with heavy-lidded eyes, swaying occasionally. Madeleine was gazing abstractedly into the fire, and Armand was thinking he had never seen anything quite as pretty as Madeleine's face with the firelight on it.

"The Lord's people may be approaching the climax of their tribulations," concluded the pastor. "We must be firm in our minds, ready to accept flight or the dungeon—whatever He sends—with meekness and joy that we are accounted worthy to suffer for Him."

CHAPTER 2

In Versailles

Armand de Gandon awoke with a start. For an uneasy moment he had the feeling that he was in the wrong place. A quick glance around the bare, windowless cell, and it all came back to him—and his uneasiness changed to excitement. He was in one of the loft rooms of the Grand Commun, the vast dormitory for the royal household at Versailles. Today he was to accompany his great and good friend the Duc de Lauzières to the court of the Grande Monarque.

It was a chill morning, a reminder of departed winter. By the light of a single candle stub, his roommate was adjusting his wig before a fragment of mirror on the wall. Through the flimsy partitions a subdued rustling, like the sound of a regiment of rats, told of hundreds of menials of greater and lesser degree also preparing for another day.

Armand swung his feet out of the so-called bed and grunted with shock as they touched the freezing planks. Shivering, he reached for his breeches and began to dress carefully. His new clothes deserved some care, for they had cost him nearly a year's income from his poor estate down south. But then one could not circulate in this milieu for nothing.

The breeches and the coat were sky blue. Bunches of ribbons ornamented the shoulders and sleeves, and there were many buttons. He wore a russet *justaucorps** as long as the coat and used as a vest. This was

---

* A close-fitting coat.

trimmed in silver lace. The full white shirt was gathered at the wrists. The coat was to be worn open, the vest buttoned. A lawn cravat tied by a ribbon was at his throat, and the opening of the shirt was concealed by a *jabot** of lace. The shoes, not particularly comfortable, were of black leather with red heels and linings. Armand thought the heels taller and narrower than was safe, but those Parisian merchants cowed one so that one lacked the temerity to suggest a more substantial model. The big silver bows on the shoes and the dandyish stiffening and flaring of the skirt of the coat made him feel a bit ridiculous also. He had to remind himself that here he was a courtier, not a soldier. On a rickety chair nearby lay a fine black beaver hat, the brim turned up at the sides. The hat was garnished with silver lace, and an ostrich plume lay within the brim. Add to all this yellow stockings, a curly black wig (he simply could not afford a light-colored one), a dress sword with a fringed knot, and a silver-headed cane, and he would be ready to face the polite world.

The other young man was now dressed and had stepped to the door.

"At the hotel," he said, and jerked a thumb over his shoulder. Armand nodded.

Before putting on his neckcloth and coat, Armand stepped over to the nightstand by the other cot. With a thoughtful forefinger he tested the water in the basin. The Huguenot fires had been burning rather low in him in recent days. As he had ridden north from Saint Martin two weeks earlier, the somber prospects of his Protestant friends had weighed much on his mind. He even speculated a little uneasily about the dangers of his own course. Would his head be turned by the vanities of the great city and the preferment of a duke?

Sophisticates knew that washing with water was dangerous. It was safer, if one *must* wash, to use watered wine, as did the king. "Just a country bumpkin come to town," he said to himself as he dashed the stinging water on his face.

There were so many things to learn. He sighed. He had never before had to concern himself with these extreme points of decorum. Here,

---

* Frill.

one never addressed anyone simply as "monsieur." That was very bourgeois. And in the Versailles chateau itself, he must remember, one never
knocked. One scratched on doors with the nail of a little finger. In the
houses of the town one never scratched but knocked. Of course, at a
lady's door one used the knocker once—no more. And if he had it
straight, it was the small end of the boiled egg one must cut, not the
large end. Truly, the opportunities to show oneself to disadvantage were
endless.

As he straightened up to adjust his cravat, he bumped his head on a
beam of the sloping ceiling. For one of his height, the ceilings on these
cubicles were not adequate at all. When the ducal party had reached
Versailles the previous evening, the duke had put up at a friend's house.
But even an influential person could not provide for most of his depen-
dents, and some had to double up around the corner in one of the
thousand rooms of the Grand Commun. Armand steadied his new wig,
which was a trifle longer than he was accustomed to, and put on his hat.
Blowing out the candle, he stepped into the fourth-floor hallway, foul
with odors of bad cooking and unwashed humanity.

Most of the tide that flowed out of the front doors of the Grand
Commun were in the livery of one of the seven services of the royal
household or of the seven services of the queen, the dauphin, or the
dauphine. But some were gentlemen like Armand who needed quarters
for the night and were now hurrying to the ceremonial rising of their
patrons, who in their turn would be expected to assist at the *levée** of
His Majesty at eight.

Big fleas have little fleas, thought Armand, *and behold the newest of
the little ones*. He rounded the corner of the Grand Commun, passed
behind the red secretariat building, and on to the Place d'Armes. A
brisk walk of several hundred yards to the Avenue de Paris brought
him to the duke's quarters. It was just six, and the sun was almost
up.

Getting up in the morning was a high point of the day when a personage was concerned. And when the *levée* was conducted in a small

---

*Arising.

chamber, such as the one where the duke had spent the night, it was very like a booth at the Palais Royal.

The great man was out of his bed now (Armand had arrived a minute late) and seated near his dressing table, hemmed in by a thick cloud of servants and sycophants. A fire smoldered in the grate, and the air was close enough to cut with a knife. His Grace, in a striped silk dressing gown, sipped tea for his digestion's sake, complained of his rheumatics in a high nasal voice, and held court for his retainers simultaneously. His bald head protruded from the neckcloth used to keep the unguents from soiling the dressing gown, and his deep black eyes swung this way and that as he followed the talk. While his valet applied the cosmetics to his wizened face and another servant held up wigs for his choice, pretty gentlemen and near-gentlemen scraped in as close as they could, begging favors, flattering, and fawning. Had the duke's gouty leg not been out in front of him on a footstool, they would have cut him off from his fire and completely submerged him.

Armand's tardy arrival caused a mild sensation. Usually it was a task to fight one's way to the center, where one could gaze respectfully upon the glistening cranium of the eminent man. But Armand was new, obviously in high favor, and therefore heartily disliked by everyone who gravitated around this ducal sun. His competitors hoped to see some sign of displeasure, and a frown for Armand would have cheered them greatly. So they allowed him to work his way through rather easily and make his reverences, sweeping the floor with his hat, his hand touching the planks. However, the duke appeared to note nothing amiss. His face crinkled in a pleased grin, and he graciously allowed the newcomer to kiss his bony hand.

His Grace then dropped a bombshell. He casually mentioned that Monsieur de Gandon would accompany him to His Majesty's own *levée* that morning that he might pay homage to the sovereign in person. The retinue was breathless with envy, and for a moment Armand himself could not speak. Only the duke's high favor with the king would make it thinkable to introduce such an insignificant person into such august surroundings. As the retinue went out of the hotel into the blessed crispness of the spring morning, it would have taken a far duller person than Armand de Gandon not to realize that he was deeply unpopular with everyone but the old duke himself.

Bearers carried the duke's blue lacquered sedan chair down the avenue, past the royal stables, through the first gate, and across the cobbles of the Place d'Armes. The swarm of clients accompanied him afoot until they reached the great gilded portals embellished with the blue and gilt arms of France. Stone sentry boxes flanked the main gate, and on top of them were marble groups representing victories over Austria and Spain. The statues gleamed pinkly in the morning sun, and already the fencing was taking on a golden glow. The whole scene struck the impressionable visitor with the unspeakable wealth and power of France— the center of the world.

At this point, sedan chairs in which one might ride in style across the court of the Chateau to a vestibule of the palace were available for six *sous.* No carriages except those of royalty ever penetrated there. Armand would have preferred the short walk but feared to embarrass the duke by some little *gaucherie,** so he hired a chair and two blue-coated bearers to take him to the plain doorway of the chateau.

On Armand's arm, the duke proceeded through the hallways and corridors of the new palace, followed by all the pack. Using his cane as a pointer, the duke kept up a constant stream of comment on the chambers through which they passed, pointing out the abilities or failures of the artists responsible for their embellishment. He mentioned who had been camping in each room, for in that overcrowded place it was a mark of great distinction to sleep in one of the public rooms, even though one could hardly be abed until early in the morning and must needs arise very soon thereafter. Only the greatest grandees could win an airless cubicle on an upper floor of the chateau.

The swarms of unfamiliar faces left Armand in a sort of stupor—he could assimilate only so much in so short a time. He did notice that they met no women, for the women's *levées* were not for another hour yet.

---

*Awkwardness.

After a number of turns, they reached a series of anterooms and some of the retinue dropped off, unable to approach farther toward the royal sleeping chamber. They would wait the reemergence of the duke and the gentlemen, for that was after all the best hope of swarms of freeloaders, or *cherche-midis*—a meal at noon and a bed for the night.

The duke, Armand, and the other gentry entered the dimly lit Chambre of the Oeil-de-Boeuf. Glancing about cautiously, Armand could see why the room had the name, for up on the right wall near the ceiling was a large eye-shaped window of colored glass that was beginning to shed a soft radiance on the throng below. One's eye was drawn up past the gilt stucco ornamentation on the cornices to the vaulted white ceiling. Richly carved and gilded doors led on the one hand to the king's bedchamber and on the other to the Grand Gallery. Pressed into the room were the great of France, clothed in every hue of the rainbow, in every expensive fabric procurable by the tailors of the world's fashion center. Jeweled rings, buttons, and sword hilts added flashing points of light to the symphony of colored silks and satins.

Though not extraordinarily sensitive or timid, Armand swallowed with sudden apprehension. He was overcome by a feeling of insignificance and presumption at trespassing here. All about him were peers, generals, and marshals, the holders of the most ancient and exalted titles in the land—arrogant men, some of whom could trace their lineage back centuries before the king's own House of Bourbon had come down out of the southern mountains. Yet it would be unthinkable for them not to be present at the arising of the monarch. In all France the gentle dew of favors and advancement came from this one source. Since but one sun shone, for a noble not to strive to place himself under those beneficent rays was to resign himself to outer darkness. Even the greatest nobles wore themselves out in this constant attendance and the deadly rivalry it entailed. How dull, how profitless was life on one's estates! Even the lesser nobility were expected to show themselves. Not to be near, not to be seen by the king on every possible occasion every day could lead to the most crushing and final of rejections: "I never see him."

Few seemed to be running that risk this morning, thought Armand, and he dazedly supported the duke as he circulated through the throng, exchanging civilities with friends and enemies.

As eight o'clock approached, the tension in the room rose, and the buzz of conversation took on a higher pitch. Even now the royal watchmaker was in the sleeping chamber to wind the royal watch, the wigmaker from the wig cabinet next door was there to leave a selection of wigs with which to start the day, and the royal fagot bearers were building a royal fire—not perhaps an important matter to a king who always slept with covers at hip level, winter and summer. These formalities were known to all the world, and it was said that one had but to look at his watch in any part of France to know what Louis XIV was doing at any particular moment.

Emotion now ran even higher. The king was being informed that it was eight o'clock, he being presumed to have slept through the preliminaries. The crowd in the anteroom swayed gently like tall grass in a light breeze. The greatest dignitaries gathered close to the door—among them, the duke, proud in the exclusive privilege of the *grande entrée*. Armand remained behind in the press of lesser mortals who lacked birth, function, or favor.

A few moments later, the remainder of the court nobility were permitted in, after giving their names to the doorkeeper. As they entered the stuffy room, the king was just putting on his breeches, a feat he performed with the dexterity and grace of one who had been doing it in public for decades. When the time came for the shirt, it was handed by the First Valet to the senior person present, who happened to be the Duc de Lauzières. Before the envious and awestricken eyes of his fellow peers, the old man then handed the shirt to the king.

As Armand stood behind the carved and gilded balustrade, he was prey to powerful emotions. That he should be this close to his king! Once before he had seen the monarch. It had been at a review, and he had thrilled with pride as the regiment had marched past while the king and his courtiers stood watching on a little mound. Armand had marched with drawn sword at the salute, just behind the colors and in front of the ranks. He had felt rather than seen the sovereign on that occasion, for the colonel-duke had instructed his men to avert their gaze slightly from the Sun King, as if his glory hurt their eyes. (The duke was clever at such tactful touches—somewhat better in fact than he was on the battlefield.) Now, with swimming head, Armand stood not fifteen feet from the greatest king on earth, the embodiment of France!

As he gaped in solemn pride, the pageant continued, with each of the players skillfully performing his accustomed role. None, however, were so well versed in the tableau as the king himself. Every one of his sixty-five inches added to the effect of superb dignity and graciousness. The nobility, traditional competitors of the Crown, were now completely his. They had no power but now prized their nearness to the throne instead—the right to hold the royal shirt, to be the first to greet His Majesty in the morning. They craved the casual, trivial word that would elevate them among their peers, repair their fortunes, or gain them additional time with their creditors.

It was not the king's day to shave nor to wash his face and hands. He did mention quite forcefully that Lent was approaching, and he would take it very ill if he heard that anyone about the court should eat meat on those sacred days—unless they were very old or had a doctor's certificate.

When he had finished dressing, the conversation turned as usual to hunting. This gave Armand an opportunity to study the magnificence of the sleeping chamber—the white-and-gold doors, the fireplaces of bluish marble at each end, and the huge mirrors with sculptured and gilded frames. The cornices were masses of gilding too, with the arms of France and the cipher of the monarch worked into the scheme. The west wall was of crimson velvet. Beneath a gilded pavilion, on an estrade, stood the king's bed. Each corner of its canopy sprouted white plumes. Out the windows, beyond the courtyard, one could see the sunlit Avenue de Paris.

The king finished his cup of hippocras* and proceeded to prayers. As he knelt on the *prie-dieu*† by his bed, the ecclesiastics present plumped

---

*Spiced wine.

†Kneeling desk for use at prayer.

to their knees also, but the laity remained standing with heads bared. Then the monarch rose, saluted the assemblage courteously, and withdrew to an inner chamber, his particular favorites flowing after him like a loose-jointed tail. The ordinary sort drifted out of the chamber to await nine o'clock mass in the temporary chapel.

As Armand's mind began to recover a little, he found his Huguenot conscience still alive, if feeble. He knew he was expected to join the duke for mass. But concentrated thinking produced a happy result, and he consoled himself with a precedent: Had not Naaman held the arm of the king of Syria in the temple of Rimmon?

* * * * *

This was Thursday, so the king granted private audiences. (He customarily met his council three mornings a week and his confessor on Fridays.) Armand was beginning to discover that a courtier's duties required a lot of standing. He tried to shift his weight from one foot to another as unobtrusively as possible. Either the marble flooring was marvelously hard or his high heels were betraying him. Sitting was unthinkable for the common herd, but they remained outside the royal chambers gossiping, criticizing, talking endlessly about hunting, fashions, and the pettiest of matters, eyeing with practiced calculation all who entered or left the Presence, estimating to a hair's breadth the standing of favorites, and scenting to a marvelous nicety any shift in the wind.

Armand had not eaten, and his head was beginning to ache as much as his feet. *How like a disorderly chicken coop as the chickens peck away at each other,* he thought. He had been shocked in the chapel, too. He could remember the Huguenot services of his boyhood, and except for a couple of times when two nobles had quarreled over precedence in the pews, the dignity and decorum had been noteworthy. Here at Versailles, the worshipers (to use the term loosely) came to be seen by the king, who did not appear to care if they chatted, flirted, or told indecent stories throughout the service.

Every so often ornate exchanges with passing courtiers interrupted Armand's train of thought. He felt himself coloring with embarrassment. *At Saint Martin,* he thought bitterly, shifting his weight once more, *I pass for a man of the world, a model of elegance and polish—yes, am even suspected of turning the heads of virtuous maidens. Here, without doubt, I have the standing of a dancing bear at a country fair. Not that I haven't met aristocratic snobs in plenty in the army. But to succeed here, one must be hard as glass and know when to be silent, when to be bold, when to scrape invisibly along the wall, and when to drop a friend. Also, one must cultivate an eye that misses nothing and an instinct for knowing what the king is going to do and how to be seen by him when he does it. I would I were out of this.*

Armand was saying this to himself when suddenly everything changed. A gorgeous gentleman usher in pink silks and a powdered wig announced the audience of the Duc de Lauzières. Before he realized it, Armand found himself entering the king's presence with the duke on his arm.

Louis XIV sat in a high-backed chair by a large table piled with papers. He had good legs, and they were crossed now to show them to best advantage. His Majesty greeted the pair in fatherly fashion. He was half a head shorter, but the calm gaze of the gray-green eyes, and the undeniable majesty of his demeanor made one forget his physical size, the protruding lip, and the pockmarks. Here was a king who had performed his role so long that he was no longer conscious of playacting when he claimed to be God's lieutenant on earth.

Elegant as His Majesty appeared, his dress was plainer than that of most of the courtiers. He wore his favorite brown. The blue ribbon of the Order of the Holy Ghost crossed his embroidered long vest. He wore no jewels save for stones in his garters and shoe buckles, but his *peruke** was enormous.

The duke presented the young soldier and dwelt on the exploit of six years earlier, which he pretended the king would recall. He tactfully refrained from any mention of the major's Huguenot background.

The king responded most graciously and seemed pleased by Armand's confusion—a reaction he rather liked in those who met their king for

---

* Wig.

the first time. Before Armand realized it, he found himself discussing the current controversy over whether pikes should still be carried in the infantry.

"Louvois is decidedly for keeping pikemen in addition to musketeers," observed the king.

"Louvois is a—"

The major colored crimson and wished he might sink between the tiles. But the king smiled. "There are times when I am inclined to agree with you, though he is one of my most capable servants. But pray proceed."

"Forgive me, Your Majesty. What I should have said was that the first thing a pikeman does on any battlefield is to throw his pike away and procure himself a musket. If all our infantry were expert in musketry, we should have no need for pikes. I fear the war minister does not have the field experience to see it as lower officers do." The king seemed interested, and Armand's confidence began to return.

The audience concluded with a discussion of uniforms. "If all ranks might wear uniforms, Your Majesty would be better served, for it would eliminate the deserter and the *passe volant** almost at a blow and would prevent some grievous errors in battle."

The king objected to the cost, and before he knew it, the major was once again arguing with him. The king seemed to enjoy it and took the difference of opinion in good humor since it was done with proper submissiveness.

What a grasp of detail! What a kindly manner! thought Armand, much impressed. *He's not the ogre we Huguenots fear, yet how can such a king be so harsh to his people? If they could but get to him—*

"You have served us well," the king was saying, "and your career promises to be a brilliant one. You are fortunate in the friendship of the duke." He inclined his head to terminate the audience.

"I live but to serve Your Majesty," murmured Armand. Then he and the duke backed from the king's presence.

---

* A civilian temporarily drafted so that an officer could display a larger number of soldiers than he actually commanded and fraudulently claim additional money from the king for their support.

As they emerged into the anterooms, Armand noted a change in atmosphere. "Here is someone on the way up!" whispered the perspicacious. As he followed the duke through the press, it seemed that the lords and ladies alike wished to be friends. What a quarter of an hour could do was really rather amusing, he thought wryly.

* * * * *

At dusk Armand stood under the chestnuts in the Versailles gardens with his hands clasped behind his back. He listened with one ear only as the duke, seated on a stone bench, was describing the building-up of the chateau from the neglected hunting lodge of Louis XIII to its present magnificence. They were on a side path near the Allée d'Eté. Close by, the goddess Flora lounged in a basin with winged cupids. A line of silent statues sloped gently down to a greater basin, where Apollo sat enthroned in a four-horse chariot. Beyond lay the Grand Canal, the fading light gleaming redly on its tranquil surface. Few of the fourteen hundred jets were on, for water was still a problem on this arid plain, and the works to bring the River Eure over to the king's gardens were not yet completed.

The cinder paths were hard on dress shoes, and it was with gratitude that one found benches among the groves. The duke was making some unflattering suppositions about the contractors and guessing at total construction costs, but Armand was reliving the high points of the day. He had been impressed, for example, by the king's *diner en public,** and wondered, with the circuitous route the food had to travel from another building, and the tasting of all dishes, whether the king had ever enjoyed a hot meal.

He also recalled the review of the French and Swiss guards in the courtyard of the chateau, right below the royal bedchamber. He especially envied the Life Guards in scarlet and blue, who were accompanied by trumpeters and preceded by their black cymbal player dressed in splendor like a Turkish sultan. These were elite corps in which even the common soldiers were gentle-born. After watching their evolutions,

---

* Dinner eaten in public.

he regretfully promised himself that here was something he would have to work on when he returned to the regiment.

The duke was still gossiping. He talked so much that he did not seem to mind if his listeners were not always with him. "Never stand when you can sit, my boy!" he cackled happily. "You have strong young shanks now, but they'll wear out fast on these marble floors. Sit down, sit down!"

Armand sat.

The light was failing rapidly. It was too dark to see the snuff discolorations on the duke's suit of plum satin. His blue silk ribbon of the Holy Ghost appeared white now in the dimness. The air was mild, for the afternoon had warmed considerably. The scent of the flowers was heavy; the king liked the more potent varieties, and he liked them renewed frequently.

"How do you find Versailles now?" inquired the old man, squinting up intently at the young officer.

"It is somewhat overwhelming to one used to the camp or the country, my lord. There is so much to learn, but it is a great privilege to be here and to see the magnificence all the world talks of."

"True, but I didn't bring you out here to listen to birds or to admire statuary."

Armand turned to look at him, a little surprised.

"I've had my eye on you for a long time, major; in fact, ever since that occasion six years ago when you proved yourself in the field," asserted the duke. Armand dropped his eyes modestly. "I have felt that you have justified your promotions many times over. I have always been satisfied that I recommended them."

The duke stabbed with his cane in the general direction of the chateau. "Now, the king, as you know, is raising twenty-seven new regiments of infantry. Why just now, with the world at peace, I don't know—but one is permitted to guess." He winked in conspiratorial fashion, which screwed his seamed face into a thousand wrinkles. Then he leaned forward and dropped his voice, but it rasped enough to cut through the tinkling of the waters. "For the time, it pleases me to remain as colonel of my own regiment, but I intend to arrange for you the colonelcy of one of the new regiments—if you think you would be interested. The king will agree, I've little doubt, though the commission might take a little time to complete."

Armand didn't hear the concluding words. His mind reeled, and he was glad to be sitting down. A regiment for the taking? He couldn't speak. The duke watched him quizzically, apparently enjoying the effect of his words. For an opportunity like this, hundreds of the nobility pawned their own and their relations' assets and flocked to court. Few were ever so fortunate. Why, just that morning Armand had overheard some talk that the Marquis de Soyecourt had paid forty-two thousand *livres* for the Vermandois regiment. A really good regiment, like one of the Swiss, might run up to sixty thousand. Armand would not earn that much in his lifetime from his estate and officer's pay put together! Stammering his gratitude, he protested his unworthiness.

"Nonsense!" snapped the duke. "I know what I'm doing. We can talk more of that later, but I thought you should know what's in the wind. If you are concerned about my kin, pray calm yourself. Those ghouls can hardly wait till I'm dumped in a grave, but we Robillarts are a tough lot. At seventy-one, I'm a mere boy! I'll have the laugh on them yet—in more ways than they suspect." He winked at the dumbfounded Armand. "A colonelcy for one of them? Servile curs and sneak thieves! They have the martial virtues of weevils in a biscuit! A hundred years ago it would have been my pleasure to hang the lot of them, but these are degenerate times and *seigneurs** no longer enjoy their rightful powers."

"But sir, you are too kind—"

"What were you going to say? Don't bother. I don't appreciate being argued with."

Armand's mouth closed helplessly.

"Would you be more interested if you had a little pocket money to live in proper style?" the duke asked.

The young major thought rather dazedly of the weary years behind and the many more he had expected as a career officer on four *louis d'or*† a month. He had always assumed that for the rest of his life he would

---

* Feudal lords.
† A gold coin.

do the work while titled loafers with purchased commissions took the credit and the promotions. He remembered the bitter snubs and insults, how he had resented their arrogance, their ignorance, their caracoling horses, their wines, silver, and fine clothes. He thought of the young officers who bankrupted themselves and turned thief trying to live up to that extravagance. He himself had long ago turned his back on competitive magnificence, swallowing his pride, or rather making it a matter of pride to live on his pay. And, of course, for such parsimony, one suffered more grievous ridicule. Well, all of that could be left behind now.

"My lord, what *can* I say? It's like a fairy tale!"

"Well then, colonel," said the duke, reading his answer in the younger man's rapt face, "let's not talk here longer. It's almost time for the *appartement*."* He heaved himself stiffly to his feet and took Armand's arm. "Since the good old days of the divine Athenais, matters run more soberly around the court—though I think there will be enough of interest to give you an enjoyable evening. Fie on that gloomy Madame Maintenon! 'Tis she who has scared our poor king so badly about his soul that if this keeps up, Versailles will turn into a convent, I fear."

The two men strolled slowly back toward the terrace of the chateau.

"His Majesty was pleased with you this morning, and we would do well to keep him in that opinion. Your *gaffe*† on Louvois was sheer genius. The great minister is indispensable to good King Louis, but he's hard to get along with—a surly churl, and lately he has ruffled the royal temper. An experienced courtier could not have improved upon your ingenuous blurt—beautifully timed, and it appeared quite sincere."

The duke laughed at Armand's discomfiture. "Oh, I know you didn't intend it. That's what made it so successful! Now, one of the ways we keep our royal master well-disposed toward us is to be present at the *appartements*. He has the rare gift of walking in on these affairs and being able to tell at a glance who is not there. I would much rather be in Paris this evening, but our gracious lord does not care much for his

* Entertainment held in the court.
† Blundering remark.

capital city, and there would be inquiries about those who presumed to steal away for entertainment elsewhere. Under the circumstances, I think I shall remain here, bored rigid probably, but visible."

* * * * *

The thin and graceful strains of Lulli's orchestra floated through the tall windows of the chateau as the soldier and the duke mounted the broad terrace. Since the old man was short of breath, they paused a moment. It was dark now, and the brighter stars had appeared. Fountains played, the waters sparkled in the light from the windows, and reflected light made pastel shades on the palace walls. Couples strolled about on the terrace, and snatches of laughter mingled with music. A jewel on someone's costume sparkled occasionally. The scented evening was pure enchantment.

This dream chateau was no more splendid than the possibilities opening before him, thought Armand. A courtier, in high favor, with a powerful patron—where might it not end? A title? A marshal's baton? What did the duke mean? He had no son now—his son had been killed in Germany in the battle that had won Armand his chance. His thoughts were intoxicating.

Armand glanced up at the shimmering stars, and a sudden twinge of guilt troubled him. What would this do to his religion? To be sure, he had never made much of it before. As a soldier he'd managed a certain suppleness of conscience. Why could he not manage just as well at court, too? No one had asked him to apostatize.

The duke turned in from the terrace toward the Salon of Venus and the Little Gallery. A portly bishop, with the jowly distinction of a Roman emperor, approached the pair at the foot of the Ambassador's Staircase. After introductions, the duke transferred his grasp to the churchman's sleeve.

"Go enjoy yourself, my boy," he said airily. "His Grandeur and I have a little score to settle, a matter of a thousand *louis* I took from him at *picquet** last summer. He thinks he can do something about it

---

* A card game.

now, and it is only civil that I give him the opportunity." He saluted Armand with his walking stick. "Win or lose, the curse will be off the evening." He laughed raspingly, and he and the bishop went off to their game.

Armand contented himself for a time by standing and admiring the staircase. Then he gazed up at the marble vault soaring to the roof of the chateau and at the superb landing with the fountain playing in its niche and the white bust of the king in its niche above. On each side more steps rose from the landing. Over the balustrades the court could look down at mere foreigners ascending the lower flight to make their submission to the Sun King awaiting them on the landing. Tapestries of the king's victories hung on the walls. The ceiling was aswarm with personified arts, sciences, and virtues.

As he drifted through the crowded apartments, he felt almost suffocated by the magnificence about him. The Salon of Venus was in marble mosaic. The goddess ruled the ceiling. She was painted crowned by the Graces, and she had the unlikely company of Augustus, Nebuchadnezzar, Alexander, and Cyrus. The draperies and the furniture were splendid in green and gold. Liveried servants piled up pyramids of fruits, flowers, and confections on silver tables. Eight-branched candlesticks of cut glass and silver illuminated the scene.

Armand passed through the stunning Salon of Diana and its crimson-and-gold décor to the ballroom, the Salon of Mars, with a marble tribune over to the left for the musicians. The god of battles rode his wolf car across the ceiling, escorted by Caesar, Cyrus, Marcus Aurelius, and Constantine. Two huge silver-and-glass chandeliers swung overhead. Silver also gleamed in the tables set between the windows, in flower baskets, candlesticks, and punchbowls. The draperies were in green velvet with gold fringes.

Tonight the card players had the chamber. Blue-liveried footmen dispensed counters and kept score. The din was fearful. Angry and excited voices overtopped the normal roar of conversation. Here was one of the few places a courtier was entitled to sit down, but from an excess of scruples and a shortage of cash, Armand resisted the temptation. He spotted the duke and the bishop hard at play. The latter was losing again. His face was red and perspiring, and his language sufficient to give respectful pause even to an infantry major.

Armand passed through two more gorgeous chambers and then through a large arch that led into the noblest spectacle of all, the Grand Gallery. The flames of four thousand candles were reflected in nineteen tall mirrors set between the windows. The hall swept 240 feet into the distance. Lebrun had dedicated four years of labor on the ceiling alone to the glory of the Grande Monarque. Because of its height, the thirty allegories of the young Louis XIV and his victories were only dimly visible, observed by the impressionable soldier through a golden haze of equal parts candle smoke and splendor.

Armand stood rooted to the spot. In the subdued light the Grand Gallery was a hall of luminous shadows, of things half glimpsed, of fabrics and marbles softly blended. The Savonnierie carpets underfoot were sensed rather than seen. There was the impression of gleaming silver, not a clear picture of tables, orange tubs, and chandeliers. He couldn't determine whether it was caused by the luster of the crystal, the white damask curtains with the royal cipher in gold, or the green-and-gold draperies. Around him milled hundreds of courtiers, the opulence of their dress softened by the effect of the candlelight on iridescent fabrics and metallic lace. Pale faces and white shoulders glowed in unwonted perfection. His ears were filled with the murmur of hundreds of voices, the rustling of satins, and snatches of distant music. He stood speechless with pride and wonder, viewing this abode of demigods.

Progressing slowly through the throng came the center of all the adoration. As he made his stately way, Louis XIV smiled graciously at this one and inclined an ear politely to the appeal of that one, leaving ripples of joy or disappointment in his wake. But he never refused or agreed on the spot. "I will see," he would murmur in his majestic but gentlemanly way. The captain of the guard pressed behind him, always at the king's back, his eyes roving restlessly to and fro.

Tall and handsome as he was, though unfashionably bronzed, Armand did not escape notice. The bashful major was taken over by a determined blonde in crimson satin. Her hair was well powdered and she wore her black beauty patches in the style called "kisses." She played her wide blue eyes on him like a battery, but neither her natural nor artificial charms breached his reserve.

She had added six inches to her slight stature by her high-wired *fontange,** fluttering with ribbons and beautified with pleated ruffles, but the top of it came scarcely to his eyes. She chattered constantly and kept him busy fighting his way in and out of the Salon of Venus to fetch her sweetmeats and glazed fruits from the huge mounds on the sideboards, and in between he made trips for her to the punchbowl. But she only secured his full attention once, and that was when he stepped on her train. For the rest of it, for his taste, she was oversupplied with conversation and pockmarks.

"My dear hopeful Countess Whatever-your-name-is," he said to himself as he returned once more from the refreshment tables, "on my pay I couldn't keep you in lace." Then he remembered that his fortune was in flood and began to realize at least one of the problems fortune might bring.

The blonde would have been even more discouraged had she realized that her taciturn target was comparing her with a tall brunette who had never been near Versailles. *If Madeleine were only here,* he mused, listening absently to the rattle of his companion. What would she think of this wonderful place—and his good luck? How would she look in a court gown, with a high *fontange* and a trialing *manteau*†? That magnificent complexion of hers—how it would be set off by candlelight in the Hall of Mirrors! *She would look like a veritable queen,* he told himself. How far would she surpass the late real queen of France—sallow, dumpy, snag-toothed Maria Theresa!

Supper was at ten, and there Armand lost the blonde, baffled but game, ready to try again tomorrow. The king put away another huge meal, eating silently *au grande couvert,*§ under the devoted eyes of the court. Feeling a little peaked, he ate only three bowls of soup, a whole pheasant and a whole partridge, some mutton with garlic, a slice of ham, a salad, some fruit, hard-boiled eggs, and pastry.

---

* A fancy headdress.
† Coat.
§ Publicly and ceremoniously.

Louis then adjourned to his bedroom, where, leaning against the balustrade before his bed, he received the curtsies of the ladies. Then he bowed, gave the password and countersign to the captain of the guard, and retired to his private chamber to be with his family. The doors were left open, and the courtiers assembling for the *coucher** stood in the dogs' room and watched the king and his brother seated in armchairs, the ladies on taborets, and the dauphin standing.

After a long hour of this, during which Armand almost went to sleep erect, he joined the courtiers massed expectantly in the bedchamber for the *grande coucher*. The king said his prayers under scores of eyes and selected a distinguished courtier for the honor of taking the candlestick from the first *valet de chambre*.† When His Majesty finished undressing, he dismissed the Court with another bow. With the majority, Armand now left the room and waited in the Oeil-de-Boeuf for the grandees who had the honor of the *petit coucher*. Eventually, the sovereign was under the coverlet and alone, except for his valet (who would sleep beyond the balustrade on a camp bed) and a midnight snack left for him on a night table—a matter of three loaves, two bottles of wine, water, and three cold dishes.

Armand did not remember much about the *coucher* of the duke. By this time he was more dead than alive, but they got the old man into bed somehow, and Armand limped back to the Grand Commun, his mind still whirling with the tremendous events of the day. His feet were on fire, his eyes gritty.

At one-thirty in the morning he reached the top of the creaking stairs and opened the door of his garret. The room was airless and stifling; the pallet hard as the wooden trestle supporting it. He would have to be up again at six, but he was too tired and happy to care. He fell asleep almost instantly.

* * * * *

When the lawyers at Versailles drew up the edict banning Huguenot services, they overlooked the picnic. The congregation of the former

---

* Retirement.

† Room servant.

church at Saint Martin gathered around their pastor in the corner of a meadow about a mile from town while he asked the Lord's blessing on their picnic lunch. Certainly no one could object to that. It was true, if any wished to quibble, that the prayer was suspiciously like a sermon in tone and length.

When Pastor Merson had finished, the group began to break up into smaller ones. The older men gathered in knots to talk, and the married women and unattached girls started to prepare the food.

"I hope the Lord is not angered by our manner of worship," said one elderly man with drooping antique mustaches.

"I'm not especially worried about the Lord," said Cortot, shading his eyes with his hand as he searched the edges of the meadow. "I'm certain He understands our predicament well enough, but I don't doubt those rascals over yonder beyond the fence are keeping good watch over us."

"I hope watching makes them good and hungry," said a plump young woman spitefully.

"Clouds!" exclaimed the pastor, glancing up. "Just a few so far. I hope it doesn't rain. The whole day free from our vexations would do us all good."

"Then you might have mentioned it in your prayer," said young Alexandre Cortot in a low voice. "You certainly didn't leave anything else out!"

Madeleine, who was standing nearby clipped her younger brother smartly on the ear. "Watch your tongue, sir," she said crisply and shot him a scorching glance.

Alexandre had been hanging around Madeleine and Mathieu, as if debating whether to play with the other boys or to stay by and play the nuisance to his sister and her fiancé. The boy had been one of the Gloomy One's pupils and had had more than his share of the cuffings and lashings that make a schoolroom move smoothly. No doubt he would have liked to even the score. But something about Madeleine's demeanor must have helped the boy make up his mind, for he elected the games.

"That takes care of *him*, I think," declared Madeleine with satisfaction. With one hand she contended with the breeze for control of stray wisps of hair that tried to creep from under her white cap. The blue skirt and red cloak billowed gently and required her other hand. She looked demurely up at Mathieu, but long lashes and blue eyes seemed to mean nothing to him that morning. His handsome face did not lighten.

The breeze also played with his hair, and the long strands tickled his face. He brushed them back with a petulant gesture. "Let's go somewhere else," he said stiffly. "The food won't be ready for a time, and I'm not hungry anyway."

"All right," she agreed quickly. "Let's go up over the rise and look down into the next valley. It's not very far."

They moved away up the gradual slope. Madeleine impulsively thrust her hand into his; he took it almost with hesitation.

"Take care now. Don't go far," Madame Cortot called to them as they started.

"We won't, Mother," replied Madeleine. "Don't worry about us. We're not hungry." She laughed. "Mother always says that," she told Mathieu.

Madeleine and Mathieu climbed silently to a low ridge between the two valleys.

"Why so glum, Mathieu?" she ventured finally. "Do you think I did wrong to reprove Alexandre? He needs as much as he gets—but I suppose you'd know that well enough! Anyone who has him for a pupil has my sympathy! Father doesn't hear half his impudence."

"I don't think I want to discuss Alexandre," Mathieu answered austerely.

In a few moments Madeleine tried again as they started down the other slope. "Did you ever think when the breeze blows this long grass in these endless, ever-changing rows that it's like ranks of soldiers constantly reforming their lines? The battle is never over."

He didn't speak, so she tried again. "The flowers scattered through are the officers trying to keep the lines straight!" Mathieu's continued stubborn silence puzzled Madeleine.

The breeze was strong, so they went a little distance down the other side of the ridge. The picnic party was out of sight, and they had the hillside to themselves. Below, vineyards stretched off to the highway and a contorted ribbon of sluggish brown river. Beyond the river were more vineyards and hills fading indistinguishably into the distant blue massif. To the left below them was an old chateau surrounded by a stone wall. Once it had been the property of a Huguenot gentleman. He and his family had long since abandoned it, and the Crown had seized it.

Madeleine sank to her knees in the grass and began to pick the little blue flowers within her reach. "They say the old Bellay chateau there is now to be a House of New Catholics," she remarked.

Mathieu didn't answer.

"It seems like there are always stories going around about Huguenot children being carried off and shut up in such places. Why, a couple of weeks ago it was all over town. Cook came home from market full of it. Mother was rather excited. Then she and Father argued again about going to New York or some such place." She sighed. "Do you think anything awful like that could happen here?"

Mathieu lay on one elbow chewing a grass blade. If he was looking toward the chateau, he was looking through it and beyond. After a silence of some length, she tried again. There was a tiny frown between her delicate brows.

"Mathieu! Do you not feel well?"

"I feel very well, thank you."

What is troubling him? Madeleine wondered as he remained glum and silent. Mathieu could be difficult at times, she reflected, but he also had his admirable side. She knew he had methodically planned each step of his rise. Attending school at Saumur, he had been one of the steady ones, eschewing frivolity, gaming, trictrac, crude pranks, riots, duels, carousing, debt, and all other forms of infamous conduct to which his fellow students were partial. Like clockwork he had won highest honors in the annual written and oral examinations, and he had good conduct certificates for each year—*fort meritoirement,** no less. As the piety prize one year, he carried off the book *Consolations Against the Terrors of Death*. And to be *proposant*† in the Saumur church for two years was not an

---

* Very meritorious.
† Candidate for the ministry.

honor that came to everyone. He had been preparing the defense of his thesis when the royal edict shut the school. Not long afterward his dead father's estate had been confiscated on a technicality, and he was left penniless. For three meager years he had been stranded in Saint Martin, bravely supporting himself as a teacher of a miserable little beginners' school, tutor for several well-to-do families, and *chanteur** of the church—when there was still a church. Plans with loose ends baffled and enraged him. Prudent planning and hard work should have been sufficient.

Well she knew Mathieu's plans for the future. Pastor Merson and Monsieur Cortot had made the arrangement that eventually Mathieu should wed Madeleine. Her dowry would be a good one. If the young minister could procure the pastorate he looked for and have no concern for his material wants through this advantageous marriage, then he would settle down to a life of preaching in successively larger churches, learned disputation, and controversial writings. In time he would become a highly respected leader of the church. He had no intention of burying himself in obscure parishes as his uncle was doing. The times were uncertain, and calamity might be expected to smite disorderly folk. But he was plagued with a growing sense of injustice that his careful arrangements should be so badly spoiled. Now his only avenue to the ministry would be by flight abroad, without possibility of return.

At last Mathieu broke the silence. "Why is Pastor Merson so cheerful?" he demanded. "He must be losing his mind. Four children, his church closed, no money, and he *picnics*! I doubt I can stand much more of this frivolity."

"Well, I suppose it's natural we should enjoy an innocent occasion together," Madeleine said quickly in defense of the pastor. "There have been troubles ever since one can remember, but the Lord has always protected us. He knows what's going to happen. Now, what good does it do to worry?"

"You just have no idea of the situation we're in," Mathieu snapped impatiently. "Your parents probably keep it from you—or else they don't think it can happen to them."

---

* Singer.

"I'm not a complete fool, I'll have you know," Madeleine declared with spirit. "I really don't see what good it does to go about so sour all the time. My father and your uncle have their worries—more than we know of, likely enough—but they seem cheerful. They feel the Lord's protecting hand over us, and they wait on Him to show us what we should do—and when."

"And while they picnic, the noose grows tighter."

Madeleine looked startled.

"How could you have any idea what it's like?" he asked, avoiding her gaze. "Daughter of the richest man in town, protected, favored. You can't imagine what it is like to have one's hopes blasted, one's plans in shambles."

"I believe, Mathieu, that I know more than you give me credit for. You are discouraged, are you not, because you can't finish your studies and you can't decide whether to go abroad or not and you've lost your father's estate and now the teaching post? You know," she interrupted herself, "I think you let yourself be badly upset by all the little certain things going amiss—more upset than some might be when a great and risky venture fails."

"This is no jesting matter," he said coldly.

"I'm not jesting, believe me, dear Mathieu," she said gently. "You are but four and twenty. You *could* go to a seminary abroad—"

"That would mean exile forever!" he cried. "Would *you* want to leave France?"

"I— I don't really know. I don't think I would, . . . I mean, unless I had to. We all may have to someday, you know."

There was no sound save the humming of insects and a trill from a meadow bird. The sun was growing hot, and the clouds had disappeared. Madeleine gazed anxiously at Mathieu. He didn't meet her eyes but gave her his profile, with tendrils of long yellow hair blowing across the high forehead.

"You must have more confidence that the Lord guides His people, Mathieu. Look around you. Some get along quite well in spite—"

"Oh, certainly, mademoiselle," he countered bitterly. "The turncoat, the apostate, does well indeed! Let him but preen himself in the king's uniform no matter what he did to earn it, and all fawn on him like he was some great thing!"

Madeleine colored and dropped her eyes. "If you refer to Armand de Gandon," she said coolly, "you do him an injustice. He is a very pleasant gentleman, and I'm sure his conduct is exemplary."

"A lackey of the Scarlet Woman you mean! How much of a Huguenot do you suppose *he's* ever been? They've been heating the furnace seven times hotter for the rest of us, and he wanders by tricked out like a, a—"

He was glaring and shaking his finger in her face. She bit her lip.

"Really, Mathieu, I cannot permit you to speak in this way of a friend of my father. I suppose I should be flattered, for you sound jealous. Of late it *has* been hard to tell that you cared very much for me. I don't know whether to laugh at you or be angry, but you are being *very* silly. Monsieur de Gandon passed through here for the first time in ten years to pay his respects. He had no interest in me nor I in him. A betrothal means more to me than that. I think you owe me an apology for your surly speech."

Under her firm gaze, he faltered. "I'm sorry, Madeleine, of course, but—but you are wrong about him. He *is* interested in you and counts on those peacock's feathers to sweep you off your feet."

"Well," she said, only a little mollified, "you must entertain a high opinion of your fiancée to think that a stranger in a pretty coat could change her mind. We *have* been promised to each other for a long time now."

Mathieu turned on her fiercely. "Yes, now," he cried. "What about us?"

"Us?"

"Why do we wait this long? You are old enough now—seventeen before the month is out. Do your parents wish you to be a spinster? Why shouldn't I 'imagine' things now and again?" He was growing vehement again.

"Calm yourself, dear Mathieu," Madeleine said, laying a gentle hand on his arm. "I—we didn't know you felt that way, but my father is a man of his word. He did not wish to seem to press you in your present situation or to hasten you."

He was taken aback. "*You* did not wish to press *me*?" He pondered a moment. "Then you are willing to go on, post the banns,* and marry a husband without prospects?"

"I was promised to you some time ago, Mathieu, and not to your 'prospects.' "

"Well, what if I took your suggestion and left the country? What about you?"

"Your wife would go with you," she said, "if she was wanted. Mathieu," she added, "you are not like you used to be when you first came here. I've given my word. I'd never look at another though he wore Joseph's original coat of many colors. If my parents set the wedding immediately, would this cure your melancholy? As for your evil circumstances, you know God can turn evil to good."

He seemed unable to discard his jealousy so quickly. "Well, I should no longer have to worry," he rejoined irritably.

"Then let's tell them," she said at last without looking up. "They will be anxious only that we are happy." She feared she did not sound particularly happy just then.

Mathieu said nothing more. Perhaps he felt he had said too much already. He rose to his feet, retrieved his hat, and helped Madeleine up. They silently retraced their steps up the slope and down the other side. They could hear the distant sounds of merriment where their friends were eating dinner.

---

* Banns were posted in a church or other place as prescribed by law to advise the public of a proposed marriage.

CHAPTER 3

Madeleine Escapes

Two weeks after the great day at Versailles, Armand de Gandon descended the slope to Saint Martin on his big bay. The late afternoon sun gilded the steep roofs of the town, touching them with a golden brightness that the narrow alleys never saw. The pastel quiltwork of the fields was growing darker, and the blackish trees climbing the gentle hills to the horizon cast long shadows. The uncertain river wandered through the rushes below the walls and glowed for a few moments in an unnatural rose. Amid its rustic setting, rising comfortably above crumbling walls, the town looked like a quaint, old colored print, far removed from strife and turmoil. "And unlike Paris, Saint Martin can't be smelled a league away," Armand reminded his horse.

As the soldier closed the distance to the town, his weary muscles and empty stomach were ready for the welcome he could anticipate at the Cortots' home. The tired horse carried him through the battered gate, where the municipal arms surmounted the arch. Sections of wall still stood behind the filled-in ditch, a reminder of the bloody days when the Protestant townspeople had resisted their king. That was sixty years before. Now grass and weeds had taken over, and even the slovenly sentry was not in sight.

Armand's mount picked its way delicately over the open sewers, through refuse piles, dodging pigs, chickens, and an occasional child, to a small square. Bearing slightly to the right, the soldier rode down a narrow side street, ducking from time to time to keep from being brained by overhanging signboards. It was the quiet time of the evening. He met no adult in the airless thoroughfare, but as he was coming up to the Cortot house, he saw a black coach round the bend ahead of him.

The Cortots' massive front door stood ajar. Armand was surprised. He dismounted stiffly, for he had been in the saddle since dawn. He called and then rapped on the door panel, but there was no answer. Still more puzzled than alarmed, he entered the foyer. The house seemed deserted. Surely, in these times, if the family had gone away, they wouldn't have left the door unbarred.

He was about to call again when he heard something like a moan. Through a doorway he saw a plain buckled shoe lying on the floor and then a stockinged foot nearby. Stepping quickly forward, Armand found one of the Cortot manservants, apparently unconscious, lying on the planking.

"What ails you, boy? Where's your master?" Armand cried out in alarm. He knelt beside the prone figure, now stirring slightly. "You're coming out of it now," he said encouragingly. "What's happened? Where is everyone?"

The servant began to collect his wits. He blinked several times and then tried shaking his head, but this made him groan.

"They got the twins," he said at last in a shaky voice. Armand helped him to a sitting position.

"O, come on, fellow. Who did? Speak up!"

"A couple of bailiffs did." The servant, now sitting unassisted, fingered the back of his head. "Got them both—Louis and Louise. Carried them off in a coach." At the moment, he seemed more concerned about the lump on his head than about the twins.

The soldier remembered a coach. "When?" he snapped impatiently and shook the unfortunate vigorously by the collar. "Where?"

"Had an order from the intendant, they said. Wasn't no one home but us. I never dreamed— Well, how was I to expect—?"

"Yes, yes!" snarled Armand. "Now quit babbling or I'll give you a knock myself."

"That's all right, monsieur. Needn't get so excited. You can't do nothing anyhow. They came in a little black carriage. They're taking them to the House of New Catholics out by the south gate, I suppose. Said they had witnesses the twins asked for religious instruction, and—"

By the time the servingman had wobbled to his feet, Armand had already dashed away, leaving the door ajar again.

* * * * *

As Armand lashed his surprised horse down the deserted street, he was overcome by a cold fury. He hadn't forgotten Versailles, the Duc de Lauzières, the regiment—they just didn't seem important at the moment. What did matter were two frightened children. Gandon, level-headed major of the Regiment of Maine and devoted servant of the king, had vanished like a spark struck from flint. Instantly, he had shed a hundred years of discipline and reverted to the mind of his Bearnaise ancestors, who thought nothing of drawing swords on Majesty itself in defense of the right.

Rounding a third bend, the bay scrambling and sliding in the loose dirt, Armand saw the black coach joggling slowly along the unpaved street. Breathing a short prayer of thanks that he wasn't in uniform and that no one else was in sight, he jammed his hat down on his ears and launched his mount on his quarry.

The coach was just about to take a sharp turn to the right when the horse and rider came up behind them out of nowhere so rapidly that the driver had no time to locate the direction of the hoofbeats. Armand drove his animal into the near coach horse just as they started the turn and simultaneously brought his heavy cavalry pistol down on the nose of the surprised horse as hard as he could. The team bolted instantly, and the coachman yelled in terror. Already too far to one side in the narrow passageway and now crowded by this apparition, the coachman had no room to turn. The fleeing horses squeezed past the jutting corner of the stone building, but the wheel of the vehicle struck it with shattering force.

In the middle of a shriek, the coachman shot from his seat into the mud, where he rolled over and over to the far side of the street. The axle snapped, the fastenings of the leather springs gave way, and the coach body dropped to the ground and crumpled into kindling and splinters. For a second the coach horses plunged and kicked, and then they tore loose and galloped off down the street. The driver cowered in the gutter, his hands over his head, still screaming as the animals clattered past him, their hooves missing him by inches. Back in the wreckage lay the kidnappers, stunned and helpless. Blood from an ugly scalp wound ran down the fat face of the head bailiff.

Armand slid to the ground and pulled the two children free. They had been riding backward and were merely stunned by the collision. Placing them on his horse's neck, he hastily jumped into the saddle and fled. It was time, for in the crepuscular glow he had glimpsed white faces at windows. Citizens ran out of doorways even as he sped around the corner. He hoped that no one had had the presence of mind to get a square look at the rescuer.

* * * * *

"I hope I have not seemed inhospitable these last ten days," Cortot protested wearily, "but it *is* dangerous for you to tarry here. You know we are grateful for your rescue of the twins and for your desire to be of help to Madeleine and Alexandre, but you only endanger yourself." He sat heavily on the edge of the bed on which Armand had been lying fully clothed.

"Yes, monsieur, I know," replied Armand. "We've been through this before, and I don't think you can change my mind. I'll go over your city wall some night; but no one knows I'm in town, and I may be of help. But what of your visit with the mayor? I see they didn't lock you up yet."

"It was most unpleasant. It was plain *I* didn't assault the bailiffs, yet they must believe I know more than I tell. The coachman swears they were attacked by at least ten ruffians." He smiled wanly. "The curé was so furious that he stuttered, and I thought he might be called heavenward any moment by an apoplexy. He threatened the mayor with the bishop, and I think that saved me. One could see the mayor's ears go back and a stubborn look come on his face."

"Do not the town fathers get on well with the clergy?"

"I suppose so—with the curé at any rate. They hate the orders, you know, because the orders are usually exempt from the *octroi** and that raises the taxes for everyone else. Our council fought this newest House of New Catholics bitterly. They didn't need to be told who would be supporting it eventually."

"I thought," said Armand, "that the idea was to carry off children of the better sort only, so the house would pay its own way."

Cortot shook his head.

"When they carried off my Madeleine and Alexandre, they took forty others as offerings to their idols, but since then, many families have disappeared entirely—heading for the frontiers, I don't doubt, to save the rest of their children. This puts the upkeep of the kidnapped ones they leave behind on the few of us who have means. If I go or am jailed, they'll have that much more trouble supporting their captives without calling on the town revenues. I can see the mayor's thought in this."

"Any word from Madeleine yet?" Armand rose and slipped on his shoes.

"Only that of three days ago, that she had expressed a desire for instruction and requested that we not be allowed to disturb her while she undertook these studies. She'll be permitted no visitors until she abjures, I suppose, or she will certainly be well chaperoned if we are allowed to visit her."

"A kindly thought of His Majesty—do not disturb her, forsooth!" Armand smiled without mirth.

"At least we know where she is, but there's no word from Alexandre. I don't know where the nearest house for boys might be."

"I'm sorry my presence has been a trial to you," said Armand. "Truly, with Madame ill also, you've been sorely tried."

"I'm confident that both of my children will be true to the Faith," said Cortot. "And I'm sure the Lord knows of the wretched condition of my wife this past week. Her affliction is mainly from the shock, I think; and though I am still uneasy for her, she seems better today and will be up soon."

---

* City toll.

A knocking at the street door sent Cortot from the room. From what he could hear, Armand judged that the pastor had arrived, accompanied by his nephew, the tall Mathieu. They were climbing the stairs now, and the voices of the two older men sounded excited. The soldier grinned at the discomfiture awaiting the schoolmaster.

"We must have a secret place for what I have to tell, Brother Cortot," said the pastor. "Walls have ears these days."

"Nay, pastor," replied the bourgeois firmly, "you wrong my servants. They are part of the family. They grumble a bit, but they are absolutely loyal."

Armand looked down upon the rosy pate of Cortot as he puffed up the stairs. Behind him came the pastor in the plain black required by law.

"Come on up, brethren," urged their host. "We'll talk in Monsieur Gandon's room. He'll be glad for a chance to do something."

At the mention of that name, the head of the third man on the stairs jerked up. In spite of the dimness of the stairwell, Armand caught a glance that was even darker. "Well met, friend," he remarked to himself ironically. "Sorry to spoil your day!"

"I hope now, Brother Cortot, that we may have a way to reach your daughter," began the pastor as soon as the trio had entered the room and shut the door.

"I rejoice to hear it, pastor. Pray make yourselves comfortable, gentlemen."

The pastor perched on a stool near the head of the bed. Cortot dropped again into a chair, and the two young men sat on the edge of the bed, somewhat in the fashion of strange dogs encountering one another for the first time. The pastor gave them a long look, smiled faintly, and turned to Cortot. "I do not delude myself that we have a sure way to Mademoiselle Madeleine, much less to rescue her. But this may lead to something."

Armand and Cortot leaned forward anxiously; Mathieu frowned at the floor.

"You remember that Petitjean who was the instrument used to bring down the temple a month ago? I have seen much of him of late, for he carries a troubled conscience for the harm he wrought the church.

Yesterday he told me that he keeps company with a kitchen maid, one Lisette, at the house where the females are kept—the old Bellay chateau not far from town."

Cortot nodded eagerly.

"I said nothing to him then," the pastor continued, "but do you perceive the opportunity that may present itself?"

Both Gandon and Cortot nodded.

"In his anxiety to repair some of the damage he has done," the pastor continued, "might not Petitjean be an intermediary, perhaps enlisting his friend in our aid?"

"It would lighten the burden on my heart, pastor, were I to hear from the girl," said the father. "But the risk would be too great."

"No, monsieur," interrupted Armand, half rising in his eagerness. "Don't use the fellow as a courier. That would be to tempt fate. Let him carry *one* message, but let it be to arrange a rescue!"

"A rescue, you say," and Cortot shook his head sadly. "That's a *very* frail vessel."

"True," countered Armand impatiently. "But we could tell Madeleine where to meet . . . us. The note would say nothing of rescue. We would need Petitjean no more."

Cortot did not look entirely convinced. The pastor smiled benignly.

"Brother Gandon has anticipated my thought in the matter—"

"Not so fast, Uncle," cut in Mathieu almost rudely. "I have more reason than anyone else to see mademoiselle delivered," and he shot a meaning glance at Armand. "But this lackey Petitjean has played us false before and in his cups would easily do so again. It will be of no help to the lady if we are all broken on the wheel!"

"Mathieu is right," conceded Cortot, somewhat wilted. "It's the house built on the sands."

"No," replied Armand with a nonchalance that seemed to choke Mathieu. "They could but hang us. It's worth a try." He laughed—probably the first time that sound had been heard in the house for days.

"If I could but get her out of that house," Cortot explained, "I would send her and the twins to my cousin in Champagne. They would be safe for a time, at least, and later—well, conditions might improve here, or, in any case, the borders would be closer."

"I would count it a privilege to escort them there, sir," Armand said as he sprang to his feet and began to pace back and forth behind the men's chairs.

"I wish," sighed Cortot, "that we might free all the children shut up there."

"I wish so, too," agreed the pastor sadly. "But it would not do. They would be rounded up shortly and the worse treated for it. There are not many with your means, brother."

"God is good to us beyond our deserts," agreed Cortot.

"If this succeeds, Monsieur Cortot," Armand stopped his pacing and looked down at the older man, "credulity will be terribly strained when a child of yours escapes twice in a row. They can play a very rough game. Have you ever been put to the question? Run, sir, and get out of the country while there is time. Even if they don't find where the twins are hidden, they'll be so suspicious of you that they'll have you locked up soon on one pretext or another."

Cortot licked his lips and his head sagged.

"Why wait?" Armand persisted. "Many have passed over into the Germanies and to the provinces of Holland—even to England."

"It's as I've said before." Cortot sighed. "This is our soil. We were born here, and our parents are buried here. I grant you the brethren in those countries have been more than kind to those of us who have fled. But, well, look at England—a king hardly better than a papist himself, cold fogs, a barbarous tongue. Once you run, you must always be ready to run again." He smiled faintly. "And the place smells of coal fire, I hear."

"You are making excuses now! Have you had a whiff of the alley outside your own front door lately? Anyway, I doubt King Charles can do much to turn the minds of Englishmen."

"I know little of such matters, Armand, but what would a man of my age do in a foreign land?"

"Fie, Uncle Isaac! This is not like you." He looked fixedly at Cortot until his host dropped his eyes.

"Well, Armand," he began hesitantly, "what I tell you, you may have suspected. Madame is quite set on staying here. To her, this is faith; I hope it be not presumption. I hope, as signs multiply, that she will be persuaded while there is yet time. I wish we had our eldest boy again. He was like you—ready for action . . ." His voice trailed off. "Still," added Cortot, "how could one feel safe anywhere? The king's reach is long. I have thought of the English settlements in America. I would prefer a French land, but only good Catholics may go to Canada."

His voice shook with sudden feeling. "If I could but get my family to Holland, these pests could have every stick of property I own, nor would I much care what they would do to me." He paused. "I've had such an easy time. So many of the troubles have passed me by. Saint Martin is one of the pleasant places, and I feel even as Lot, reluctant to flee Sodom and it about to burn about my ears. My wife, that is . . . well, it is hard to know what to do. Sometimes I think one thing, sometimes another." He raised his hands in a gesture of futility.

"Then shall I broach the matter to Petitjean with such caution as I can?" the pastor resumed. He looked sharply at the two younger men. "If mademoiselle can win free of the building itself, surely you two nimble fellows could spirit her to a city of refuge."

"Surely," Armand agreed without consulting Mathieu. "If I—we— are caught, it would not be the ruin of an entire family but just a prank by addled gallants. If it is successful, I rejoin my regiment with no one, I trust, the wiser for my sojourn here. And perhaps Monsieur Bertrand might wish to keep on going to Holland. Prospects for preachers hereabouts must be poor." He turned cheerfully to the glowering Mathieu. "Are you with me?"

Mathieu's agreement, when it came, sounded a trifle forced. "I assure you, gentlemen, that I would do all in my power to arrange for the safety of mademoiselle, for surely you understand my sentiments for her. But any plan must be drawn up with care. We must, ah—avoid, recklessness and—and bravado—and plan very carefully," he ended lamely.

Armand looked at him quizzically and said nothing.

* * * * *

Madeleine lay on her pallet in a crowded room on the second floor of the House of New Catholics. It was pitch black, chill, and damp; but she was not shivering entirely from the cold. Outside the glassless windows, the rain hissed against the sloping tiles of the roof. It had been raining for hours, and the wind was rising. She had no idea what time it was. Had it been ten minutes or an hour since the sister had removed the candle after her last look around the roomful of girls?

Never in Madeleine's short and comfortable life had she wanted to do anything as desperately as she wanted to escape from this house. It wasn't one of the fashionable convents where exhausted reprobates retired to tidy up their spiritual affairs before death and indiscreet ladies might spend an enforced vacation from the court. This one was newly opened and still in some disrepair.

That it was cold and comfortless might help to break the wills of its young inmates, but it was not physical discomfort that Madeleine Cortot had quickly learned to hate and fear. Every day brought home to her more strongly what a lifetime in such a place would mean. Sometimes, it was true, stubborn cases were released in a few months if the sisters felt conversion was hopeless, but then an order from the king could shut such a one up in a regular convent for the rest of one's life—and force an endowment from a father as well. This might easily happen to her, for her father was wealthy, and she would be too valuable a prize to relinquish.

That she would suffer her faith to erode never seriously occurred to her. It was a question of living a life of unending gray under a ceaseless drizzle of ritual and "instruction," of unrelenting pressure that at times was outright intimidation. No physical mistreatment to speak of, but unrelenting "charity" and mechanical repetition until one was ready to go out of one's mind. The work was hard, and it wasn't difficult to keep one's mind numb during the day. But at night, in the dark, with a vivid imagination at full gallop, she came closer to losing her grip on hope.

Two days ago, while she was on her knees scrubbing the kitchen flagstones, Lisette had suddenly loomed over her. Madeleine, now used to the heavy hand of the big peasant woman, had automatically flinched.

Lisette seemed especially to dislike Madeleine—perhaps because the Huguenot girl had the book learning and strong opinions that so scandalized the Romanists and made the heretic women more difficult to deal with than the men. Madeleine disliked almost everything about Lisette also, from her coarse red hands to her mustache.

Madeleine had not looked her in the face but stared instead at the heavy ankles and the purple veins above the wooden shoes. She gritted her teeth and waited for the blow, but instead, a tiny wad of paper dropped in front of her. Madeleine's heart had leaped crazily. Instantly she placed one wet hand over the paper and continued her brush stroke with the other. Lisette lumbered away without a word. A hearty smack resounded a moment later and told Madeleine that Lisette had caught some Huguenot girl dawdling. None of the other captives or servants in the room appeared to have seen anything.

Madeleine scrubbed herself into a corner and surreptitiously unfolded the bit of paper. It was wet, and the writing was blurred and hard to read: "Be at back wall Wednesday midnight."

She caught her breath. Who could have sent it? Was it a cruel joke? Was Lisette an ally—perhaps a secret Protestant? She felt so excited that the room spun for a few seconds. She hoped her face didn't betray her.

Then she straightened her aching back and risked a glance at the square, sallow face. The slatey eyes were as expressionless as ever. Not a flicker of understanding or complicity there! *Lisette wants nothing to do with this,* she mused as she resumed her scrubbing. *So be it! But how do I get out of the building?* Later, at her first opportunity, she had swallowed the note, though it nearly gagged her.

The next morning Madeleine had made a special point to look out the window of the second-floor room she slept in. The windows had been hastily barred by wooden slats—sufficient to restrain young children and girls until something more permanent could be devised. Underneath the window, the tiled roof sloped off to the hillside rising in back. Over to the right a projection of the roof covered the kitchen storerooms, and there the roof came closest to the ground. To leap to the ground from that place shouldn't be hard. Then it would be uphill fifty yards or so to a tall stone wall at the rear of the garden. Certainly there would be no way over the wall from the inside. Beyond lay the grassy slopes where only a week before she had lain in the spring sunshine and talked marriage with Mathieu. It seemed ages away now. Mathieu must be the one who sent the note. A rush of affection and homesickness swept over Madeleine. She strangled a sob and wiped two tears away quickly with the back of her hand.

The day had dragged on routinely—orisons at half past six, catechism at a quarter after seven, mass at nine. Then sessions of work and study, always under close supervision and with silence usually imposed. Madeleine's mind kept busy, however mechanically her hands might work. If she could but lay hands on some implement to pry the wooden bars off the window!

Not until almost time for the litanies at four o'clock did she find her opportunity. She had been peeling turnips for supper, and as she turned away from the table with a panful, she pretended to trip on the uneven flagstones and cascaded turnips over the floor. She had immediately dropped to her knees to pick them up and slipped the knife she had been using inside her shapeless gray blouse. Her "accident" attracted attention, but not the reason for it, so she hardly minded the cruel slap from Lisette or the parting shove through the doorway toward the chapel.

Now she was wondering if the blade would prove strong enough. If it broke, that would be the end of the matter. To try to slip through the ground-floor areas, where the sisters had their quarters and the windows were grilled with iron, would be hopeless—as hopeless as trying to unbar the great front door.

At supper she choked down a little of the turnips and mashed chestnuts, keeping her eyes lowered modestly lest anyone read her face. The mother superior usually seemed to be in a world of her own, but that heavy opaque gaze might take in more than one suspected. Madeleine was still dreading a last-minute summons. Was it all a cat-and-mouse game?

After nine o'clock prayers, the flock were shepherded to their cells. It didn't take the girls long to prepare for bed. They wore only the simplest blouses and skirts of peasant gray.

When the light had been removed, the girls whispered their prayers—their real prayers. They had to be careful, for there would be extra work as punishment if they were overheard, and one could never tell when someone might be listening in the hall.

Madeleine lay in the dark, overcome by a feeling of meanness and misery she had never felt before. She had no assurance that she could escape, but just the hope had renewed her courage. She had felt responsible to the younger captives, who were equally frightened but understood less than she why they had been suddenly torn from their homes. What would happen to the little ones who had no hope, no outside friends? Must they stay here and be taught that their parents, their loved ones, were irremediably damned? Yet she couldn't organize an escape of all forty of them. That would mean disaster. Was it her duty to stay or to go? Would the others be punished if she escaped? Would they be encouraged or dismayed if she succeeded? She wrestled with her doubts until she unintentionally dozed off.

Now she lay awake, listening to that incessant rain and wondering if she had overslept and thus ruined all. There might be no time to lose. But was everyone asleep? Long after the faint gleam of the candle had died away, the rustlings and groanings and sighings of restless children would continue. Some were not far from nightmare; some would lie awake in the cold dark, listening to the rain and the wind as they whipped against the big house. How soon would it be safe to try the window?

The monotonous downpour continued.

It must be midnight, she thought as panic seized her. *I can't stand this any longer!* She sat up and tried to see the other beds in the dark. It was as black as the inside of a boot. *If I can't hear them above this storm, perhaps they can't hear me either,* she thought.

Madeleine eased herself off the mattress to the stone floor and crawled toward the window, guided more by sound than by sight. Twice she touched the corners of straw pallets, but the sleepers did not stir. Reaching the window at last, she rose cautiously and experimented with the edges of the boards. Working as carefully as she could and praying that the slight squeaks and scrapes of the knife would be drowned by the noise of the elements, she finally worked one end of a board almost completely loose. She stood and listened a moment, oblivious to the spray that had already drenched her head and shoulders. Then she began on the next board.

After what seemed like hours, all three boards were loosened at both ends. And the knife remained unbroken. There was no telling what might be waiting for her out there in the dark. A knife might be a handy thing to have. She pushed with all her strength on one side of the loosened boards, forcing the nails out of their holes and bending the boards outward on the nails of the other side as if they were hinges. When one screeched suddenly in protest, her heart jumped against her front teeth, and she waited a long moment before she dared breathe again. At last all three pointed outward.

Madeleine climbed through the opening. She was taller and slimmer than most French girls, but it was not easy. The protruding nails took a heavy toll of her skirt and blouse. Standing on the tiles outside the window, she carefully pushed the bars back in place as well as she could, hoping that they might seem normal—at least at first glance. Then she turned and began to inch her way down the slippery roof in the darkness. The rain beat on her, and the wind ripped at her. It blew her cap off almost at once, and her hair went across her face. She was thoroughly soaked.

A loose tile slithered down the slope and went over the edge. It made only the faintest plop as it struck the sodden ground below. Here was another advantage of the storm, Madeleine realized. If she should fall, the mud down there would reduce the chance of injury.

Step by step she felt her way and at last reached the edge of the roof. She explored the void with an inquiring toe. Rain, wind, and darkness blurred everything in one indistinguishable pall. The wind-driven drops blinded her, and the moaning of the wind made a nerve-racking setting for the nameless terrors lurking below.

At last she felt she had reached the extension of the roof that covered the storerooms, and she proceeded more boldly. The drop from that part of the roof to the ground would be only a few feet. Reaching the edge, she took a deep breath and, commending her safety to God, jumped, accompanied by several tiles. She landed on hands and knees in a slough formed by the runoff from the steep hillside flowing along the back wall of the building. She had hardly been jarred.

Unable to see anything, Madeleine followed the steepness uphill toward the invisible stone wall. By now she felt sure there was no trap. In the drop she had lost her knife. It was just as well, she told herself, for she doubted that she could bring herself to use it. She remembered that when the bailiffs had broken into the Leblanc home and laid hands on her, she had been too paralyzed to move. Alexandre, on the other hand, had fought like a fiend until two of the officers had wrestled him to the floor and one of them sat on him. The other was nursing a very bloody nose. She wished she had Alexandre there at that moment. He had often been a painful nuisance, but she promised herself she would never speak unkindly to him again if the Lord permitted them to be together once more.

Bushes and low, swaying tree limbs clutched at her, scratching her face and arms and completing the ruin of her skirt, now almost rent in two. A short while later she bumped into stone and knew she had gone as far as she could. Collapsing on the muddy ground, she buried her face in her soggy skirt. The rain continued to come down in sheets, and a small river ran down her neck. She realized she must have cut her foot in the climb, for it was paining her now. Whether she had arrived too early or too late she did not know; she felt so tired she could hardly force her mind to consider the question.

* * * * *

For the fourth time, Mathieu Bertrand tripped over a root or stone and fell flat in the darkness. The storm lantern he carried flew from his hand and disappeared. But the slight injury to his knees and the additional mud on his clothing were as nothing compared to the damage to his self-esteem. The nonchalant bearing of his companion made it no easier.

"No matter," cried Armand de Gandon above the storm. "We're getting so close to the house now that we'd have had to put the lantern out soon, and in all this slop it wasn't doing much good anyway."

Mathieu said nothing as they struggled along, the wind tugging at their cloaks, the rain stinging their faces in spite of turned-down hat brims. He had agreed to this mad business because he did wish to have Madeleine rescued if it was at all possible. But he had to admit that he had been dragooned into it partly at least because he was so sick of the way everyone fawned on this soldier. Certainly if everything didn't have to be done in such a mortal hurry, something more practical could have been worked out. He hadn't imagined it would be like this, blundering about blindly in a torrential downpour. He simply was not at his best in this sort of thing, and he suspected Armand knew it. But his uncle had been so anxious to push the matter.

"Let's bear a little down the slope," called Armand. "We don't want to overshoot the wall in the dark." He drew his sword and felt ahead of him like a blind man with a cane.

Five minutes more of groping and they fetched up against a wall. By stumbling along for several yards, they determined that it ran at right angles to the slope and not with it. They knew then they had the rear wall. From the outside, climbing would be no great matter. The problem would arise in attempting the return trip, for the ground falling away downhill made the wall taller on the inside than on the outside. One of them would have to stay on top of the wall to assist in the escape. Both were tall and sturdy; it wouldn't matter which one went over the wall.

Armand seemed to undergo a sudden attack of delicacy. "Here's the rope," he said. "Jump, and I'll pull on your signal."

Mathieu froze. Perhaps Madeleine was waiting on the other side of the wall, and perhaps she wasn't. Who knew what might be in ambush for one foolhardy enough to drop off the wall into nothingness. Suppose the note had been discovered, or Petitjean or Lisette had played the traitor, or Madeleine had been caught and forced to talk? For a second the rain lashed at his face and he stood speechless. He couldn't see Armand's face, but he was certain what its expression would be: a leer of triumph or contempt. A wave of self-pity flowed over him, and tears of rage stung his eyes. It wasn't a fair contest. He couldn't help feeling ridiculous.

"I imagine you are more expert at such ventures. *You* jump, and *I'll* hold the rope," he said at last.

Mathieu's answer was actually prompt enough, and Armand seemed not to notice the hesitation. He needed no second urging and dropped off into the convent yard, landing with a splash that was audible above the downpour. Mathieu, teetering on the top of the wall, found himself toying guiltily with the wish that this debonair one would walk into the arms of waiting papists and *then* see what his cleverness would get him.

It seemed an age, waiting, holding the rope's end. Mathieu felt as conspicuous as though he were standing on the top of the wall in broad daylight, though it was black as the pit down there. What would that crazy soldier do if Madeleine had been unable to get out of the building? Go in after her? The very thought so stirred up his terror that he nearly fell off the wall. He was trying to master his vertigo when he felt a sharp tug on the rope. Armand, or someone, was below him now, though invisible in the darkness.

"Hold it firm," hissed the someone. Mathieu braced himself convulsively. Suddenly, Armand was beside him, gasping for breath.

"Pull!" urged the officer. Madeleine came up with the rope looped around her hands and wrists. They tried to keep her swinging in the clear, but, encumbered by the sodden skirt, she bumped and scraped the stones until she was atop the wall with the two men. She made no outcry when her knee, unprotected by the remnants of her skirt, was gashed against the rough stone.

Armand then dropped to the ground on the outside of the wall, and Mathieu without a word grasped Madeleine's wrists and lowered her to the ground were Armand waited. They stood there a moment to get their bearings. Armand coiled the rope. Madeleine began to cry quietly. Mathieu could think of nothing to say meet for the occasion. Each man then grasped an arm of the girl, and they half carried, half dragged her through thickets and over rocks.

After endless weavings to and fro, they felt themselves on level ground and proceeded along the deserted highway, past the old Huguenot cemetery to a stone bridge half a mile distant from town. They crossed over, turned right, and in a few more yards came to a carriage hidden rather unnecessarily behind a screen of oaks and bushes a hundred feet from the road. A hoarse voice hailed them anxiously from the coach box.

"Did you find her?" It was Moïse, the senior servant of the Cortot ménage.

"Yes, thank the Lord!" responded Armand. "She's a bit damp but will be good as new when she can change into something dry. How do the twins?"

"They're asleep," said a new voice. A leathern flap of the coach window was disturbed, but the face at the opening could not be seen. The petulant voice belonged to Rebekah, daughter of the Cortot cook, impressed for duty as Madeleine's maid. "Dry, did you say? Monsieur is indeed witty for so late at night! If only I could be dry again I wouldn't mind being hanged."

Rivulets of rainwater were running down the sagging spots in the leather roof, going inside as well as outside the coach. Armand and Mathieu lifted the dripping girl to the step of the carriage.

"Will you both be coming, too?" asked Madeleine, pausing a moment on the carriage step and pushing a wet strand of hair from her mouth.

"I'll be with you all the way to your cousin's place in Champagne," replied Armand. "I've been trying to convince Mathieu that he'd best come too, before all the world knows just where he's been tonight. I must mount now, mademoiselle," he said, stepping back, "and we must be on our way before every catchpoll* south of the Loire is on our scent." He disappeared in the darkness.

Mathieu had not released Madeleine's hand. He tried to see her face in the darkness. "I shall never forget your bravery, dear Mathieu," she said earnestly, "and the terrible risks you have taken tonight. I shall ever be in your debt."

"It was nothing," said Mathieu, clinging desperately to her hand. "I would like to come, of course, but I must remain in Saint Martin to allay suspicion. I do hope you understand. It would never do if we should disappear at the same time. But I have your promise to wait for me?"

"Yes, I'll wait for you, Mathieu, till the end of the world if necessary."

He kissed her hand while the relentless rain continued to soak them both. Almost he decided to go with her now—but to flee all across France?

---

* An exactor of taxes or other officer with power to arrest.

"We will go on with the wedding when this furor dies down, shall we not?"

"Yes, dear Mathieu," she said tenderly. "But do come soon!"

Armand rode up, ready to go. Moïse, aware of the scene at the carriage step, sounded worried, cold, and impatient.

"How long are we supposed to sit here and gargle rainwater?" he complained. Armand undoubtedly had the same question but forbore to ask it aloud.

"I cannot say how grateful I am, monsieur, for what you have done," said Madeleine. "The two of you have saved my life and I think my sanity, too."

"Our pleasure, mademoiselle," Armand returned politely. "I have been sufficiently rewarded already, but we must share your gratitude with your father and the good pastor. It would be most agreeable to remain here and converse with you both, but we are not yet safe, and there is a long way to go."

Armand turned to Mathieu. "Changed your mind about coming with us? No? Well then, *au revoir.*"

He swung his horse around. The animal was excited and hard to restrain.

"God grant you a safe journey, mademoiselle," said Mathieu. Taking her hand again, he kissed it fervently. "I will tell your parents you left in good courage."

"I pray He will protect you all at Saint Martin," she replied. "I fear what may happen when it is known I am missing. Be sure to tell my father that he and mother *must* leave Saint Martin—at once, you understand? I shall not be easy in my mind until I hear that they have gone."

"Yes, yes, I will."

"Tell them to forget the property. It makes so little difference really."

"Yes, my dear."

"You will come soon, too, won't you? We'll be waiting for you. Don't delay for anything."

The coach started with a jerk and vanished almost immediately in the gloom. Mathieu could hear it bumping and lurching along the edge of the brook as it headed for the highway.

With a heart as clammy with apprehension as his clothes were sodden with rain, he turned to mount his horse. He would ride back and forth till dawn. It would never do to rouse the guard at the gate at two o'clock in the morning.

* * * * *

For the next eight days the fugitives pushed relentlessly on through the foul weather, bouncing over rocky highways, slewing through mudholes, and fording swollen streams, always wet, never stopping longer than to change horses or, rarely, to eat or sleep. Madeleine and the twins stayed in the coach at most of the stops, and it was the cranky Rebekah who was sent on errands for her mistress. All the party were well worn down by the pace when they at last approached the borders of Champagne.

On that morning the sun broke through in a tentative manner and sent feeble rays through the branches of the forest aisles. Steam rose from the sodden ground, and rays of light played strange tricks with silhouettes of trees and bushes. Armand, dozing over his horse's neck, repeatedly thought he saw ghostly phantasms that turned out to be imaginary when he came closer. Emerging from a patch of woodland, he spied a stream rushing over a rocky bed. The sunshine was gaining in brilliance, and the boulders along the water's edge looked dry. The twins were restless; the maid increasingly sullen. Madeleine had not complained, but Armand thought she looked haggard. What with the downpour and the fear of pursuit, they had hardly exchanged a hundred words on the journey. Surely a halt would do them all good. Armand drew in his horse and hailed Moïse.

"It can't hurt to stop a few moments in this place. There's little likelihood of passersby, and it would be good to feel solid ground again. Let's catch our breath here in this pleasant spot."

The coachman brightened immediately and without a word drove the light vehicle off the tracks that passed for a road. He leaped to the ground, and in a few moments the horses were grazing, the twins were in the reeds throwing rocks into the stream, and the maid, perched on a boulder, was nagging them in her fretful way, though neither paid her any attention. Eyes closed, Moïse lay on the moss not far from the horses.

Madeleine reclined on a canvas from the coach, one arm propping up her head. Armand sat on his saddle blanket with his back to a tree, studying her profile as if trying to commit it to memory.

"It's good to see the sun again, mademoiselle," he said. "I feared it had gone out entirely!"

"I'm glad, too," she replied with a charming little laugh. "I find that the whole universe is not still shaking. In that wretched coach I feared I would curdle."

"I'm sorry for the discomfort," replied Armand, smiling. "Coaches are not the most comfortable way to travel, but I hope we have outdistanced the news of your escape."

"I keep thinking of the folks at Saint Martin," Madeleine said worriedly. "I hope they are safe. The papists will be furious!"

"It depends on the zeal of the authorities. I tried to persuade your father to leave. He will be a marked man—three children missing!"

"It wasn't entirely his fault," she said sadly. "I'm so glad to be out of that—that place, but it wouldn't be worth it if anyone suffers on my account."

"Don't worry about Mathieu," said Armand. "That gentleman has nothing to implicate him if he keeps his mouth shut."

Madeleine looked quickly at the soldier and studied his face for a moment.

"Now, don't be unfair to Mathieu. It is not his *forte* to take desperate chances." A touch of defiance entered her tone. "He is not a man of war, and these midnight goings must have been torture to him. I think he did admirably. Of course, monsieur," she added quickly, "I am most grateful to you. It was assuredly most generous of you to go to such trouble just to help a friend of your father. But Mathieu and I are betrothed. Perhaps you did not know?"

He smiled down at her. "Had you not been, I would have been astonished."

She stared at him, uncertain what to say. He studied his fingers.

"Monsieur Bertrand seemed surly, or perhaps I should say, unhappy, on my short acquaintance with him. Is he always thus?"

"Oh, no," she replied quickly. "He is most kind and considerate always. Of course he is naturally grave and dignified, though on occasion he sings very sweetly when I accompany him on the clavecin."

"It is my unlucky star again. I have missed this treat."

Her glance was definitely suspicious this time. "Well, monsieur, I have noticed this manner you speak of, but it is only lately that he has been thus. You are not to conclude that this is his true nature. If you knew him better, you would understand and pity, not ridicule."

He made a gesture of protest and tried to speak, but she would not let him. "Since his college was closed and he couldn't finish his studies, he's been melancholy. Then just this year they closed the little church school, too. Don't you think his melancholy is forgivable?"

Armand shrugged his shoulders. He regretted he had brought up the subject. They remained silent for a time. Madeleine nibbled a grass blade absently.

"He really should have come with us," she said finally. "He needs a new start. I know I could help him—he's so devoted to me." She looked at Armand pleadingly. "He'll be coming after us soon, don't you think? One who has suffered so many disappointments needs sympathy and understanding. Have your plans never gone awry?"

Armand raised one eyebrow and affected a continued interest in his fingers. "Now and again, but some people are not in nearly as desperate a plight as they imagine themselves."

She colored and changed the subject.

"Now, what of you, monsieur? Will this affair not injure your prospects?"

"Oh, I doubt I'm in any danger." He shrugged again. "No one knew I was in Saint Martin, save our friends. I'm on leave from the regiment and just happened to be passing through town when the kidnappings took place."

He found himself telling her of his visit at Versailles. Flattered by her rapt attention, he was encouraged to go on and describe the palace and its ceremonial in detail.

"You can imagine how these prospects affected me," he continued. "My father left me little but a good name and perhaps a parsimonious nature. I grew up with our peasant children in the duck pond by our chateau. 'Chateau' did I say? That tumbledown relic of the last century, moldering, collapsed chambers, dingy tapestries, and rushes on the floors? It was a hopeless grind to be of the country *noblesse.* My pedigree is as long as any duke's, but my mother salted her own pork and kept her own accounts. She had one fine gown—a brocade inherited from her grandmother. We wore homespun like the peasants, and I grew up on sodden meat and soup. I had a tutor for a while, but we saw little money, and what there was kept losing its value. When my mother died, my father and I gave up in despair and went back to soldiering.

"Surely, I could repair to my estate, or what's left of it after ten years under a rascally bailiff, and I could stay home and wear my tattered serge to market and proudly advertise my gentility by carrying my sword as I peddle my turnips. Or I could go off to the wars and hope for advancement."

His tone was becoming bitter.

"Advancements? Precious little these days without a patron or royal favor. All the country nobles flock to Versailles and compete for secretaryships and commissions from the royal bounty. But I told myself I'd starve before I would beg! To live around a barracks is a boring life, and one can hardly exist on the pay and stay honest. But I've tried. At least it was better than that dreary farm. Now the kindness of the duke has changed it all, and I haven't had to sell myself to do it."

Armand became aware that he had been talking a good deal and stopped abruptly. Madeleine seemed much impressed and gazed at him for a long time. He detected doubt in her eyes nevertheless, and he bridled uneasily.

"Well," he said, "I did not mean to deafen you with my complaints, but what are you thinking?"

"I don't know," she replied thoughtfully, still staring at him as if seeing him for the first time. "Really, monsieur, it would be impertinence for me to advise you."

His feeling of discomfort grew, and when he met her eyes, he dropped his. She seemed to see right through him—to read his doubts despite how carefully he had tried to hide them.

"As a client of the duke, with rank and income assured," he said defiantly, "I could be of far greater service to the brethren than as an obscure officer without hope of advancement."

"What will be the good of this for yourself?" Her voice was low. Again he tried meeting her eyes, but the collision with their violet glow gave him an almost physical jolt. He wished above all things to seem unconcerned right now, but he felt flustered by her question.

"You must forgive me, monsieur," she persisted, "for presuming to speak a little plainly. Perhaps it is due to *my* pedigree that I don't know any better. It would be wonderful for you to have these well-deserved rewards and be able to help the brethren, too; to put behind you all the vexations you speak of, yet . . ." She hesitated, looked at him pleadingly, and summoned up more courage. "Yes, monsieur, I—I cannot but tremble for your soul in such a place as Versailles."

"Mademoiselle, I have tried to explain . . ."

Her level glance was still difficult to meet. He turned quickly to see what the children might be doing. They had stopped throwing rocks and were examining some creature they had scooped from the water.

"I suppose," said Madeleine as she sat up and stretched gracefully, "that with all this good fortune will come a consort? What are the ladies like, there at Versailles?"

"Nothing has been said about that," Armand returned, staring into the leafy branches over his head. "In truth, the ladies of the court are nothing special except in their wardrobes and their headdresses. Even the king abominates their headgear, which creeps higher each year; but, I'm told, he can't do anything about it." He thought of the little blonde at the *appartement* but decided this was not the time to mention her. He hastened on. "I recall when I was a youngster that we could tell who we'd marry. You go to a pigsty on Saint Andrew's Eve and knock on the gate. If the sow grunts first, you'll marry a widow; if it's one of the piglets first, then it'll be a maid!"

"And is this the fashion at Versailles?"

"Truly some of the sleeping quarters are but sties, and if you'd seen some of the sights I saw, you'd vow that the sows are there, too. I've not tried my luck."

He started to rise but remained on his knees beside her.

"Let's not be concerned about the harpies at court trapping me. Rather, let's see to it that I dance at *your* wedding. We ought to reach your cousin's place by nightfall, and then you'd best start writing urgent letters to that lethargic gallant of the blond locks.

"You might wait too long, you know," he added wistfully. "I'll give you my address should there be need for more traveling. The regiment is stationed in Flanders now, but in May I am on detached duty to the cavalry encampment on the Saar—three thousand men under St. Ruth—for which I am glad. Most of the infantry find themselves on the Eure, landscape-gardening for the palace. The royal waterworks, you know. I'll be in Flanders again afterward. You have but to call me and I am at your command—if only to dance at this wedding!"

"No," she said firmly, shaking her head, "you have done quite enough. You are most gallant and thoughtless of yourself to offer such service to one who can mean nothing to you. It would not be right to endanger you a second time."

"I wish . . ." Armand said suddenly. "Wouldn't you like to come to Versailles for a visit? I could show you much the like of which you could see nowhere else on earth."

"It would be marvelous, monsieur, but hardly wise—for either of us."

With a sigh he rose to get the horses.

"You are certainly a chivalrous hero," he told himself, "to do so much out of filial piety. Would you have done as much if she had been homely? The witch of Endor rather than a damsel out of the Song of Songs?"

He untied his horse and poked Moïse into wakefulness with unnecessary vigor. Soon they resumed their journey.

CHAPTER 4

Catholic or Dead!

The bare walls of Saint Martin's town hall were decorated with a few faded tapestries, portraits of former magistrates in heavy ruffs, and a copper plate inscribed with the municipal privileges. Above the dais at the end of the hall was a painting on wood of the city arms, surmounted by a large crucifix. The table on the dais was draped with green, and chairs embroidered with the city arms were ranged in front of it in a row. Over all was a pale light that seeped through dirty windows high up the walls. And standing uneasily in the stuffy chamber, the two hundred patriarchs of Saint Martin's Huguenot families awaited the moment they had dreaded for nearly five years. Only the occasional shuffling of feet or clearing of throats broke the oppressive silence.

Outside, the red roofs and the merchants' signs sparkled in brilliant sunshine. The August sky was bright and blue, but no Protestant faces reflected the brightness. In their sober best, they had come in answer to a summons by the town crier. Before he could beat his drum and bray his message in more than a couple of the town squares, every household had heard the news: They must be at the Hotel de Ville at nine o'clock. The intendant would be there to demand of the adherents of the PRR, the Pretended Reformed Religion, that they renounce their faith at once, all together, or face the consequences. The consequences had become well known in many French communities since the day in 1681 when Intendant Marillac over in Poitou discovered that quartering dragoons in Huguenot houses was the quickest way to bring wholesale conversions. Now Saint Martin might have its turn at the *dragonnades*.*

The crier did not mention that several squadrons of the Queen's Regiment of dragoons rode within hours of the town. He did not have to specify such details—the birds of the air told of the matter. And they mentioned that six companies of the Touraine infantry were en route also, though it would take the foot soldiers longer to arrive. The French army, it was well known, was not recruited among the good angels.

In contrast to the drawn faces and drab garb of the Huguenot burghers was a smaller group, composed mainly of the intendant's staff and the churchmen, standing by the main door. They affected to ignore the unhappy audience. Resplendent in ribbons and laces, dress swords at their sides, the young aides exchanged gossip of Paris and the court, laughing and simpering among themselves as they preened their gaudy plumage.

The bishop arrived, tall, pale, aristocratic, with prominent black bows and graying temples. His iridescent reds and purples contrasted with the brown of the obsequious knot of missionaries in his wake. The scene was an old one for them, for they traveled ahead of the dragoons and performed the baptisms that welcomed the heretics back to the bosom of the Mother Church. Whether this took place before or after the ministrations of the soldiery mattered little to them. They had come to help the local priests with the extra business. Father Chabert, exhilarated by the prospects, chattered happily with the clerics and fawned upon the bishop.

At nine the bell in the tower rang the opening of the assembly, and before the dull throb had died away, the intendant made his entrance and ascended the low platform. The tall, thin mayor, twisting his chain of office nervously, entered next. The councilmen draped in their robes of blue and violet with gold chains of office about their necks, followed

---

* Persecution by dragoons.

at a slower pace. They looked uneasy, though no avowed heretics had served in the city government for some time.

The intendant, a barrel in tight yellow silk and a tremendously full chestnut wig, carried a long, silver-tipped staff in his hand. His aides and the military officers ranged themselves behind him. He stared arrogantly about the room, his square face red with heat and suppressed emotion. Several uniformed noncommissioned officers of the intendant's escort filed in last and took stations by the doors, staring insolently at the Huguenots and spraying the adjacent floor and civilians with brown streams of tobacco juice.

After a tense moment of silence, the mayor gave a slight nod to the *sergeant de ville,* splendid in a colorful costume embroidered with the arms of the town. He rapped for order and in a quavering falsetto declared the meeting open. Then he scuttled back to safety. The mayor produced a parchment of welcome and stumbled through the loyal banalities under the contemptuous blue eyes of the intendant. The aides continued their conversation in only slightly lower tones. The clergy listened with polite condescension, but the soldiers, plainly bored, shuffled their booted feet and clanked their accouterments.

The mayor finished at last and stepped back awkwardly, almost tripping on the hem of his robe. The town council instantly retreated a step. The intendant inclined his massive head in acknowledgment of the mayor's concluding bow. Then he began to speak. He mentioned a *lettre de cachet** he held from the king for his "dear and well-beloved subjects" in Saint Martin. He suggested strongly that His Majesty was offended by the misuse of the civic freedoms permitted in the municipality and on that ominous note called on the bishop to address the assembly.

The bishop, reputed to be one of the better court preachers, discoursed for some time on the love of the king and the church for their erring children. His melodious, beautifully modulated voice swelled soothingly, almost hypnotically, as he invited the heretics to humble themselves, to put behind them the error that enchained them, and to

* Sealed letter, usually authorizing legal procedures.

return to the fold. Then it would be well for them in this life, and it would certainly improve their chances in the life to come.

No one, he pointed out, could reasonably expect a liberty of conscience that authorized equally a lie and the truth. Was it not effrontery to claim an equality for their false religion with that of Jesus Christ, which was sacred and holy? It was lonely and cold outside the church, he reminded them. Dawn had come, dispelling the mists of error. Many of them might actually be grateful for the visit of the dragoons and missionaries, for it would enable them to be converted and yet save face. Of course, the church deplored anything smacking of violence and hoped those assembled would recognize the spirit of love in which this invitation was extended to them.

The intendant then resumed in a different vein. In harshest tones he assured his hearers that impudent heretics who too long abused the king's graciousness were traitors to God and could hardly, therefore, be loyal to their king. If they withstood their sovereign's order and stubbornly resisted the Holy Ghost, His Majesty would consider himself discharged from any responsibility for the pains and calamities that might befall them. Those who were reasonable would be exempt from billeting for two years, and he would not permit the intractable to intimidate the wise and prudent.

Sweeping the crowd with a glance that defied anyone to answer, he turned his back pointedly on his victims and stepped to the largest chair on the dais. There he slouched as on a throne, his legs crossed insolently.

A thundering silence followed. Even the aides stopped talking and gazed at the Huguenots. Each heretic could, no doubt, hear the pounding of his own heart. All remained numb. To his credit, the mayor was the first to recover.

"If your excellency would perhaps allow a little time for consideration, a little time for these gentlemen to discuss—"

The intendant's face crimsoned alarmingly. The veins in his forehead stood out, and the tips of his moustache quivered. He struck his fist on the arm of the chair and curled the mayor up with a single tremendous snort. "These rascals have had twenty-five years to consider and discuss!" He leaned forward as if he might bite the unhappy mayor. "Do they think His Majesty's patience is inexhaustible?"

No one spoke.

"Enough of this trifling!" he roared. "His Majesty is not interested in seeing who can be the last one to abjure!"

Still no sound.

"Conversion today or troops tomorrow," remarked an officer softly but distinctly.

"Speak up, confound you!"

There was a rustling, a stirring in the Huguenot ranks. Cortot was aware of many eyes on him. Since the transfer of the pastor, he was the moral leader as well as the head elder. It was a crucial moment. The wrong word, the reading of assent in a brother's eye, and the whole group might collapse in a panic. It had happened elsewhere. Cortot knew that many were in agony of indecision. Each would have to make his own decision eventually, but Cortot was determined that the Lord must not be dishonored by mass cowardice. With an unspoken prayer for the right words but with death in his heart, he replied in a firm voice.

"Our property, our bodies, yes, our lives belong to the king, and reserving but our consciences, which concern only God, everything we have is devoted to His Majesty's service."

The moment of wavering passed. The Huguenots straightened almost perceptibly and looked boldly at their tormentors.

"I've heard a lot of fine words lately," sneered the intendant when he could trust himself to speak. "We have ways of dealing with such insolence. Has anyone else anything to say?"

The group remained silent. Nothing else needed to be said. One of the soldiers by the door laughed nastily.

The intendant rose and without a further glance at the recalcitrants, strode out of the room, followed by his retinue. The Huguenots dispersed with scarcely a word, each man alone with his own forebodings. As was the custom, a tolling of the bell ended the assembly. What had in other times seemed a comforting sound now rang brazen and ominous in their ears.

* * * * *

The Cortot household prepared for the onslaught like a fortress expecting a final assault. Isaac Cortot made his dispositions calmly, in the knowledge that most of his precautions would be useless. The better silver and a few keepsakes he buried in several spots in the garden. Not much could be hidden or the house would appear suspiciously bare. The family laid in quantities of fresh and preserved meats and lined up baskets of vegetables by the cellar door. Many unwelcome guests would come for dinner. Cortot summoned the servants into the parlor and began counting out silver pieces from a small iron coffer he had taken from its hiding place behind the books.

"There is no reason for you to remain here for this unpleasantness," he said matter-of-factly. "You have been good servants, and it would be no reward for your faithfulness to keep you here. I'm going to give you your wages for the next month, and then you had better be off before the callers arrive."

There were five of them. They stood silent and stricken. Moïse, majordomo and sometime coachman, recovered first.

"Nay, Master Cortot. That would be a fine thing to do, to run off and leave you and madame with these fiends from hell. Anyway, where would we go?" He shrugged eloquently.

"Moïse is right," said Sara, the cook. "There is no safety anywhere, and the Lord can protect us as well here as hiding in a ditch."

"I am grateful, my friends," said Cortot with tears in his eyes; "but I beseech you to think of yourselves and leave while there is yet time."

After a brief argument, the stable boy and two maids decided to risk trying to leave town. Moïse and Sara refused even to consider the idea. Even if one could get past the guards at the gate, the countryside would be swarming with peasants looking for fugitives.

The hot August afternoon wore on. The town seemed abnormally quiet. The four remaining in the Cortot house spent much of the time on their knees. Sometimes they just sat together in the parlor taking comfort from each other's presence. They said little. Monsieur and madame both felt thankful that none of their children would have to go through the experience. If they had regrets that they had not fled sooner, no one spoke of them aloud.

From time to time, Cortot read certain of the psalms for their encouragement. He had read two verses of Psalm 130 when they became aware of a barely audible humming or buzzing sound, like a swarm of bees in a warm noontide. As it grew louder, it resolved itself into a murmur of many voices, punctuated with shouts and the scuffing of many feet. Hesitating a moment, Cortot resumed his reading from verses 3–8 with only a slight tremor in his voice: " 'If thou, LORD, shouldest mark iniquities, O Lord, who shall stand? But there is forgiveness with thee, that thou mayest be feared. I wait for the LORD, my soul doth wait, and in his word do I hope—' "

A splintering crash came from not far down the street. They looked at each other ashen-faced.

" 'My soul waiteth for the Lord more than they that watch for the morning: I say, more than they that watch for the morning. Let Israel hope in the LORD: for with the Lord there is mercy, and with him is plenteous redemption. And he shall redeem Israel from all his iniquities.' "

Now the tramping and the shouting came nearer. The dragoons, followed by a good representation of the town rabble, were chanting discordantly, "Catholic or dead! Catholic or dead!" A heavy and continuous pounding began at the door.

Madame Cortot sat with her eyes closed and her hands folded in her lap, lips moving. "Remember," her husband admonished, " 'It is the LORD: let him do what seemeth him good' " (1 Samuel 3:18). Then he leaped to open the door before it could be battered in.

He flung the door open and was almost struck by the butt of a pistol with which a villainous-looking dragoon had been hammering on the door. At the side of the trooper stood an officer in a red coat. He had a paper in his hand.

"Cortot?"

"Yes, monsieur."

"You are required to provide billets for me and twelve dragoons with provision for our horses until further notice. His Majesty's command.

You are to provide daily expenses for me of fifteen *livres,* three *livres* each for my men. I require a bed, three chairs, a chest of drawers, commode, and a bed for my valet, according to the regulations approved by the minister of war."

The officer strode in, bouncing Cortot to one side. An orderly, with a small monkey on his shoulder that belonged to the officer, followed. A light brass chain ran from the monkey's collar to the soldier's belt.

In seconds, it seemed, the house filled with horsemen, who stamped about from attic to cellar in their heavy boots. At the back door, the family dog was shot dead before he could get to his feet. The cat departed in a flash of gray, dodging several pistol balls.

The intruders set to work at once, smashing open cabinets and desks in search for valuables. They wasted no time in asking for keys before even seeing whether such were needed.

The officer, a captain, established himself in the library and requisitioned the chief bedroom as his own. He immediately ordered dinner. The common soldiers made themselves at home in the other rooms according to their peculiar humors. They were hungry too, and though a number of them seemed fairly well exhilarated already, they suffered from a raging thirst. Discovery of the wine cellar followed in due course. The trembling cook worked as fast as she could, assisted by blows and oaths, while Moïse and Cortot were set to work watering the horses for the visitors. Madame Cortot, a huddled brown figure in a state of near collapse, was ignored by the intruders except for an occasional rude remark.

The troopers had brought only fourteen mounts, the officer having two, but the way they shoveled Cortot's feed and hay about the stable yard and into the mud, one would have thought they were providing for an entire squadron. One sentimental drunk decided his animal was too good for the stable and with difficulty got it into the parlor, where it plunged about in fright, with sad results for the furnishings.

Awaiting dinner, several soldiers engaged in target practice in the parlor. Soon the room was filled with a haze of gunpowder and the floor littered with bric-a-brac and glass. Cortot, passing a bedroom door, happened to see a solitary cavalryman, hat in hand, his thin face tight with concentration, slashing the bed hangings into ribbons of equal width with his sword. In the room where the children had kept their toys, the floor was covered with headless dolls, trampled lead soldiers, and smashed carts. A small drum, perhaps considered contraband, lay by the door, completely stove in, and the remains of Alexandre's violin lay scattered near his bed. At least that's one loss the boy would be able to bear with courage, thought his father.

In spite of terror and bruises, the cook produced an enormous dinner, much of which the guests deliberately wasted. Their hilarity and violence seemed to increase by the hour. The house rang with oaths in three languages, the smashing of crockery, and the splintering of the lighter furniture.

In the street outside, a gang of loafers assembled, for the looting of the Cortot mansion promised more entertainment than usual. Of course the soldiery would not allow the civilian riffraff to infringe upon their prerogatives, but the mob waited, assured that the cavalry would put on a good performance.

Cortot had to help move his furniture, bedding, and clothing into the street. His horses were brought out from the stables. Crying, "We'll beat your old pewter for you!" a trooper flung an armload into the gutter. An impromptu auction got under way amid much horseplay and clowning. Expensive iron chests, mattresses, and kitchenware were knocked down for pennies, while passing members of the missionary order beamed benevolently on the fun. The big black wooden chest with the experiences of the children of Israel carved on it, a family heirloom for four generations, went for three or four *livres.* Cortot felt like weeping.

The evening ended at last. Except for the chamber where the officer lay, scarcely an undamaged stick of furniture remained in the house. The master, mistress, and two servants took refuge in some of the scattered hay in the stable, for the cavalry mounts had better manners than their masters. Though weary beyond description, Cortot could not sleep, but lay in the straw looking at his house dark in the pale moonlight. It seemed to be staring blindly from black, eyeless sockets. The door stood ajar, and window frames and panes were smashed. The cellar, he knew, was awash. From within could be heard heavy breathing, snores, and mutterings of the dragoons as they slept off the fatigue of a pleasant evening's work. Food, wine, and filth littered the floors, and some of the guests were sprawled on the planks, oblivious to everything, including their own discomfort. It was poor consolation to recall that normally the men would have been hanged for such conduct.

Cortot suspected that worse would be coming in the morning, for if destruction did not bring him around, tortures would soon follow— restricted only by the king's limitation that none of the heretics were to be actually killed. Soldiers were known, however, to miscalculate how much of the softening process a feeble frame might be able to stand. Though several of the missionaries had looked in on his house during the afternoon, they had made no effort yet to engage him in disputation. With them was Father Chabert, who appeared to be in the seventh heaven of delight. Vengeance might be the Lord's, but His self-appointed servants found it sweet indeed to participate. While Cortot pondered these matters, Sara called to him in a low voice. In alarm he crawled over to where his wife lay, an indistinct bundle in the hay.

"Monsieur," the cook whispered with a note of panic in her voice, "listen to madame breathe! It's not right. I can't wake her. Do you suppose it's an apoplexy?"

Cortot had to agree she looked ghastly; something was terribly wrong. He had feared something like this. He tried to remember what he had heard of brain fevers. "We must get her away from here before *they* wake up," he whispered hoarsely, an icy hand clutching his heart. "This ruination has been too much for her."

"There's no place to go," whispered Moïse, who had come up silently. "All our people are in the same fix."

In his mind Cortot ran up and down the street. The most hopeful prospect might be the Delarge sisters. They were maiden Catholic ladies at the end of the street, always good friends; but it would be asking much to shelter a Huguenot woman with these devils loose. There was no use taking her to any Protestant house, and they could not get her out of the city. He, at least, had better be here in the morning to make explanations for Mathilde. If she was dying, he knew the priests would keep him away from the bedside, but she could hardly be in a worse situation than she was lying here. If the Catholic ladies had sufficient courage to take her in, they would still have to report her, but so would any doctor or apothecary he might summon.

Cortot made his decision quickly. With a word to the others, he slipped out and down the alley to make his appeal. He decided as he warily crept from shadow to shadow in the deserted street that he would die before he would beg for help. But if he could find any help for his dear Mathilde, pride no longer mattered.

* * * * *

While Cortot was assisting Sara with the debris after the morning meal, he was approached by a surly dragoon, who ordered him to report at once to the officer. Wiping his hands hastily on his breeches, the Huguenot hurried to the library.

For several moments the great man studiously ignored him. He pretended to be wrapped up in lighting his pipe, a long churchwarden, using for a spill a page out of one of Cortot's devotional books. The officer had a handsome, aristocratic face and was evidently of gentle breeding; but his mouth was thin and cruel, and the eyes as sympathetic as stones. His monkey sat on his shoulder, shrilling jungle talk and crumbling a biscuit on the floor. The officer was at his unbuttoned ease, though he wore his spurs this early in the morning, as the scars on the tabletop bore witness. He wore a ruffled white shirt and blue breeches. A magnificent red coat with huge blue cuffs and silver buttons was draped over a candelabra. On the table lay his white *jabot* and his red stocking cap with blue trim and long white tassel.

Eventually, he deigned to notice his host. "We are not swineherds, my good man," he drawled softly, "and we do not wish to eat like swine. Kindly convey my compliments to your cook and inform her that if she serves us any more of this refuse, I shall have her basted before her own fire, and you too, for good measure. At first I thought it was a plot to poison us, but now I am inclined to credit it to provincial cooking. Now, pay attention while I place my order for dinner. I am in no mood to sample the delicacies of the region—these mashed chestnuts and such fare." He shuddered delicately.

For a long moment the captain sat and thought as Cortot stood silently.

"Let us see this time that the table is properly set," began the officer, shaking the ashes of his pipe onto the carpet. "Bread and knives to the left, napkins to the right. Then let us start with a soup, let us say a *potage** of finely hashed chicken, distilled with barley, dried roses, and cinnamon. There will naturally be hot and cold *entremets*,[†] which, trusting soul that I am, I will leave to you. As for the entrée, I can't really decide between a suckling pig, or should it be spiced duck, or perhaps pheasant, or maybe partridge in cabbage?" He paused to think the problem through. "Well, then let's have them all. It will be less trouble to decide. Serve the roast with oranges, naturally, and I prefer my sauces flavored with rose water. There will be fruits in season, hors d'oeuvres—shall we say roast beef spread with kidneys, onions, and cheese—and desserts—a good variety to choose from."

Cortot continued to stand there for a time, silently awaiting dismissal. He was trying desperately to remember all that he had been told. The officer suddenly looked at him as if seeing him for the first time.

"You know, of course, that I have eight more men coming here shortly. Several of your more intelligent *confreres*[§] have already seen the light. The dull ones like you will have the honor of more and more of my splendid fellows until you also achieve wisdom."

"May I ask you, monsieur," said Cortot with a sudden boldness, "do you not think it sacrilege that we are asked to abjure and accept the solemn mysteries of your religion without sincere belief?"

The soldier jumped as if stabbed. He bared his teeth in a snarl.

"If I heard you correctly, you heretic pig," said he in his softly menacing way, "you have a truly imperishable crust. It sounded like you were questioning the will of His Christian Majesty. I hope that I have misunderstood you, for otherwise I should feel an obligation to run you

---

* A thick soup.
† Side dishes.
§ Comrades.

through. Pray do not bother your pretty head about such matters. If the king wishes us to convert you to Islam, we will do so. In fact, we shall labor with you folk until the sight of a single horseman will send you running to abjure. We have all the time in the world; we'll work with you until you comprehend."

"With God's help, *that* I shall never do," said Cortot firmly but respectfully.

"You have a pretty good opinion of yourself," sneered the captain.

The conversation languished. The house was not exactly silent, however, for from the other rooms could be heard loud argument and a scattering of pistol shots. Suddenly the house trembled. Two quarreling troopers were rolling down the stairs locked in each other's arms. The officer blinked and raised his eyebrows.

"Are you still here, civilian? Your presence is making me unwell. Be so good as to remove yourself at once and carry out my orders exactly and immediately. None of your stringy merchant's tricks! I know you take me for a kindly sort, foolishly indulgent and easily imposed upon, but I warn you, don't trifle with my natural good nature!"

Accompanied by a bleary-eyed trooper whose slight stock of French words had a strong Westphalian overlay, Cortot set off for the market. His escort unsheathed a saber, but Cortot knew better than to try to run away. He was sweating profusely, and not entirely because of the warm morning.

Cortot made his rounds with the shaggy and unclean shadow unpleasantly close behind. In some shops he was grossly overcharged by proprietors who leered at him knowingly; others gave him frightened looks of sympathy. A baker impulsively thrust several extra loaves upon him with a wordless grimace of understanding.

Soldiers, both horse and foot, filled the streets of Saint Martin. Sometimes they were shepherding miserable civilians to the church at sword point. Many of these Cortot recognized as friends and neighbors. Most were the worse for wear. As the saying went, "Twenty-four hours from torture to communion." A bedraggled Petitjean trotted by unseeing, with a pitchfork at his backsides and once again an apostate. The brethren were crumbling, Cortot noticed with a sick feeling in his stomach, but he could not find it in his heart to blame them; there was nothing like a long summer evening with the dragoons. Eventually, after all had been ruined or devoured, the soldiery would move on to fresh victims. The bishop and his assistants must be very busy.

Cortot wished that some outstanding phenomenon might occur to mark nature's outrage at this treatment of God's faithful people, but the sky was clear and beautiful. "I must be steadfast," he told himself. "No matter what man may do to the body, the soul is to be saved. I shall be reunited with my children in the next world if not in this one. We are not tempted above that we are able to bear," he reassured himself.

His meditations continued. The children must wing to a foreign land. Mathieu had gone south with his uncle, but surely at the first chance he would be going to Madeleine and the twins. Madeleine would be almost penniless now, but that would make no difference to a splendid fellow like Mathieu. He thought also of Armand and was grateful he had escaped from Saint Martin. He would probably have got himself shot, and to no purpose. He recalled the young man's tales of his prospects at Versailles and breathed a prayer that the soldier would prove worthy of his Huguenot father and not succumb to the snares of the world.

The trooper and his victim passed the Delarge house. Cortot stopped suddenly. The dragoon pricked him brutally in the back with the point of his saber and drew back his foot for a hearty kick. Cortot hastily dropped his bundles in the street and emptied his pockets. The soldier greedily accepted the handful of copper and silver.

At Cortot's knock, one of the sisters timidly peered through a little crack and opened the door a full six inches when she saw who it was.

"Oh, monsieur," she cried and burst into tears. The fear Cortot had been resolutely pushing out of his mind all morning suddenly leaped to the fore.

"Please, madame," he begged in a strangled voice, "I have so little time. Control yourself, I pray you. Is she—how is Mathilde?"

The Catholic woman made an effort, wiping her face with her apron. Then, glancing fearfully over her shoulder, she spoke rapidly, hardly above a whisper. "We've done everything we can, but she's very poor.

She breathes harshly, and all the signs are bad. The doctor has been here, and she has been bled and purged. We have shut the room up tight so no air can get in, but he shakes his head. The apothecary has been called, and he has chopped up two puppies and they are on the boil with the other ingredients for apoplexy, but they must seethe for twelve hours and—I fear she won't last that long, monsieur. And I can't let you in. You know it's strictly forbidden. The friars came; the doctor told them. Please don't blame him, monsieur. You know the law about sick heretics, and they are with her now, but she has been unconscious all the time."

"I thank you, Madame Delarge, and your sister, for your great kindness. Heaven will reward you. I will go. I want to cause no more trouble for you."

The trooper was nowhere in sight, and the stricken husband went on to his house without him. It was an impossible thought to accept, but he knew that he would probably never see Mathilde again. He knew what the law prescribed for the bodies of dead heretics and tried not to think of that either. "If she must go," he prayed, "Lord, let her go without regaining her senses." The missionaries would be waiting to hound the dying woman to abjure her religion to save her immortal soul. He stumbled up to his back door, his heart a leaden lump in his chest. The soldier was still missing—probably drinking up the *pourboire** in the nearest cabaret.

The gray kitten approached timidly and rubbed against his calf. "Did you come back?" Cortot muttered as he fumbled with the door. "Leave while you can, poor beast. You'd best abjure, Protestant kitty, and learn to meow to St. Gertrude. She's the patron saint of cats, they tell me."

He stopped. "I must be out of my head. I'd best pull my wits together; it bids fair to be a grim day."

---

* Tip.

CHAPTER 5

Difficult Decisions

"In my opinion, the 'Fence' will soon be down," said the white-haired man with the harsh voice. "The preparations are about complete I'm told."

Jean Claude, once called by Louis XIV "the best preacher in my kingdom," wiped his mouth with his napkin. It was Sunday in October 1685, at Charenton, the nearest Huguenot church permitted to Parisians. The Arbaleste Inn was filled with the clatter of crockery and a mannerly hum of voices as the faithful consumed the noon meal between services at their largest temple.

Pastor Claude was an unprepossessing man, neither brilliant nor dramatic in manner. But his skill and vigor in debate had made him the best-known Huguenot minister. Ever since his collision with the redoubtable Bishop Bossuet, he had typified the defense of the Religion better than either of the *Ruvignys*.* Now he sat in a large chair with his fingertips together, frowning over his spectacles. His plate lay empty save for a neat pile of bones. His table companions, preachers save for the two, were dispatching the last morsels from the nine or ten platters before them. Most diners in the room were also subdued in color of clothing and in manner.

Pastor Jean Merson leaned forward with his elbows resting on the

---

* Official Protestant commissioners at the court.

table. "Do you suppose I will have time to return to the south ere it happens?"

"It would be something of a risk," replied Claude in his judicious manner. "It's no secret that the Chancellor Le Tellier is failing rapidly and is using every argument to compass our undoing before he leaves this world. Louvois, as a dutiful son, and Madame de Maintenon are also said to be working with him for an end to the edict."

"No one can claim it is a surprise," sighed a cadaverous minister from Picardy. "The 'Fence' has had missing planks for a generation, and they pull out more each year." He pushed his plate away gloomily.

Claude nodded grimly. "If a revocation is coupled with measures to muzzle the ministry, then our public work in France is finished."

Armand de Gandon, in civilian clothes, silently nursed a glass of lemonade and followed the speakers with his eyes. Except for an elderly deacon, he was the only lay person at the table and felt tongue-tied in the presence of so much gravity. Pastor Merson had spied Armand as he entered the inn and had insisted that he join the ministers at their table.

"You are recently from the south, Brother Merson." Claude turned to the slender figure on his left. "There have been strange tales out of Nimes, my old church. Are they true?"

"I know not what you heard, but the news is bad," replied Armand's friend, shaking his head. "Pastor Cheiron preached a vigorous appeal to stand fast, and the congregation protested its determination with groanings. Yet when the soldiery appeared a few days later, the collapse was general; and though I regret to have to say it, the pastor abjured with most of his flock. It is said that after Bâville threatened them of Montpellier, eight thousand bowed the knee to Baal."

The other ministers looked stunned. "The end of all things is truly near," whispered one.

"It is the falling away foretold for the last days," agreed another.

Armand spoke timidly. "The king has sent Bourdaloue, his best court preacher, to exhort the new converts at Montpellier. The king has said that his own courtiers wouldn't mind mediocre sermons but that the heretics expected well-presented sermons with good doctrine."

"A dragoon makes a better apostle than the best court preacher," said Merson.

"We teeter on the edge of a precipice," said Claude. "It has been months since we have been able to deliver any sort of protest to the king, and the old commissioner has been told plainly that no more of our addresses will be received. The bishops who surround the throne denounce the edict day and night. The Bishop of Albi said—and I think I quote him correctly—that it is 'the most cursed edict imaginable by which liberty of conscience was allowed to each and all; the worst thing in the world.' Of course Pope Clement VIII said this eighty years ago."

The deacon, a little man with a watery blue eye, shook his head. "I'm sorry to have lived to see this day," he quavered. "I remember when I was a boy, back in 1621, when the first Charenton church burned. What a calamity we thought that was, and like the elders of Israel, I always held our present building to be inferior to the old one. But how precious this one seems now!"

"God defend us!" said one of the others.

"Amen," agreed another.

"We live in the fearfulest age Christians have ever seen," another pastor said sententiously.

"Would you counsel one to stay for the afternoon service who must be in Paris tonight?" Merson inquired. "I am told it is not wise for those of the Religion to be out together after dark these days."

Claude, who was eating chunks of cheese off the point of his knife, took his time answering. He looked to see where the waiters were and lowered his voice.

"I do not know that we shall ever worship here again after today, brethren. The hour is even later than we think. We are privily warned that next Sunday the congregation will be filled with worshipers ostensibly one with us, but it is plotted that royal officials will appear and urge us to join peaceably with the king's religion—whereupon these interlopers will set up a cry of 'reunion' hoping that we may lose our heads and embrace the papistical confession *en bloc*. If we determine this is indeed afoot, it would be better to close the church today than to have the last service marred in such fashion."

106

He turned to Pastor Merson. "Do not be overly concerned about the police. La Reynie has arrested a few in Paris, and he keeps several of us in the Bastille at a given moment to prove he is properly zealous. But he is first a policeman and no fanatic. Let us all remain for the Communion this afternoon."

After the murmur of assent, one diner arose, made his reverence, and replaced his hat. "It is about time for the first bell," he said. "Would you excuse me? I should like to stop by the bookstore." The others rose, bowing and shaking hands.

As the men passed out of the inn door into the sunshine, beggars clustered around seeking alms. "They'll have changed their tune by next week," remarked Armand to Pastor Merson. "Likely, they'll be crying in the name of Our Lady by then."

The old deacon tugged at Armand's sleeve. "Do you return to Paris tonight, brother?"

Armand nodded.

"Then might I impose upon your good nature and ride with you? What Pastor Claude says of the police may all be very well, but I have seen too much of late to feel bold." Armand's size and armament were comforting.

"I would be honored by your company, brother," said Armand politely. "I have been to Paris several times, but I am ashamed to say this is the first time I have worshiped at Charenton. You can show me the best route to the city."

"Then let us meet at the outside gate after the last service," replied the deacon with evident relief. "We should be able to reach the barrier by closing time." He bobbed a quick bow and hurried up the avenue.

Pastor Merson waited until the deacon had gone and then guided Armand to one side of the stream of worshipers moving up the wide paved street to the temple. They turned off on a path leading to the cemetery of the nobility.

"Well met, Brother Armand," said the pastor. "You are in health?"

"Yes, thank you, pastor," said Armand. "It was a pleasant surprise to meet you here. Have you any particular news of the south—of Saint

Martin? I know nothing except that the dragonnades reached there two months ago."

"It is not a pretty story." The older man shook his head. "I am no longer there, as you know, but I passed through about two weeks ago on my way here. The brethren suffered cruelly in body and goods, and, I fear, some also in soul. Madame Cortot is dead, poor woman. She was felled of an apoplexy. Brother Cortot is in greatly reduced circumstances, but I marvel at his good courage. His house was well-nigh destroyed. When he is less closely watched, he hopes to escape from the country. Madeleine and the small children are yet in the refuge where you left them last spring. Nothing recent has been heard of the older boy, who was in the House for New Catholics. Our brother's great worry now is that harm may befall Madeleine and the twins before he can arrange their escape."

The pastor glanced at the soldier's impassive face. "And how goes it with you, brother?" he asked softly.

"Well enough. One exists." Armand felt his reply was a little lame.

The pastor didn't press for details. "I pray the Lord will bless you and your plans," he said. Was there a hint of reproof in the tone? Armand dropped his eyes and was carefully noncommittal.

"Your nephew, Mathieu Bertrand? How does he? I had understood he was affianced to Mademoiselle Madeleine and was to join her ere this."

"He went south with me to Cette but is presently near Nimes. Poor lad. He has taken our reverses much to heart. At present he hesitates to go on with the marriage." Merson sighed. "I would I might inspire him with more hope, but there is indeed little surety for God's people in these times."

The temple bell began to ring slowly, as if for the last time. The two turned back toward the main thoroughfare. Armand was deep in thought, and the pastor eyed him speculatively. They walked in silence until they were joined by Pastor Claude. Armand dropped back politely and bowed his leave-taking. "It was most agreeable to have the honor of your acquaintance, messieurs," he said, "and you were most kind to permit me at your table."

"The pleasure has been ours," Claude assured the officer. "You must make my home yours whenever you are in Paris."

With further civilities they parted, and Armand backed into the throng and was lost to sight. With a quizzical look on his face, Merson watched him go.

"Well, old friend," remarked Claude with an uplifted eyebrow. "You look pleased with yourself. Have you performed your good deed for the day?"

"Yes, I think I have," replied the other with a satisfied smile.

* * * * *

It had been a good Sabbath at Charenton. After three services, which included the reading of thirty-two chapters of Scripture, the delivery of one hundred and sixty-seven pages in three sermons, the singing of nineteen psalms, and the recitation of two hundred verses, the worshipers departed satisfied. Armand found the old man at the agreed place, and they turned their mounts toward the capital. When they reached the open meadow, the horses settled down to an easy trot. Armand perceived that his companion wanted to talk. There were worse ways of spending a late autumn afternoon. Already the browns showed in the landscape, and there was a nip in the air.

"It's hardly to be believed," the deacon reminisced, "that this may have been my last trip out here. I've come by land or water these sixty-five years, sometimes twice a week. I know every foot of the way. I'm seventy-six, you know.

"Paris has always hated the Reform. I've wondered if it be Rome or Paris that is the Scarlet Woman, for the cup of filthiness can certainly be filled in Paris too, and she is bespattered with the blood of the saints. She burned Louis de Berquin at the first, and then there was St. Bartholomew's Day. Even now our services may not be held in the city limits, but I suppose insult is better than murder.

"It's two leagues from the Bastille to Charenton," he went on, his eyes far away. "On a Sunday there would be three or four thousand come to a service. Some of us would ride, a few in carriages, but a lot more came by shank's mare. Hundreds came by river. We had trouble once in a while at the *octroi** when entering or leaving the city, but the roads were more trouble—mud in the spring and slush in the winter—so it was hard on the old, no doubt; but it was great adventure when one was young.

"Long ago, the *seigneurs* would race their carriages—oh, the excitement! We behave more seemly now—the times are so bad, perhaps, and the nobility have fallen away. I remember once the Duc de Guiche tried to kidnap the beautiful young widow Madame de Harambure on her way to church. Richelieu himself put a stop to that one.

"I remember how we boys preferred the river route. Only a *sol*† it cost for the trip—two hours it took—with sixty in a barge. The riffraff on the Ile de Notre Dame might pelt us with stones when we passed under the bridges. You never knew.

"How we used to sing on the river! I can hear it yet. In the fog we could hear them coming—until four years ago an edict stopped singing even in open country. The fog was dangerous. I remember once a collision during the seventh verse of the ninety-second psalm. Some had to swim for it that time."

He fell silent for a time, revisiting a world peopled by friends long since dead.

"Great men, men of renown, were common in those days. Any pastor could handle an entire book of the Bible for a sermon—none of the sickly custom you see in some pulpits today of confining the Word to a few chapters. . . .

"You saw the temple today. Have you ever seen the like in all your travels? I wouldn't think so. It holds four thousand on the three floors with the balconies; yet all can hear perfectly. And it is well lighted with those tall windows—eighty-one of them." He fell silent again.

"Truly," he sighed at last, "we shall never see the like again this side of the heavenly city." He began to recite in a high, thin voice:

---

* Boundary where local taxes are collected.
† A French coin worth about a penny.

110

Now as the ark was saved from the Flood
>When God placed His church there for safety,
As also saved by receiving the church
>Was little Zoar, hard by Sodom,
So God will keep Charenton
>Under His wings.

Armand turned in his saddle. "And do you plan to flee Sodom?"

"It is much on my mind. If the edict is revoked, it may be too late. There are many ways, though, that one might try: by land over the frontiers or by sea to England. From Paris to the Lowlands is the most direct, but the water journey is usually easiest. In any case, it is dangerous."

"I beg you to discuss these possibilities with me."

For some time they discussed the various routes to Protestant countries, by land and by sea, disguises, forged papers, guides—honest or rascally, but indispensable nevertheless—the venality of frontier guards and sea captains, and the dreadful penalties on those taken in flight. They were now passing the country houses of the wealthy Parisian bourgeoisie, and the villages came closer together—Paris was near. Armand, both intrigued and aghast at his companion's disclosures, loosened his pistols in their holsters and made certain that his scabbard was swinging clear.

"It seems then," mused Armand, "that from Paris, the best way is to head for a Channel port, but what if one had to start from Champagne?"

"Then such a one should strike for the nearest border. It would be well to avoid the thicker parts of the Ardennes, but one should also keep in mind that to arrive in the Rhine principalities is not always to win safety, for our troops range far into the empire, and those petty princelings dare not protest. One must have a guide, and, with a good one, heading for the Netherlands might be wiser.

"When fleeing, one should avoid towns and villages like the plague, but circling around through forests and thickets requires a guide unless you know the country well. It is hard to say how long the border guards will remain as complacent as they have been until now, so good passports and a letter from a bishop attesting one's orthodoxy are very useful."

"How does one come by such trifles?" asked the soldier as they neared a gate.

"You are serious?" asked the old man, lowering his voice.

"Well, yes," said Armand, after a little hesitation. "Not immediately, perhaps, but in a month or so, after some arrangements have been made."

"Who can tell what the situation may be in a month?" muttered the old man out of the side of his mouth, his eyes on the guard. They passed unchallenged through the gate. "But it may be that long before I myself can go, and if I am yet here, I may be able to be of service to you. I will tell you where to find me. But, I implore you, be discreet, for these are troublous times, and among the flock are ravening wolves in sheep's clothing."

Saying no more, they fought their way through the holiday crowds in Sunday serge, past the wine and lemonade shops, shoving aside brazen-voiced peddlers and beggars, cringing as a coach driven by a madman plummeted down the narrow lanes with no regard for the lives of foot passengers. Armand saw the deacon safely to his little basement shoe shop and once again edged his cautious way through the pullulating humanity to the safety of the Duc de Lauzières's town house, more than ready for a good meal and a soft bed.

* * * * *

Armand de Gandon stretched his weary legs while his horse was led to the watering trough by a strikingly unclean urchin. It had been a hard and boring week in October out on the Eure, where the infantry of France dug ditches for their king's waterworks that would eventually make his gardens at Versailles bloom. Armand had ridden to Paris with routine papers for the duke, his colonel. He was tired, and the horse was hot, so he paused after entering the gate.

He bought some raisins from the least noisy of the street peddlers who thronged about him and, ignoring the maledictions of the others, strolled toward the window of a print seller to see what was new. He was feeling quite cheerful in spite of the tedium of his current duties. In the past month of shovel work, the regiment had lost only thirteen by desertion, six dead of the fever, and scarcely thirty men in the hospital. True, the duke did not much concern himself with such matters, that being what he had professional officers for, but Armand felt a solid sense of satisfaction for a job well done. It would not be long now, surely, until his commission for the new regiment came through. He felt he deserved the promotion.

His face and spirits both dropped as he saw a royal proclamation on the wall of the shop. Grimly he read the opening words: "Louis, by the Grace of God, King of France and of Navarre, to all to whom these presents shall come, greeting. The King Henry the Great, our ancestor of glorious memory—" At last the Fence was down!

The proclamation declared the Edict of Nantes revoked since "the greater part of the Pretended Reformed Religion" had embraced the true faith. The edict was therefore useless. All ministers of the PRR must be out of the country within fifteen days; all Huguenots who had previously fled must return in four months; and any who tried to flee in the future would be consigned to the galleys for life if men or suffer loss of body and goods in a convent if women. No meetings could be held. All Huguenot children born hereafter must be baptized in the Roman confession, but otherwise those not yet converted were not to be molested "until it pleases God to enlighten them like the others." At the bottom of the sheets it concluded, "For such is our pleasure," and was signed "Louis," followed by the chancellor, Le Tellier, and "*Par le Roy,** Colbert."

Furious, Armand urgently elbowed past an unsavory saleswoman of chestnuts in order to see in the print seller's window. He needed a moment to control his emotions, but the samples in the window were no help.

An engraving, entitled "The Pretended Reformed Religion at Bay," showed a very ill person, evidently Huguenotism, on a bed with a horrible dragon lurking underneath. A doctor was taking the patient's pulse, and a man busied himself raking Protestant books into a fire.

---

* By the king.

Several doggerel verses were included, of which Armand scanned the last two:

Your books and your writings are burned on the spot,
　　Error and heresy are reduced to ashes;
The sun that shines uncovers to your eye
　　The naked truth, your greatest enemy.

The worship of your gods is abolished,
　　The thunder and lightning that smash your altars,
Your idols stricken, your temples demolished,
　　Are the eternal witnesses of your entire ruin!

Grinding his teeth, Armand glanced at the other engraving. It showed a grim Louis XIV brandishing a sword over the ruins of Huguenot temples. "Not without cause does the king carry the sword—" This was supported by some close theological argument: "Heretics! If you still doubt the Most Holy Sacraments, listen to Jesus Christ, for St. John, chapter six, says 'I am the LIVING bread—!' " The fine print was hard to read through the streaked glass.

Armand turned back to his horse, his mind seething with half-formed intentions. Certainly it was dangerous for Madeleine to remain in the country, yet it would be a desperate matter to try an escape now. Was it not Mathieu's affair anyway? The Revocation specifically said that Huguenots who kept their mouths shut should not be bothered until it pleased the Lord to enlighten them. The regiment would soon be his, and the duke had been trying to encourage him in a tender interest at court. There were some indications that the lady, though of highest birth, might be a little interested herself. Was it sensible to throw everything away now for a sentimental gesture—and for the fiancée of another?

He took his horse's bridle, checked his saddlebags, and for good measure felt to see whether he still had his purse. The barefoot urchin held the horse while he mounted. There was something about the impudence of the boy's expression that reminded Armand of Alexandre

Cortot. Though he did not wish right then to be reminded of the Cortots, perhaps it was to stifle his conscience that he put the *deniers* back into his pocket and threw the boy an entire *sou** instead.

* * * * *

The November fog had lifted to treetop level as Mathieu Bertrand, cold and wretched from his long journey, jogged down a poplar-lined avenue. He hoped he was nearing Hauterive, the country house east of Troyes where Monsieur Cortot told him he would find Madeleine. Around his waist, concealed by his black jacket and riding cloak, was a leather belt that contained just about the last coin Cortot had been able to scrape up.

As Mathieu's nag shambled along between the dripping trees, he recalled his joy at receiving the letter from Cortot. Now, hunched over the neck of his Rosinante, he wondered what had possessed him. When the edict had been revoked, he and his uncle had lost everything, and the latter had been expelled from France. Now Mathieu found a starveling livelihood as a clerk for a new convert draper in Nimes. The royal net had large holes in places, and a small fish like Mathieu was not disturbed. Cortot's urgent appeal had been welcome, he admitted to himself, as an excuse to break away from a futile trade; but with this northern damp chilling one to the bone, courage also froze, and even the dusty draper's shop could be seen to offer advantages.

Mathieu viewed the future much as he did the road ahead of him now—as obscured by wisps of uncertain fog. When a vision of Madeleine's face flashed through his mind, the dimness dissolved; but when he dwelt on the precarious prospects of one's daily bread, all became murky again. If only they had not made that fool rescue from the convent, he and Madeleine could have settled discreetly on her father's land and waited for the storm to pass. Officially, Protestantism might no longer exist in the kingdom, but in fact, each made his own terms with Caesar. The zeal of officials, the fanaticism of the clergy, and the spitefulness of neighbors varied from place to place, but a heretic who did

---

* A small coin.

not outwardly defy the law was not likely to be disturbed. For safety's sake, Mathieu had sent no messages either to his uncle in Holland or to Madeleine since the Revocation.

When Mathieu had located Isaac Cortot, he found him existing with Moïse and the latter's sister in a cottage in the foothills two leagues from Saint Martin. It stood on an eroded little plot with a few vines and fruit trees and a great many weeds. It had once been a herdsman's hut and a minor part of Cortot's properties. He had given it to Moïse after the dragonnades, hoping the property was insignificant enough to escape the cupidity of the enemy. His town house had been confiscated shortly afterward for "taxes," and he had slipped away to live with his former servant, trusting that he had been forgotten in town.

As Cortot embraced Mathieu, he had cried over and over again "How fortunate that I was able to reach you!" Mathieu had been shocked to observe how much the older man had aged in the three months since he had seen him last. The face once so round and rosy was heavily lined, and the wattles hung loosely. "I doubt I will ever see my children again in this life," Cortot had said. "The fury of the persecutor will not be satisfied until I am in the grave, like my dear Mathilde." The tears rose in his eyes and spilled down his cheeks. "But the young ones must make their escape from Babylon even if they take away but their souls for a prey. Lord willing, I may try later, but it would be madness now. However, this is what I wrote you for, my dear Mathieu!"

In his money belt Cortot had almost three hundred *livres* in gold and silver coins. He had pressed it into Mathieu's hands. The younger man's heart had beaten suddenly faster as he divined what this was leading to.

"This I hid from the dragoons, my boy. Go up to Champagne. I will give you the directions. Madeleine and the twins have been there six months now, and I don't know how much longer they will be safe. I grieve that matters have worked this way, my son. Indeed, I had hoped you would be my son in truth ere this, but the Lord in His providence has planned all for our good. You will no longer be marrying the daughter of a rich man; you will have only my blessing. But you and Madeleine are young and of good courage and you love each other; and with this, all may be accomplished. You will take your abode in a foreign land, but take heart from Ruth the Moabitess. I have a few more *livres* with a banker in Amsterdam, and Madeleine has my letter of credit. It will help, but my children will still have to labor for their bread. However, I trust the Lord's arm is not shortened nor does He need silver or gold. 'The LORD gave, and the LORD hath taken away; blessed be the name of the LORD' " (Job 1:21).

Mathieu had not forgotten the still-sturdy figure standing by the doorway of that windowless hut as he rode down the path toward the highroad. "I hope that you children will enter the terrestrial Canaan," the old gentleman had said, "but at least we shall surely meet again in the heavenly. I shall be forever in your debt for this service."

The long journey on a poor horse had fatigued the spirit as well as the body. Constantly on Mathieu's mind were the threats in the Revocation edict—galleys for the men and convents for the women who tried to flee the country. He had heard a good many escape stories: the journey by sea hidden in bales of merchandise, or drifting in an open boat without food or water; slipping over the line in disguise as priests, peddlers, or peasants, or even fighting one's way through. Truly, none of it appealed to him as making sense just then. Later, the watch on the borders would be less rigorous. To wait discreetly—would not that be the better part of wisdom? Would not the Lord be better served by live worshipers in secret than by dead ones or ones driven insane in a dungeon?

Not that he couldn't endure a dungeon as well as the next one, he assured himself, but what kindness would it be to drag Madeleine from the comparative safety she now enjoyed and expose her anew to a convent? She would never be permitted a second escape. Suppose they were apprehended together and his part in her first escape became known. Might not he be devoted to the wheel rather than the galley? In spite of what they said about galleys, he thought he would prefer them to the painful certainty of the wheel. There was something so final about having one's limbs broken by the iron bar! When nursing such thoughts, he would ride in a cold sweat for miles.

He found himself entertaining the thought at times that a marriage without a dowry was not a particularly intelligent venture. Perhaps he had been misled, and recent changes in the fortunes of the Cortots were a divine leading he shouldn't ignore. By the time he had reached the gates of Hauterive, he had come to some decisions.

Mathieu followed the porter to the main entrance of the modest chateau. It stood in the midst of ambitious formal gardens.

"Madame is not here today," the majordomo informed him, eyeing his bedraggled raiment with unconcealed suspicion. Mathieu took the news with admirable fortitude and studied several prints of saints and an apotheosis of Louis XIV on the walls of the antechamber while the servant sought Mademoiselle Cortot.

A door opened behind him, and he wheeled to greet his promised one. He fell to his knees and kissed her hand fervently. Her eyes glowed with excitement. Standing up again and feasting his eyes on the familiar beauty of her face, his troubling thoughts vanished like smoke. He became aware that she was speaking, and her warm, low voice brought back such memories that once again he felt all courage and devotion.

"You look so fatigued, Mathieu. There's hollowness about your eyes. It has been a hard journey? I'm so glad you've come at last. And my father? How did you leave him? Where is he living? He hasn't answered my last letters. Do you bring word from him?"

"I do," he whispered, and looked questioningly about the white paneled room, especially at the open door into the hall.

"It's beautiful outside," she responded instantly. "Let's go into the garden. I think the children are out there. They'll be so glad to see you!"

In a moment she reappeared with a flame-colored cloak thrown over her shoulders. It had a peaked hood, but she left her head bare. They went through the French doors and walked slowly up the graveled paths without saying a word. She leaned on his arm, while he gazed solicitously down at her happy face. They put several hedges between them and the house before he began to tell her of his visit to Saint Martin and of her father's instructions. When he had finished, Madeleine had turned white.

"I had no idea matters had come to such a pass," she said, almost in a whisper. "He has written but once since Mother died, but we did not guess from his letter how matters really were. We really ought to go at once to him, but we must do as he wishes. We can be ready any time, dear Mathieu. Cousin Diane has been most kind, but our being here has been a frightful worry to her. If one of the servants should talk, for example! And she's so anxious for her husband's promotion to the *noblesse* of the robe that she'd die if it became known she had heretic kin. She has really been most patient."

"Oh! I have a surprise!" she said, suddenly changing the subject. "Alexandre is here!" Mathieu shuddered, but she went merrily on. "The monks found him too intractable and let him go!"

Mathieu was the pale one now. He could sympathize with the unfortunate monks.

"It will be good to be *doing* something again," Madeleine went on. "For months it has been the same—up at six and housework and entertaining the children until family prayers at ten in the evening. I have embroidered until I am cross-eyed. And those youngsters! I have hunted the slipper, hid and seeked, loved my love with an A, and read Lafontaine's fables aloud until I have them all mixed up in my sleep. In revenge, I have made Louis and Louise learn most of the psalms and much of the long and short catechisms. Since Alexandre has come, I've played a little chess with him, but we are indifferent at it. You should have been here, Mathieu. He has forgotten his Latin in shocking fashion. We are bored with these woods and this weather. Truly you are a welcome sight! Let's go into the house, and when Cousin Diane returns, we will give her the news."

She noticed Mathieu's suddenly stony face and halted, surprised.

"Whatever is the matter, Mathieu? You look like a thundercloud!"

He sucked in a deep breath. Now was the time.

"It appears to me, Madeleine, my dear, that it would be best for the twins and Alexandre to tarry here a season." He saw her mouth open in instant protest, but he hastily plunged on with his speech, avoiding her eyes.

"Now, it stands to reason that it is harder for five to pass over the frontier than two. A family group attracts more attention and must move more slowly. When children are observed, it is assumed immediately that a family is escaping. They will not be in any great danger, but *you* will as long as you remain in France. Alexandre will be able to watch out for them. Of course, at a future time it will doubtless be possible for them to follow us."

Madeleine looked steadily at Mathieu as he made his case. She said nothing immediately, but he felt his heart sink. She was viewing him as if he were something strange and unpleasant she had just discovered. He looked briefly into the violet eyes and found it more comfortable to drop his gaze to her intertwined fingers.

"Indeed!" she commented finally. "That was as strange a speech as I have ever heard. And to hear it from you! You should know perfectly well that I would never leave them here. I trust you are saying this as some sort of a pleasantry, though it is a strange time and place to amuse yourself so. If the matter is so difficult, then let us pray and plan the more."

Mathieu had never been much of a humorist, and he was not joking now. He dug in his mental heels the more solidly as he relished the discovery that her protests had not overthrown his determination. He spoke again, condescendingly and patiently, but firmly, as to an unreasonable child.

"I could not be responsible for you, Madeleine, if we have the children with us. As I just said, it would make a larger party and draw dangerous attention to us. You cannot risk being captured a second time. There would be dangers enough for the two of us, but twins are easily recognized, so all perils would be multiplied. You know I would never suggest such a course unless it were absolutely necessary. Trust my judgment, Madeleine. We will not be abandoning them at all. We merely plan that they shall follow later when times are better."

The more he talked, the more persuasive he felt he sounded. But Madeleine was facing him with her fists clenched at her sides, and she appeared to be struggling for self-control—her eyes blazed and her lips trembled. For an instant he feared she might burst into tears, and he steeled himself to remain firm. However, when she found her voice, it was steady enough.

"Monsieur Bertrand, I am indeed surprised at this unworthy proposal. You do not seem to jest, but the idea is preposterous. I have no intention of leaving my brothers and my sister behind as prey for the papists. It appears that I am all they have left in this world. They may indeed come to some sorry pass, but it will not be because *I* stole off to safety and abandoned them to make their way alone! No, I shall remain here with them."

"Now, mademoiselle!" Mathieu expostulated. "You are not using your reason. They would come later. It would increase the chance of success for us all."

"What arrangements did you have in mind for 'later'?"

"Well, that would have to be determined according to the circumstances at the time. You can hardly—"

"No! I stand by what I have said. I'm not leaving here without them, monsieur. Now, unless you have something different to discuss, I feel I am wasting your valuable time."

"Listen to me," he cried in exasperation, grasping for her hand. "How can you even think of getting away by yourself?"

She fell back a pace, avoiding him and tossed her head defiantly. "Some have managed it, I am told, and perhaps I may yet find someone with the ingenuity to arrange for my brothers and my sister, too."

His temper was fraying badly under the scorn in her voice.

"Oh, indeed? And who might you have in mind?"

"No one at the moment, monsieur, but I'm willing to wait."

Mathieu's self-control dissolved, and the words tumbled out: "That apostate ribbon merchant, that dandy from Versailles, I suppose? That bowing, scraping gallant out of a romance—that salon pimp!"

Madeleine's retort sounded icy rather than agitated. "If, as I suppose, this is your picturesque way of referring to the Sieur de Gandon, I may say that I do not even know where he is. However, I doubt that he would expect me to abandon my own flesh and blood."

"The perfect chevalier, eh?" he cried furiously. "So we must risk mortal dangers so one may make comparisons with this hero of the opera? Perhaps we may expect him later in Holland, this debonair one?"

She turned away abruptly.

"If I am not good enough for you, mademoiselle," he continued hotly, "it is time we understood each other. If you are to prove a dutiful wife, it is time we discovered this, too. I take my leave."

Madeleine turned back with her anger mastered. This time she pulled at his sleeve. "Mathieu, you are beside yourself. This jealousy is unworthy of you. I've been faithful to you. It is *I* who has waited all these months for word from *you,* which never came. I knew the times were evil and that you were likely in danger, and I've been praying daily that we would soon be reunited. I have not seen or heard from the *Sieur* de Gandon nor any other. I fear your worries have unhinged you, Mathieu. Be reasonable. How could we be happy together remembering the children left here forlorn and in peril? You should not insist I do a thing like that. Don't we mean any more than that to you? Now let us talk calmly, without this shouting."

"I am *quite* reasonable, mademoiselle. You will not reconsider?"

"No, I can't. Don't ask me to, Mathieu."

He pushed her hand away, but from the expression on her face, he might as well have struck her.

"Then all I have to say is that your blood be upon your own head, mademoiselle. Goodbye!"

He bowed low, very formally, and turned away, wrapping his cloak about him. He walked slowly, his head held proudly, his boots crunching loudly on the cinders of the pathway. He half expected to hear her call him back. Her tone had been pleading, almost despairing. That was encouraging. Perhaps she was beginning to realize what she was doing. She was just a spoiled child who had always had her own way. But as he approached the iron grille at the end of the garden, she had still spoken no word.

As Mathieu reached the gate, he found the twins and Alexandre staring at him round-eyed. Alexandre, he of the missing teeth, gave tongue. "Hey!" he cried in that piercing tone that brought back so many unhappy memories of the schoolroom at Saint Martin. "If it isn't the master himself! Have you and her highness had a spat? What's going on? We couldn't hear all of it."

Mathieu pushed by them brusquely. Behind him he heard Madeleine's voice, chilly and authoritative: "That's enough from you, sir. If Monsieur Bertrand wishes his horse, see that Gervais brings it to him at once."

A few moments later, feeling spent and somewhat ill, Mathieu found himself again astride his miserable white horse and moving down the avenue toward the highway. He was outside the gate before he remembered the money belt and that he had forgotten to say a word about it to Madeleine.

* * * * *

For three days Mathieu wrestled with his thoughts. His horse plodded obediently eastward, for his tentative destination was Strasbourg, the new French bridgehead on the Rhine. If he could reach that city, adjoined as it was still with the princely states of the Holy Roman Empire, it should not prove too difficult to slip across to safety.

But this was not his immediate worry. He debated endlessly whether he should return to Hauterive. Would not this be tantamount to surrender? Would it not give Madeleine the idea that any whim of hers would rule him? The more he thought of leading a familial parade through the frontier zone, the more clearly he realized how sound his judgment had been. The emotions of a woman, yes, a young girl, were no sound basis for action. To go with all those children—unpredictable, fidgety, irreverent—preposterous! He felt a positive relief to be quit of the whole affair.

But when he recalled how he had allowed himself to become irritable and how, in particular, he had been goaded into blurting out that remark about Gandon, his skin crawled with shame. It was frightful the way that fellow seemed to be hovering over his shoulder all the time. Having seen Armand at his quixotic escapades, Madeleine seemed to expect *him,* Mathieu Bertrand, to be as giddy. Even if she never laid eyes on Gandon again, no doubt she would always be judging her husband by him. She was probably spoiled now to the point where she could not properly appreciate sense and discretion. It was well he had been firm. If she had prevailed, what a wormlike existence he would have led! Perhaps this quarrel was a providential leading.

But then there was the matter of the money. It was not his, and he had no intention of considering it so. Yet what should he do with it? He could hardly make the long journey back across France to Saint Martin. It would be somewhat difficult to explain the situation to Cortot anyway. Perhaps after he had escaped into the Germanies or found his uncle in the Netherlands, he could hire professional guides to rescue the Cortot children. Of course, three hundred *livres* would hardly stretch that far, and a number of things might go wrong with such a scheme. Should he retrace his steps right now? If she were still obdurate, he could always leave the money with her and she could use it as she wished. But there was always the risk that she might overwhelm him with tears and entreaties. He decided not to turn about just yet. It was growing late, and he was very tired. He would spend the night at an inn in the next village and think the matter through once again when he was rested. Surely the border could not be far now.

His mind had been so busy that he scarcely noticed the four nondescript mounted men under a bare-limbed tree some distance from the road. Not until he had passed them did he suddenly discover he was no longer alone. The disappearance of the sun behind the Alsatian hills was not the only reason for the chill that shot through him. The horsemen drew up beside him. His horrified thought was that they were highwaymen, but a quick glace at their arms and accouterments told him that it was worse, if possible.

One rascal, with a single malevolent eye, evidently a brigadier of cavalry, put his gloved hand on Mathieu's bridle. "Where away, my fine fellow?"

"To visit my—my cousin in Strasbourg." Mathieu gulped feebly.

"Now, how about that?" jeered the soldier. "It has a cousin in Strasbourg!" He turned to his companions and winked. "It has the plumage of a psalm singer, too. A coincidence, no doubt."

Mathieu's heart stopped beating; his viscera knotted in sudden agony. He had no passport or other document, and he was carrying three hundred *livres* in coin. The injustice of it all—that he should be in such a ghastly predicament through no choice of his own—robbed him of speech.

"Well," observed the noncommissioned officer with another triumphant wink, this time at his victim, "let's go see about this. We have ways of making birds sing, even such molting specimens as thou. I think I know a songbird when I see one!"

* * * * *

Dinner was over. The table had been cleared, and the servants had left Armand alone with the Duc de Lauzières. Neither said much for a time. The dark reaches of the duke's apartment were lit sporadically by the writhing flames in the fireplace. If they reminded Armand of the discomforts of a soul in torment, it was because he felt a similar unease himself. The wood hissed and spat, and the shadows reflected in the mirror over the mantel lent a curious effect to the figurines standing there, as if they were dancing in the uncertain glow.

During the dessert, Armand had advanced the hesitant suggestion, the possibility that he might find it advisable to resign his commission and withdraw from the service. The old man had said nothing, and in the eloquent silence Armand had not enlarged on his proposal. The duke had been more friendly and fatherly than ever of late. It was clear what *he* counted on. But nothing would be gained by waiting longer. Armand must find the words tonight.

The duke, almost hidden in his high-backed armchair, sat facing his protégé, his hands resting on the gilded chair arms. The most visible portion of his anatomy was his gouty leg on a brocaded footstool, thrust toward the fire.

"I'm flattered that you prefer my company to the charming Princess of Lorraine," he said, apropos of nothing. He always sounded a little sarcastic.

"Perhaps it is because you have better manners, my lord."

"Pray don't count on my restraint," returned the duke acidly.

Again they sat silently, the officer gathering his courage and rehearsing his arguments. The clock at the center of the mantel struck the hour.

Suddenly the duke cleared his throat and began to speak. His usually nasal tone was curiously softened, and as he gazed into the fire, it was as if he talked to himself, unaware of a listener in the room. Armand sat with head bowed, his legs crossed, staring at the flames also.

"There was once a young man, the only son of his father," mused the duke, "and heir to one of the oldest and proudest houses of France. He was a youth of great promise—handsome, devoted, brave, and endowed by admiring nature with all the gifts of body and spirit usually distributed among mortals in stingy fashion. The gods themselves must have been jealous, for on an autumn afternoon several years ago, this golden youth rode with his father at the head of the regiment he would one day inherit. A large force of the enemy surprised the column, and in a moment he lay torn and dead, his blood soaking into the thirsty German soil like that of scores of his comrades and most of the superior officers.

"Then it was that another young man, also of ancient lineage but of humbler station, sprang forth from an infantry company, formed a battle line, beat off attacks by the enemy horse, inspiring his men by his steadiness, and led the attack that recaptured the banners of the regiment and not only saved the day but also saved the honor of the distraught father.

"It was fitting that this young man should have been promoted, and indeed he was. But as the bereaved father-colonel observed the competence and formed an appreciation of the character of this young man, who never presumed on his good fortune, an idea formed in his mind— an idea that this excellent young man must surely have fathomed by now."

Armand said nothing, nor did he look at the speaker.

"This young man of whom I speak has had some doubts, perhaps. But surely he has realized what is open before him as the adopted son of a duke? A colonelcy worth twenty years of his major's pay is but the start, a bagatelle! Glory, standards to take, fortresses to storm, and down the road a few years a marshal's baton! His Majesty would graciously consent to a patent for a title. In the peerage one day, in the inner circle about the royal sun, with the reversion in due time of the titles and offices of the 'parent.' Where need one stop?

"Would some resent an 'interloper'? Only distant kinsmen—witless buffoons with the virtues of their lineage bred out of them, without credit at court and with no teeth to bite."

Armand silently wondered whether he would in time also become a buffoon, or, in the miasma of the court, breed buffoons himself.

"Now what might make such a favored young man restless? Almost certainly there is a petticoat mixed in somewhere. One needs remember that such affairs have a way of turning out differently than one expects. A match could always be arranged with a suitable family—not a difficult matter as the young man's prospects become known."

The duke leaned forward and sought the younger man's eye.

"Nor need one fret about the past," he continued. "No one is excited these days if a Huguenot officer makes an accommodation to the present situation. Take Marshall Turenne as an example. The past slips unobtrusively into the shadows. The court and the army are full of such discreet ones. No one demands a change in one's mind—just a decent show of devotion to the king's church. If the body is conveyed to chapel, who asks the whereabouts of the mind?

"The prince's religion should be that of all respectable men. If the king is *devot,** then all gentlemen should be *devot*. If the king is atheist, then let all his courtiers be atheist. But for the tranquility of the state, church and government must support one another. One must learn with equal fervor and adroitness to sing a litany or to gamble. Louis XIV has missed mass just once so far in his life, that is the cue!"

Armand stirred uneasily and seemed about to speak.

"Now, as I say," the duke resumed, "one may believe as one likes. There is nothing too serious in the past of this young man of whom I speak, nothing that cannot be glossed over by his military record. That rescue from the convent was just a youthful peccadillo."

Armand started violently. *How did he find out about that?* he asked himself in consternation.

"These are good days for New Catholics. It rains rewards for those who make graceful submission. For fanatics—only trouble." The duke's voice became urgent. "An exile's life is bitter, my son."

They sat in silence again. Armand's rehearsed speeches had come apart before he could use them, but he could still recall the verse "For what is a man profited, if he shall gain the whole world, and lose his own soul?" (Matthew 16:26). But what duty did he owe his father's religion? Could he live the sham the duke suggested? Many

---

* An extremely pious person.

did. Must one be a fool to be virtuous? Yet it would be a hard thing to walk with the Lord and go hand in hand with the persecutors of His people.

Before Armand's eyes passed visions of the regiment that for so long had been his life. Camped, perhaps by a country roadside, arms and banners stacked, the soldiers about the fire, the pots bubbling, and the aroma of garlic hovering like a benediction as the trumpet notes died away in the twilight. And there were those rare but supreme moments when one shared the intoxication of victory, and drums rolled and banners flew white and free, their brilliant quarterings gleaming in the sun over serried lines blazing with red and blue, gold and steel. Trade this for the life of a hunted fugitive, grubbing for charity among foreigners? He sighed.

"My lord, I thank you for the parable of this young man. I pray you not to inquire closely, for I am not at liberty to tell of a matter I must attend to. But it were better I did not belong to your regiment while it is done. Fool I may be, and, in fact, most certainly am, but I must answer to myself. You were always more considerate than I have deserved, and I would that you could find one more worthy of your great kindness."

"See! I grant you the leave you require before you ask for it," exclaimed the old man, shaking his head gently. "What could be fairer than that? Do what you must, but come back. Then ask for 'instruction'—that's just a word to pacify simpletons. It will smooth your way, and we can forget the jots and tittles of doctrine. Take three months—take a year, if need be—and then report to me again."

Armand's heart smote him. "My lord," he said haltingly. "I have not been a good exemplar of my faith, but even so, it is not something I could wear hidden guiltily under my coat. I fear that to ask for 'instruction' would be a commitment to be 'converted.' I cannot do this, but I will accept the leave you offer me so kindly, and I will endeavor to be prudent. But, my lord, I beg you, do not strain your great credit with the king trying to save a disobedient soldier—an ingrate. You know that is one thing His Majesty cannot abide. I feel I must obey a Higher Power, but the king will never see it that way."

Armand rose uncertainly. His words had been firm enough, but he knew a guilty relief that his decision did not have to be irrevocable. The door was still slightly ajar and would remain so as long as the duke could manage it. The old man would never quite understand a sacrifice for religious faith or a young man voluntarily leaving Versailles behind.

The soldier knelt and kissed the withered hand of his benefactor. "If I do not see you again, my lord, I shall always remember your kindness and what you have sought to do for me. Your devoted servant, sire, always."

The old duke sat with bowed head without speaking. Armand crossed to the door, paused with his hand on the knob, bowed deeply, and let himself quietly out.

* * * * *

With his decision made, Armand wrapped himself in his riding cloak, checked his pistols, and set out on foot for his destination, the house of the old deacon, from whom he must get the passport. The duke's town house was near the Luxembourg, and it was necessary to cross the Pont Neuf. Armand had always found it comforting when crossing that bridge to see the gallant equestrian figure of Henry IV overlooking the Seine. But tonight, as he trudged along the pavement, unbidden thoughts came to mind—that the Protestant hero himself had found it necessary to take "instruction" and for good and sufficient reason had changed his faith. All around the base of the statue, on the point of the Ile de la Cité, were shapeless bundles, barely discernible in the poor light. They were the legless, the blind, the scabrous beggars. He wondered where he might be sleeping on some future night, and a persistent voice told him to turn about and go back to the duke while he still could. He argued with the voice while his legs did their duty and advanced toward his destination.

The old man Armand sought lived near the Tripe Market, not far from the Rue des Sevres. It was a dark trip, and the night was full of rustlings and stirrings. Especially as he walked under the covered gallery between the Pont au Change and the Pont Notre Dame, he kept a hand on his sword hilt and stayed away from walls and the mouths of alleys. The noises were usually rats after refuse, but he met some human scavengers, too. They were an ill-favored lot, but they gave him a wide berth. A man of his size did not promise easy pickings.

At last he found the little lane he sought. No one was in sight. The buildings rose four and five stories over the street. All were dark, but how many eyes and ears would there be as he tried to rouse the old gentleman at eleven at night?

He knocked softly. The small leaded panes of the windows gleamed eerily in the moonlight. The old man might be dead, gone, or deaf. He knocked more loudly. He was beginning to perspire in the chill night air when the door opened slowly and a frightened face became dimly visible.

"Who's there?"

"Major de Gandon—you know, from Charenton."

"Come in quickly," the old man whispered, "and not so loud."

Armand followed him down a narrow flight of steps into a little room. It smelled of old food and sour bedding. The host sat on the bed, barely visible in the uncertain light of a candle stump guttering in a dish.

"Forgive my rudeness," said the deacon, rubbing his eyes, "but the night has ears. I have sold my business and will be gone in a week, I hope. I was afraid you might be from the police. One can't be too careful."

"Certainly, I understand," agreed Armand. "I, too, have decided to depart."

"Not so loud," and the old man looked around at the bare walls apprehensively.

"As you said, I'll need a passport and a letter from a bishop," Armand whispered, seating himself on a rickety stool.

"You're just in time then, for I'm having my own made up right now. I can't stand it here any longer. I hope they need shoemakers in Brandenburg, for that's where I'm going." His voice cracked in something almost like a sob. "You know, a week after we were at Charenton, the edict was revoked and those sons of Belial tore down the temple—razed it flat!"

"So I heard," Armand nodded. "Now about the passport?"

"So it *was* the last Sunday, just as Pastor Claude said."

"Very true," agreed Armand. "How about the passport?"

"Oh, yes, yes. Now, where was it you wished to leave from?"

"From Champagne."

"Then you'll be heading for the Spanish Netherlands. I think that would still be best. They're watching the ports more carefully these days, but it is rough country to the northeast, and winter, too. A good guide should get you across. But be careful, for men's lives are in danger when too many know too much."

Armand nodded grimly.

"I suppose you would do best to coach out through Sedan, but if that is impracticable, you will have to walk. Then ask at the Green Sow for one Rahab. Tell him—now get this—'Our life for yours, if ye utter not this our business.' Tell him Joshua sent you. His name is Baudin, but write none of this down."

"And the passport?"

"I can't take you there, but I'll carry your instructions. Call here in three or four days and I'll have it for you, and a good letter as if by a bishop testifying to your orthodoxy. In fact, in better French than most bishops could command."

"Very good. How much does this come to?"

"Twenty-five *écus** should cover it."

The old man groped for a ragged quill and sharpened it briefly with a penknife.

"What are the particulars for the document?"

Armand looked up at the ceiling for a moment before replying.

"Make the passport to cover Legrand, Anatole, a major, shall we say, on His Majesty's service to the Estates of Holland in the retinue of His Majesty's ambassador Monsieur d'Avaux."

"Yes."

"The passport will include Madame Legrand and the twins Louis and Louise."

---

* Coins with a shield (écu) design.

Chapter 6

Time to Travel

"It was very good of you to trouble yourself about us, monsieur," said Madeleine Cortot. Again she stood with a visitor in a corner of the formal garden.

"It would make me very happy to be of service to you, mademoiselle." Armand de Gandon bowed again and shot a glance at the girl's face. Yes, it was thinner, rather grave.

"We had hoped ere this to be in a city of refuge," she replied. "My father has sent us word that we should go on without him, but we do not know where to turn for trustworthy guides. The Gospel says to pray that your flight be not in the winter or on the Sabbath day, and I have hesitated to start out at this time of year with the children."

She glanced at the leaden horizon through the naked trees. The first snows of November would not be long in arriving.

"Mademoiselle has a trustworthy guide for the taking," Armand replied in gentle reproach.

"We could not risk exposing you to the fury of the prosecutors again, monsieur." She shook her head firmly. "Once before we—I—put you in dreadful peril, but it would not be right to have you risk the galleys now. I didn't realize my father had written you."

He shook his head and started to speak, but she raised her hand.

"It's like your generous nature to wish to help the children of your father's friend, but it is really the responsibility of another."

132

"Mademoiselle mistakes me," he protested. "I met Pastor Merson several weeks ago at the Charenton temple, and he told me of your father's circumstances. He also told me that Monsieur Bertrand was in the south and that possibly he could not be reunited with you for some time. If, of course, you expect Monsieur Bertrand, I would be happy to give him any assistance I can. I only regret I could not have presented myself at once, but there were matters I had to take care of first."

"I don't expect Monsieur Bertrand," she replied with a peculiar expression, "but that is neither here nor there. It is not right that you again risk your life, your future, and the esteem of your notable friends. Your nature is chivalrous to a fault, but I must refuse to take advantage of it."

She drew the heavy cloak about her more tightly and looked him in the eye.

"It is true," he said, "that I had some silly dreams once, and was fool enough to prattle of them overmuch. But you and your father and the rest of the brethren are my notable friends now. I have said farewell to the others. Believe me, mademoiselle, I have no future in France except as I may help my friends. I would like to be of help to you, if I may."

She bit her lip and dropped her gaze. There were tears on her lashes.

"But, monsieur, what of your regiment, the favor of the king, and all the wonders of Versailles you told me of last spring? Is all this to be sacrificed for a—a *beau geste*?"*

"I beg you, mademoiselle, to believe that I speak simple truth. I think I understand some matters better than I did six months ago. Did not Solomon say, 'Better is little with the fear of the Lord than great treasure and trouble therewith'?" (Proverbs 15:16).

"I wronged you, monsieur," she said softly, but her face was radiant. "It is very good news. We had all hoped for this!"

Neither of them spoke for a while. The wind was rising, whipping the bare branches of the trees outside the garden wall.

"I've been anxious to leave here for a long time," Madeleine said a little later. Her demeanor was more relaxed now. "My poor cousin here has been in torment since the edict was revoked. She and her husband

---

* A fine gesture.

are trying *so* hard for a title. It would not look well if it were known he had heretics on his premises."

"We'll try to put the good lady's mind at rest speedily." Armand smiled.

"Please understand, she has not asked us to go. But she will be much relieved, I know."

"Let us allow her to think we are going south to rejoin your father. I'm sure she would not intentionally hurt you, but the less she knows the better—is it not so?"

"I have a little money," she said. "It isn't much, for I sent most of what I had left to my father recently. Moïse is not able to work, you know, and my father's health has been none too good."

Armand nodded. "I have a little also, and we'll not use yours unless it's necessary. I'll be able to earn my way more easily over on the other side than a lady will. But what we need now is a plan of campaign. I have a beautiful passport I procured in Paris. It is a veritable work of art and should permit us, God willing, to pass out in fair comfort by a coach as the family of an army officer assigned to our embassy in the Netherlands. I hope," he added hastily, "that you will forgive me for my presumption, but it seemed the best idea at the time. I didn't realize that Alexandre was here with you, but no doubt he can pass as a lackey or the like. If the passport fails, then we shall have to run for it. We may be wallowing in snow soon by the look of that sky. But in any case, I agree with your cousin. This is no place for any of you."

"How much should we tell the children?" Madeleine asked.

"As little as possible until we are on the way. One may hope they are good soldiers. They must realize we are in for an uncomfortable time."

"How soon do you think—"

"As soon as the next coach for the north is due. The longer we wait, the more suspicions will be aroused. Let us not be concerned about baggage."

"We can go any time," she agreed. "The coach for Troyes will pass through the village tomorrow afternoon, if you think we ought to go that way." She glanced toward the house. "Now I think you should come in and meet my cousin. She'll remember you as the one who brought me here last spring, so your arrival will not seem so extraordinary."

Armand offered her his arm. The wind was growing colder and stronger as they strolled up the gravel path.

As Armand started to open the garden gate, the other three Cortot children materialized from behind a clipped hedge. The twins smiled shyly. Louise, with downcast eyes, curtsied to the officer, and Louis bobbed a little bow. They were plainly pleased to meet their old friend again but too embarrassed for speeches. Alexandre grinned from ear to ear.

"Haven't you lost some front teeth since I saw you last?" asked Armand genially. "Was it when you escaped from the House for New Catholics?"

"Escaped indeed!" Alexandre swelled proudly. "I was thrown out!"

"Surely not!" The officer feigned incredulity. He and Madeleine paused by the open gate. She wore the resigned look of one who has heard a story before.

"Oh, they never got far with us. There were about fifty of us in the house, and we encouraged each other. We wore those teachers out. They didn't know what to make of us. We were disorderly at services. We sat crosslegged when we were supposed to kneel. We burnt our devotional books and broke the images of the saints. Once we pretended to learn our catechism, and when they brought in all the devout from the town to show what they had taught us, we gave our own answers! We told them the pope was antichrist and that they worshiped idols and that their church was mystic Babylon, spiritually named Egypt! They got so angry they kicked a dozen of us out."

"Well, they have my sympathy," said Armand with a laugh.

"So then we wandered through the country and spoiled the Egyptians. We knew it wouldn't be good to go home again, so some of the fellows went abroad. But I knew Father had thought of sending Madeleine and the twins to Cousin Diane, so I came by to see, and here they were!"

"What about your teeth?"

"Oh, them. Well, we were getting pretty ragged on our travels, and we were decorating ourselves with clothes from a line in a little village hard by Metz when some of the village chivalry tried to stop us. I got a rock in my face, but it's hardly noticeable now, do you think?"

"Someday, maybe, one might break you in as a musketeer."

"Really! I'm thirteen now. How long would I have to wait?"

"Calm yourself, hero. These are times for craft and cunning. You must obey orders like a good soldier."

"Yes, sir. I will, sir." Alexandre saluted elaborately and fell in behind. The procession approached the chateau.

"This wind cuts right through one," observed Armand. "If the frontier guards are as well frozen as we are likely to be, they may not give us much trouble after all!"

* * * * *

Cousin Diana bade the Cortots farewell with a decent show of regret. No one volunteered any information about their destination, and she was careful not to ask. She prattled blithely of the pleasant weather to be expected and the joy of Madeleine's father at their reunion.

The travelers looked like a family of petty nobility accompanied by a servant boy. They made a leisurely progress into Troyes and before dawn the next day took the mail coach for the east.

All that day and most of the next they pitched back and forth in the coach as it crawled up the road to Sedan. Twenty leagues a day was the usual progress, but this trip was not usual. Snow had not yet fallen, but it was bitterly cold.

Madeleine had attired herself in a gray traveling suit, which was cut similarly to a riding habit. But the cold made it proper for her to wrap up in her red cloak and even hide most of her face. Armand wore a brown suit with a little lace and his old gray riding cloak. He also wore a broad-brimmed black hat and a traveling wig, and carried his sword and pistols. Louis and Louise, silent and big-eyed as always, dressed as smaller counterparts of their elders. Alexandre, in raffish glory, rode on the roof, proud and free.

The other passengers offered nothing alarming. A stout merchant, evidently an experienced traveler, had lowered the level in his flask so effectively that he remained virtually insensible to discomfort or to anything else for much of the trip. Two Carmelite nuns sat in the middle of the same seat, and their other seatmate was a well-to-do lady of uncertain age returning to Brussels from a visit with her married daughter. She tried at first to make conversation with Madeleine, but Mademoiselle Cortot pleaded indisposition, doubtless genuine enough in the circumstances. So the lady chattered with the sisters of devotional matters, heretics, fashions, herbals, and other such things. On occasion she appealed to Armand as arbiter, and he replied good-humoredly, as he became a representative of the Parisian *haute monde.**

On the second day even the Belgian lady's mill began to run down. A miserable sleet set in, which chilled the passengers to the marrow. The leather curtains of the coach impeded the cold very little. The travelers and the men aloft huddled in their wraps as best they could and endured.

It was becoming evident that this would be one of the last trips of the season; anyone foolish enough to travel after that would have to go horseback. The ruts were frozen hard, and the horses had a difficult time on the slippery road. The coachman endeavored to supply the missing traction with a liberal use of the whip and a constant stream of exhortation to the suffering beasts. On the steeper grades the passengers had to get out and walk. This restored the circulation to some extent, but it made for slow progress.

The stops worried Armand, for any observant loafer or stableboy was another possible link in a chain that might bar their passage at the last minute. He fumed inwardly when they paused for meals or a change of horses. As hour limped after hour and the frontier of the Spanish Netherlands came closer, his spirits began to rise.

Trouble with a coach wheel delayed them the second afternoon, and the party had to put up at the inn in a small town halfway between Montmedy and Sedan. After a discouraging supper, Madeleine and the twins retired to a dank chamber Armand procured for them by a little bribery. They lay huddled together in their cloaks on a bumpy mattress of husks. Armand and Alexandre settled themselves in a common room on a bench against the wall as close to the fire as possible. Alexandre dropped off to sleep instantly, but Armand was still nodding in the unaccustomed warmth and closeness when the optimism he had been

* High society.

permitting himself received a mortal blow. Suddenly he found himself wide awake, listening anxiously.

The coachman, several peasants, and a number of soldiers were restoring their courage and sharpening their intellects at a nearby table. As the liquid precaution against the cold began to take effect, their voices rose.

"They make it well worth your while," one peasant was saying as he hoisted his tankard. "Just last Thursday, Etienne Duclos got thirty-six *livres* apiece for three of them he caught near Souchard's cow barn. That's thirty-six *each,* mind you. He and his hired man threatened them with pitchforks until they gave up all their money; then they turned them in and got the bounty besides. I call that pretty clever! Etienne won't be sober again, I expect, till after Easter."

"They're under every fallen leaf these days," agreed a little soldier. "No one knows how many slip through, but it'll be less now. The guards at the border are doubled, and they're checking passports more carefully. I don't know where all the forged ones come from, but they'd better be pretty good, I tell you."

"It's spoiled a good thing for us guards," put in his taller companion. "We're changed so often that one hardly has a chance to make arrangements with the guides anymore, or so I hear."

"God's curse on all heretics, of course," added the other soldier wistfully, "but it's hard to see how letting a few of them out of the country would hurt much, especially if they left their cash behind."

"If they leave it with honest infantrymen and not with the king's lawyers, you mean?" cackled an old peasant. He found his joke so clever that he had to laugh some more, and continued until he choked and had to be beaten upon the back.

"They won't even be reaching the border as easily as they used to," observed the little soldier when the whooping had finally ceased. "Our patrols run clear back here, and we go as far inside Spanish territory as we wish, until we meet *their* people sometimes. The king of Spain knows better than to complain. And we really sift all travelers passing through Sedan, afoot or horseback or in the coaches. If we have any suspicions, a few days in jail loosens their memories in a wonderful way—especially if you separate a party and question them one by one. The heretics that get through now will have to have special help from their father the devil."

The coachman got up and stretched. "You'd better not delay me. It's getting pretty thick when the mails are held up for such nonsense. As if I don't have trouble enough with these roads!" He yawned gustily, lurched over to one of the benches muttering, and composed himself for sleep.

Then the taller soldier rose. "It grows late," he said reluctantly, "and I've a long walk back to Sedan. I'm on duty in the morning, and if I'm not on time I might as well be a Calvinist myself. The lieutenant eats them raw. He's just out of cadet school, and I think he has an eye on Louvois' job. He acts like he's the minister of war already."

"Why all the fuss?" yawned a farmer. "Not even a Huguenot would travel in the weather we're going to have before morning."

"That shows *your* ignorance my man. If it snows, they'll be thick as snow rabbits before you could get through a couple of *pater nosters.* Why, just this afternoon the lieutenant was warned that a family of five of them was heading this way—an officer, his wife, I think it was, and two or three children. A bunch like that ought to be easy to spot. I wouldn't be in their shoes tonight for all the wine in France."

Armand suddenly had trouble breathing. Had Madeleine's cousin reported them, or had someone else told on them?

"Wait till the lieutenant runs this coachful through his sieve," the soldier continued with a glance at the snoring coachman. "They'll spend the day sitting right there at the Sedan gate, I'll bet."

The soldier gave his baggy trousers a hitch, wrapped a faded cloak about his shoulders, and opened the door. "Worse luck! It's snowing!" he cried in dismay. But he plunged out anyway, followed by his short friend.

The party quickly broke up, the others leaving to get home before the snow became deep. A number of travelers remained, stretched on benches in the common room. The host, seeing his services were no longer required, thriftily drained the rest of the mulled wine, removed his apron, barred the door, blew out the candles, and retired upstairs to his bed.

In time the fire burned low. Armand hunched motionless and pondered the turn of events. The passport on which he had set such store was worthless. He made his decision. Rising carefully, with his scabbard in his hand for quietness' sake, he took a candle stub from a table and lit it in the embers in the fireplace. Then he shook Alexandre gently and motioned him to follow. As daintily as possible in his heavy boots, he tiptoed across the room, trailed by the wondering Alexandre, up the four or five steps to the door of Madeleine's room. The ill-hung door creaked alarmingly as he opened it. He paused for a moment to listen to the reassuring variety of snores, whistles, and heavy breathing behind them before entering.

For a moment he stood looking down on the sleeping Madeleine. In the dim light all he could see was the curve of her cheek and the long dark lashes, for her head was partially covered. The twins had burrowed out of sight in the pile of covering. Then he realized her eyes had opened and she was looking at him with apprehension. He leaned over and whispered the bad news. Her eyes widened, but she nodded. "What now?" she murmured with a quick look at the door.

"Before I left Paris," he said softly, "I was told of an inn in Sedan where guides might be obtained. If they have not been uncovered yet, this would be our best chance. Certainly better than for me to try to find our way through these woods. Sedan is about a league away. If we follow the road, we ought to be there by morning and all may yet be well. Let's hope the snow will keep the peasants and the patrols indoors."

She carefully roused Louis and Louise while Armand stood there with the guttering candle. He was grateful that they awoke quietly, for in his state of mind, every roach that rustled across the floor and every creak of aged timber sounded like a cavalry squadron crossing a bridge.

The children sat for a moment rubbing their eyes. As he whispered, they didn't look at him but stared instead at his tremendous flickering shadow on the wall and the low ceiling. "It's snowing," he said, "but if we walk along quickly, we won't be too cold. Remember, no matter what happens, not a sound!"

They nodded, their eyes enormous. None of the four Cortots questioned his judgment. Armand felt a little awed by such complete confidence.

"Before we start, we should ask the Lord's protection," said Madeleine. The twins knelt by the bed, and Louis recited a short prayer in his solemn way.

> The good child nothing begins,
>> But he prays to God first.
> The perverse child is accustomed
>> To do everything without praying to God.

"We'll go out the window," Armand directed. "I'll go first, and Alexandre will hand the twins down."

It would have been too risky to take them through the common room and try to unbar the door in the presence of so many sleepers. As the bedroom window was too high to reach from the ground and opened on an interior court, it was not barred. Armand launched himself into the void, praying that there would be nothing dangerous underneath. He landed hard in a rubbish heap and went to his hands and knees. After a moment of testing for anything sprained or broken, he stood erect and hissed at the dark square above.

Catching the children wasn't difficult, but when Madeleine climbed out and dropped, lissome as she was, he thought he had broken his back, and perhaps hers too. Once the shock was past, she wriggled free, almost indignantly. In the meantime, Alexandre dropped unassisted.

Taking Louis by the hand, Armand felt his way to the gate, followed by Madeleine and Louise, with Alexandre as rear guard. Muffled by the falling snow, the noise he made fumbling with the catch was hardly audible, and the quintet passed out into the deserted street.

* * * * *

The night went better than Armand had feared. Thanks to the weather, their journey was a solitary one, and the snowfall, though not heavy, was enough to cover their tracks. They traveled along the edge of the road, ready to take cover if anyone approached. Madeleine's shoes were not made for walking in snow, however, and her skirts became wet and bedraggled.

Just before dawn they approached the town of Sedan. Armand settled the Cortots behind some bushes several hundred feet from the road. Then he set out for town to find a guide. As he approached the stone gate, he remembered the old deacon's warning against going into towns, but there was no help for it. Anyway, he reasoned without much conviction, it was folk fleeing from towns that they would be seeking.

Seizing his chance, Armand strode boldly in the gate beside an ass laden with firewood. The guard didn't bat an eye at the gentleman afoot but pounced on the peasant with the animal. While they haggled over the duty on the wood, Armand slipped out of sight in the narrow streets and began to breathe normally again. He didn't want to ask questions in such a small place nor to loiter about the streets once the citizens were abroad. A few years before, Sedan had been a Huguenot bastion and had a college besides, but then had come apostasy. Now, one couldn't tell.

Some tramping along the riverbank brought him under the faded wooden sign lettered crudely "The Green Sow." The creature depicted thereon had been blue at one time and the artist's conception of a sow was only indifferently successful.

Armand hesitated outside the door. It was as villainous a place as he had ever seen. The row of houses, of which this cabaret was one, appeared to be leaning upon each other, and it looked as if the one at the end might at any moment be pushed into the Meuse. It was not a place in which a Huguenot would have been seen in normal times. Still, he was more conspicuous standing outside than he would be within.

He pushed the door open and almost strangled in the rancid atmosphere inside. When his eyes adjusted to the dark, he realized he was alone save for the host, who was warming his back at a discouraged little blaze in the fireplace.

The two men drank each other in for a long moment. In the light from the fire and the few rays coming through the windowpanes, Armand took in the filthy apron, the fishy eye, the face shining with old grease, and a mouth half open and filled with bad teeth. It was not a face to inspire trust. It could have been loved only by an extraordinarily broad-minded mother.

"Monsieur," began Armand with a polite little bow, "perhaps you will do me the service of directing me to Mademoiselle Rahab? I am informed that she may be reached through this inn."

The proprietor scrutinized the visitor unblinkingly.

"Who sent you?"

"Monsieur Joshua."

"Oh? Well, what's he say?"

" 'Our life for yours, if ye utter not this our business.' "

"He's likely to be most anywhere—maybe even out of town," the man whined. "I can't be running all over the place looking for him."

Armand divined that an application of the universal remedy was in order, so he fished out one of his precious silver *ecus* and tossed it in his palm. The innkeeper's glance flickered to the coin. Armand flipped it to him. The innkeeper caught it without a word or a smile, bounced it on the counter, and looked it over carefully. Then he put it in his pocket and left abruptly by the back door.

At length the unlovely face reappeared, and Armand was beckoned out the door into an aromatic little alley deep in garbage and frozen slush. They went around a corner and down several steps to a small door set in the masonry foundation of a crazily built wooden tenement. Armand had to stoop to pass through, and he had no sooner started down the damp stone steps when the other slammed the door behind him. For a moment he felt panic in the darkness, but then he realized that a feeble light shone ahead. A few more steps took him down into someone's wine cellar, cold with sweating walls. A small lamp with a burning rag for a wick, as used in the very poorest homes, weakened the darkness. It allowed Armand to find an upended cask to sit on without letting him see how dirty it was.

He was mulling over all the cases of murder and betrayal he had heard of and marveling at what religion might get one into when the door opened and a slight, wiry young man about his own age came down the steps. The newcomer had a ferret face and a nervous manner. His clothes told of a clerk or apprentice. He spoke so rapidly, it was hard to understand him.

"Monsieur Rahab?" asked Armand.

"Who sent you?" said the other.

"Monsieur Joshua," said Armand, and added the passwords.

"Let us suppose that I am Rahab," said the young man. "What do you want?"

"I understand you travel at times to see kin at Namur. Would you be going again soon?"

"Well?"

"I'd like to accompany you."

"Are you alone?"

"No, I left a woman and three children outside town."

"Rahab" Baudin chewed lightly at his nails. In the dim light it was hard to see his expression, but his tone was hardly encouraging.

"I doubt I'll be going for a time. The weather, you know." He shot a calculating glance at Armand. "It complicates travel."

"How much?"

"Greatly for women, very difficult for children. Accommodations are mediocre, you understand?"

"I quite understand," sighed the soldier. "But assuming the lady and the young persons are experienced travelers, what—or how much—is needed to render the journey, ah, practicable?"

The young man thought this over, perhaps estimating the reduced chances of a group of mixed age and sex in a winter crossing. Doubtless he had seen guides hung in chains when their luck had run out. Armand waited anxiously, for the rates ran from a *pistole** per head on up.

"Two *louis*† each," said the guide finally.

The rascal! Armand thought to himself bitterly. *Two hundred and forty* livres!

Haggling was fruitless; Armand had to agree to the sum though it was twice the going rate. One had to assume that this Rahab was indeed a Rahab and not the Judas he so strongly suggested. All one could do was to pray that the man wasn't one of the breed who led fugitives into traps and then shared the rewards with the soldiery.

---

* *Pistole*: a coin worth ten *livres*.
† *Louis*: a gold coin equivalent to four or five dollars.

"You won't get far prettied up like that," announced Baudin, all business. "I'll bring you clothes that'll fit the part. You have to look like peasants or the game's up before you start."

He mounted the stairs, and Armand heard the door close again. He waited as patiently as he could for another hour. Soon after Baudin returned, Armand emerged into the weak sunlight in a threadbare gray cloak that covered brown peasant serge. He had reluctantly yielded his suit, cloak, boots, and gloves. When he handed over his wig, he bade goodbye to a two-hundred-*livre* investment. His bitterest moment came when he had to surrender his sword, his only remaining memento of his father. But he had to agree that a peasant with a sword was a contradiction in terms. In spite of a painful disagreement with Baudin, Armand steadfastly refused to surrender his pistols, arguing that he would carry them concealed. Baudin had profited handsomely enough already. Disposal of Huguenot gear must be a most profitable sideline for these fellows, Armand concluded morosely.

*   *   *   *   *

It was afternoon when Baudin and Armand reached the waiting quartet outside Sedan. While the guide unpacked a bundle of old clothes, the cold, hungry fugitives lunched on black bread, cheese, and melted snow, saving half the loaf for later.

Madeleine did not look overly entranced with the gray peasant blouse and skirt offered her. She said nothing but made a *moue** of distaste when she discovered that the garments were not very clean and a number of small creatures had previously laid claim to them. But Alexandre was frankly enthusiastic about the masquerade, and the twins caught some of his excitement. The guide gathered up their old clothing and disappeared toward town while the refugees strove to perfect their disguises.

Madeleine sniffed. She surveyed the skirt of peasant shortness somewhat doubtfully, and then gingerly began to knot the dingy kerchief under her chin.

---

* Grimace or frown.

"I feel half dressed," she mourned. "And this bodice is twice too large."

Armand looked alternately at Madeleine's fine features and slim ankles. "There would be no difficulty in making you appear a lady of quality," he commented, "but you make a most unconvincing peasant."

She rocked on her heels to test the wooden shoes, her teeth chattering with the cold. "Oh," she said, "I can take care of that, I think." She stooped and pried at the frozen ground with a stick. "A little more dirt on the face and hands and perhaps some scratches." She began to apply the dirt like a cosmetic. The twins watched with interest and then imitated her.

"I don't know," said Armand critically. "You're going to have to stoop a little and look more broken-spirited to convince anyone. What is good carriage for a lady is insolence in a milkmaid. See if you can learn to waddle—no, you are not endowed properly for that—shamble, perhaps?"

Under his stare, she blushed and turned away impatiently.

"You might look at yourself," she retorted. "You'll have to do better at Jacques Bonhomme. Right now you look like an officer in disguise— rather poorly done at that. You've got an aristocratic beak that doesn't hide well; you've shaved too recently; and your spine is all parade ground."

He shrugged amiably and refused to argue further. "I wonder what is keeping our profiteer," he said. "I think I'll take a look by the road."

Alexandre had been following the conversation closely. "You know," he said to Madeleine in a low voice, "this should be the test! If you can snare him looking like that, then it's true love."

"You hold your tongue, you loathsome boy," she hissed between clenched teeth. "You're not even to *think* such things."

"And I can add two and two!" he hissed back, mimicking her.

"You are absolutely insufferable!"

"And you are so beautiful when you are angry!"

Armand returned at that moment. "Our Rahab approaches," he said cheerfully. "We'll let him judge our masquerade. It's his neck too if the disguise isn't a good one. He must know his business or he had been hung long ago!"

* * * * *

They didn't go far that afternoon. The sun disappeared early behind clouds and refused to come back; obviously, more snow was on the way. The guide conducted them to a stone barn at the edge of the hamlet of Floing, about a mile from Sedan, where the travelers spent a snug night in a haymow. Half a dozen other fugitives hid there too, but they had little opportunity for visiting.

Well before dawn several guides appeared and led their charges off into the dark. As Armand and his party trudged through the trees, they found themselves wondering who the other fugitives were, where they had come from, and what their experiences might have been. Except for murmured greetings, there had been no talk. They wondered especially about one man who had coughed uncontrollably most of the night. As they left, they had paused for prayer. The guide had stood aloof, perhaps offended at an appeal to a Competitor.

The officer and Alexandre would have had no great trouble in keeping up with the guide, but with Madeleine and the twins it was difficult. Baudin had discouraged conversation, and throughout the day he seemed to become more sullen than ever. By midafternoon it began to snow again, and travel became harder. Much of the route led up and down rough, forested slopes. When the youngsters began to falter, Armand carried them by turns on his shoulders. Alexandre spelled him manfully, but he could not carry them for as long a time. Madeleine had not said a word for hours, but she was beginning to breathe in gasps and to find her wet skirts increasingly an encumbrance. The guide, however, permitted no stops. He seemed to think they should cover the ground as nimbly as he.

The party avoided roads and cut through the forest of Mazarin and the King's Forest by almost invisible trails. At one point they crossed the River Semoy in a leaky rowboat. This put them in or near Spanish territory, but they would not be safe yet, considering how often the French violated the border.

About dusk, Armand could stand it no longer. He didn't wish to handicap the guide, but they couldn't continue at this pace. He called for a halt. He was positive the guide heard him but took no notice. The next time, the officer snapped his request as an order. The guide stopped about twenty feet away and half turned.

"A little rest, I beg you, for the sake of the young ones," said Armand.

"I thought monsieur was in haste." His attitude was ugly.

Armand fought down a hot retort. He reminded himself that they needed him but he didn't need them. And he had some right to be touchy. "Certainly," Armand replied evenly, "but the little ones are exhausted, and we shall make better time with a quarter of an hour's rest."

The guide grunted, and his glance wavered between Armand and Madeleine. For two *sous* he'd leave them in the lurch, thought Armand grimly. And for five he'd whistle up the troopers. For all Armand knew, he'd been leading them in circles all afternoon.

In the meantime, the four Cortots had sunk down in the snow a third of the way down a steep slope. Below them, scattered small trees and bushes cut off the view from the valley below. At the bottom wound a narrow trail visible from where the guide stood. There was no screen of growth directly below him.

Baudin stood there, one hand in his coat pocket, one leg bent to steady himself on the slope, watching the fugitives silently. It was getting too dark to see his face clearly. Suddenly the man turned his head as if he'd heard something. Then Armand heard it too. Something was moving on the trail. With one accord they looked downhill. From where he crouched, Armand could see nothing, but he could hear the murmuring of men's voices and the muffled jingle of harnesses. It was a cavalry patrol.

The guide must have felt exposed, though in that dim light his figure would have been hard to distinguish from a bush even had anyone below thought to look up that way. Perhaps some other idea crossed his mind. In any case, he suddenly leaped away from the refugees and started to run across the opening toward the shrubbery a dozen yards away.

One of the horsemen shouted, and almost immediately came the dull report of a carbine. Monsieur Baudin seemed to pause in midleap, spun halfway around with his mouth gaping open, folded up, and rolled down the slope.

Armand sat for a long moment, his jaw dropped in sheer incredulity at the unlikely shot in that light and distance. Madeleine and Alexandre stared in horror. The twins, lying in the snow, were too exhausted to know what had happened.

Suddenly gathering his frozen wits, Armand grabbed Madeleine's wrist and dragged her to her feet. He then scooped one child from the snow and Alexandre scrambled for the other. They shuffled desperately up the slope in the direction from which they had come. The men at the foot of the grade were doubtless dismounted by now and would be climbing up to investigate. If the little party could get out of sight, the deepening darkness would cover their footprints for now, and the falling snow would complete the job during the night.

Soon they were over the top and panting down the other side. It was now completely dark, and they were lost. Armand decided it would be useless to blunder about in the blackness. They had to have rest, and he would need sunlight or at least daylight to guess in which direction to go.

They hollowed out the snow under the low, overhanging boughs of a huge evergreen. The snowfall stopped after a while, and it seemed to get colder. Huddling together for warmth under the two cloaks they still had, they spent a night of fitful dozing. The children were tired enough to lie there and peacefully freeze, but Armand insisted that everyone be awakened at intervals to rub feet and hands.

Conversation on such occasions was desultory and wandering. They discussed their late guide and speculated about his intentions, uncertain whether to regard him with pity or to see in his fate divine retribution. Howling wolves brought them to consciousness twice. And once, Madeleine began to search about in distress. She had lost her miniature psalter, and this seemed to upset her particularly, for it had been a gift at her first Communion. It was the first and only time on the journey Armand heard her cry.

When fatigue threatened to overcome them entirely, Madeleine kept the younger ones awake by putting them through the Ten Commandments, the Apostles' Creed, the Little Catechism, and assorted prayers for special occasions. It was hard work, for her charges were sleepy and resentful. Armand dozed, coming up every so often and hearing the soft murmur of voices in a dark dream world.

"Now recite the 'Mirror of Youth' from the *Christian A B C*," ordered Madeleine. Alexandre yawned and mumbled haltingly,

> The good child fears the Lord
>> In reverence and all honor.
> The perverse child fears not God
>> And nothing does without constraint.

He faltered.
"Good, good. Go on."

> The good child fears anything to do
>> Which might God displease.
> The lax one always himself will plunge
>> In dishonesty and lies.

"I've forgotten how the rest of it goes, and I don't see what difference it makes anyway," Alexandre grumbled.

"You have it mixed up," his sister replied with a patient yawn. "That part about the 'lax' goes somewhere else."

She prodded Louis and started him on the second verse. He recited purely by rote and so faintly Armand could barely hear him,

> The good child fears anything to do
>> Which might God displease.
> The perverse child in all he does,
>> Wishes only his own will to do.

* * * * *

Voices wakened the fugitives soon after dawn. Through the branches they watched a long line of foot soldiers climb slowly past them. The men were clad mostly in civilian clothes, almost in rags in some cases, but their bandoliers and pikes or muskets identified them as infantrymen. They were moving reluctantly, grumbling as they plowed through the soft snow. They looked, thought Armand, like men who had not had their breakfast. The lieutenant, a serious-faced stripling in full uniform, was climbing at the right of the line. The stick he was swinging hit a branch of the tree under which his quarry was hidden, and a small cascade of snow fell on the breathless watchers. The officer and the line padded on, accompanied by aureoles of steam from their labored breathing. In spite of the grave danger, Armand couldn't help smiling. Not too many years had passed since he had been a new lieutenant and much of the world's burdens had rested on *his* shoulders.

The hidden ones had just expelled their breath in relief when they suddenly tensed in horror. Two men at the end of the line had been dropping farther and farther back. Unseen by the sergeant at the left rear, they slipped unobtrusively over to a snow-covered log not ten feet from the Huguenots and sat down. The older man laid his pike in the snow; the other leaned his musket against the log, muzzle uppermost. They sat for a few moments beating their blue hands together while the younger one with sincerity and thoroughness gave his views on the army, the sergeant, the lieutenant, the Huguenots, and the weather.

The veteran soldier remained calm, cracking his knuckles and blowing on his hands. "It may be warmer where you come from, my young friend," he said reprovingly, "but I think it's going to be a good bit warmer yet where you're going!"

The young soldier glared at his companion. "At least in Montpellier they're not idiotic enough to chase themselves through the woods on an empty stomach! That dog's head of a lieutenant! He takes it as a personal insult that those heretics disappeared last night."

"Maybe they were witches," grunted the other.

"Well, they weren't witches that Baudin fellow was with when he got shot! He wasn't out running around in the snow for his health—not at that time of night with a pocket full of gold. Everybody along the border knew he was guiding PRRs." He swung his arms angrily. "What a miserable business! If I ever see that recruiter who told me all those lies about the army, I'll cut his throat! Up before dawn. Not a chance for a bite or a swallow of something warm."

Madeleine pressed her upper lip, fighting desperately against a sneeze.

"It's all stupid anyway," the young man concluded. "This isn't what I enlisted for."

His senior yawned and stretched. "That's where you're wrong, my boy. Take the word of one who was a soldier when you were still in dresses. It's not for you to say what you enlisted for. If it's the pleasure of His Gracious Majesty that you're to be shot by some Dutchman in the Low Countries while wading in muck up to your elbows, then that's what you enlisted for. If, on the other hand, His Majesty has been seeing less of Louvois and more of the bishops and of Madame de Maintenon, why, then you enlisted to beat the bushes for those who don't go to the right church. It's as simple as that.

"Be calm and reflective, my boy. If I had my choice, I'd take this over that. *This* is cold, and we've had nothing to eat since yesterday afternoon, but *that* is wet, and the Dutchmen shoot at you besides. I will therefore overlook the frightening simplicity of your conversation."

"Why don't you hold your jaw?" interrupted the other rudely.

"Listen, my son. Don't always expose your folly and inexperience. Even if you made marshal someday—what a dreadful thought for France—even then you'd find you wouldn't be able to decide what to do with yourself. Even then there'd be someone to help the king make up his mind, so you'd be just as bad off as you are right now, a very homely private soldier with missing buttons and a runny nose."

The younger man favored the philosopher with a frosty regard. "If you elderly bores fought as well as you talked, we should have had the Lowlands these twelve years and the heretics would have no place to run."

It was the other's turn to be offended, and they sat in silence for a moment. The younger man snapped a brittle twig from a bare bush protruding from the snow and switched it listlessly. Then came a halloo from somewhere up the white slope behind them. Both soldiers turned their heads, looking unhappily at the line of footprints disappearing into the trees.

"Our martial babe has discovered that the expedition is not up to full strength. Even now he asks the good sergeant to count the lambs." The soldier rose and brushed caked snow from his coattails.

The younger one picked up his musket. "There are thirty of us," he said scornfully. "That big ape can't count beyond five. What they've missed is that big red lantern you carry for a nose. It's like a fifth flag for the regiment."

A second yell, more urgent than the first, echoed among the trees.

"It has ever been the fate of wisdom and experience to be sneered at by callow youth," observed the veteran as he began to move, trailing his pike behind him.

"My apologies. Certainly, if promotions were earned in tavern affrays, *you* would have made marshal by now." They trudged away quarreling, slipping in the snow.

The fugitives remained huddled for a long time. Finally they looked at each other somewhat sheepishly, and tense muscles relaxed.

* * * * *

Over the next two days there was a sameness to their torment that made it hard to remember what occurred during a particular day. When the feeble sun appeared for a few minutes, Armand tried to set a course for the north. He felt that the border would not prove far away if they could go in a straight line. But all they had was snow, trees, cold, and hunger.

Later, they halted at the edge of a small clearing. Ahead was the modest cottage of a forester, with stable attached. While Armand debated what to do next, the twins flopped in the snow in a stupor. Armand and Alexandre had been carrying them by turns much of the time, but it was increasingly hard to keep mind and will obedient. The white wilderness numbed more than fingers and toes. Madeleine knelt by the youngsters and looked up frightened.

"They can't go any farther this way. They're hardly out of bib and gown. I can't see them starve here in front of my eyes! I'm going to ask for food at that house."

Armand was equally positive. "We're lost if you do. They'll hold us and call the troopers. Let's not give up now. It *can't* be much farther!"

"Well, one mile or twenty—they can't go on without food."

Armand was stupid with fatigue and hunger himself. He shrugged.

"Perhaps so. Maybe we were led this way for their sakes. If just the children and you . . . God grant that they are folk with kind hearts."

However, he made them wait until it seemed certain that the man of the house was not in. The afternoon was waning when Madeleine half led and half dragged Louis and Louise to the cottage door, followed by a subdued Alexandre. Armand lay in concealment and watched them.

Madeleine had to knock twice before the door opened an inch and a frightened young peasant woman peeped out. She started to close the door again.

"Please!" Madeleine's voice was so despairing that the woman reluctantly opened the door a little wider. The Cortots entered the single room with its great bed in one corner, the chest in the other, and the fireplace with copper kettles gleaming dully on the wall above. The floor was earthen.

The woman, blond and sturdy, wore plain, threadbare clothing. Three towheaded children clung to her skirts. They looked frightened too, for they probably saw few strangers in this isolated place. But what instantly drew the attention of the visitors was the iron pot with a vegetable stew bubbling on the hearth. The smell along with the closeness of the room made Madeleine dizzy. The forester's wife noticed her pale face and helped her to a three-legged stool.

"We've been on a journey," Madeleine explained unnecessarily. "I think we have lost our way, and we saw your house among the trees. Could I beg you to feed the children? They are spent. I'll need nothing if you have but little."

The woman looked uneasily at the door. Her mind was not hard to read. *Her husband is out hunting us right now,* Madeleine thought in despair. *Armand was right. I've ruined us—but what else was there to do?*

Madeleine's anguish was so plain that it seemed to help the woman make up her mind. She swung the door open and, speaking in the local dialect, murmured, "You are welcome, but we don't have much to offer." Then she brushed aside her brood, took down four wooden bowls, and filled them with the stew. It was mostly turnip, for such people did not often see meat. But it was hot. She had them sit at the trestle table while she hacked off coarse hunks of blackish bread. Madeleine furtively concealed her slice, thinking of the famished Armand outside in the snow.

With the sudden relaxation and the warmth, Madeleine felt such a lassitude creeping over her that she wished she could lie down and sleep for a century. She looked longingly at the feather bed behind the green serge curtains and wondered if she would ever luxuriate in a real bed again. But they must not tarry and compromise their hostess. Either the woman had decided charity was permissible if one did not know the identity of the guests or she expected her husband soon.

She firmly refused any money and insisted they take the rest of the loaf. She held the door for them as they filed out into the winter again, and she gave them a pitying look as she closed the door. Madeleine had, however, left a gold coin under her bowl, and she felt that never had she received such value for her money.

* * * * *

That night they spent a little more comfortably, this time in a straw-stack. In the morning they struck a forest path and followed in the direction Armand hoped was north. The thick snow showed their prints remorselessly, so they struggled along the roadside, ready to dive for cover if anyone appeared. When sure they were alone, they softly sang some of the psalms of Marot. Again the rests tended to become longer and more frequent. The bread gave out, and courage began to slip.

In the early afternoon, they had one close call when they collided with a cavalry patrol. Armand and Alexandre leaped to shelter, but Madeleine and the twins, lagging a little behind, their hearing dulled by fatigue, didn't run in time. The girl had the good sense to keep walking as if indifferent to the horsemen.

The trio no doubt looked as gray and ragged as any other peasants, and the bored troopers, wrapped to the nose against the cold, showed no curiosity. Armand held his breath as the soldiers passed, for he knew better than the brave Madeleine what a slug from a carbine could do. Only her tattered rags looked the peasant, he decided. Her carriage was as defiant as ever; she betrayed no peasant in her features.

* * * * *

Late in the afternoon, coming over a rise, Armand halted dumb-founded. Before the travelers stood a hut, a wooden barrier, and the river flowing by the side of the road. Wooded slopes rose on both sides. It was a French border post. They must have wandered back into France again, perhaps into the finger of land pointing north from Givet.

They sat down behind a tree and held a council. They could cut off into the forest and hills, but then they would lose the road and the river. The children were in no condition to begin that all over again. The Lord had brought them thus far, said Armand, and though by no means as self-confident as he had been a few days earlier, he was for attempting to brazen their way through. This time it was Madeleine who protested.

"We'll see," Armand said. "If the Lord will provide but a single sentinel, and a venal one by preference, all may go well yet."

He stood up and looked down at his charges. Their faces were pinched with hunger and fatigue, their lips blue with cold. Even Alexandre said little.

On the occasion of that battle seven years before, he reminded himself, the odds had been nearly hopeless. If the Imperialist colonel had known his business, Armand and his men would have been picked up in blankets. Now he felt the same dryness in his mouth he had known that day when the enemy horse came bearing down on his wavering company and he realized that the French cavalry on his flank was oozing to the rear. He had done all he could do and left the rest with the Lord. His musketeers had held steady until the moment to fire, and the tide turned. Now again he must hold steady and leave the rest to the Lord.

"You remain where you are," he told the Cortots. "I'm going down to try to persuade the guard to let us through. Let us each have a bundle of sticks as if we have been gathering firewood. If it goes all right, I'll signal you to go through the barrier. Go without stopping, mind you, or saying a word, no matter what I do. If I'm seized, keep your heads. Hide here till dark and then try to go around through the woods and regain the road as soon as you can. The Spanish border must be very close now. Truly, I had thought we were there already. I'll go now and see what the Lord intends for us." Straightening up, he threw them a debonair half salute. Louise began to cry.

Smoke was rising from the guard hut some yards from the road.

Sounds of drunken quarreling inside could be heard. The sentry at the barrier was stamping his feet and singing softly to himself a current ditty good for a sentence in any Paris jail.

> If you want to know why
>> La Chaise is the king's confessor,
> It's because this sneaky priest—

Armand approached, trying to look as humble as possible. The singer stopped abruptly and wheeled on the newcomer. Under the scrutiny of the sentry, Armand attempted to amble peasant-fashion. It was not too difficult, for he was weak from hunger.

The soldier was short and slight, with bright black eyes set close together. He had missing teeth. His hat brim was folded up on each side, revealing the face of the younger of the two soldiers who had been quarreling in the snow several mornings earlier.

Armand removed his hat and tried to cringe as became a ragged inferior. This was difficult, for the border guard was a head shorter.

"Who goes?" snapped the soldier.

"I'd like to go up the road yonder," replied the bogus peasant hesitantly. "I came down this morning to gather wood, and it's shorter home this way. I'm from the village right up the road." *If I were alone,* thought Armand, *I'd have a try at clubbing him, for my pistols are surely too wet to fire.*

"Well, let's see your passport," demanded the soldier, leaning his arm on the musket barrel.

"Passport? I never needed one before to gather wood!" Armand tried to strike the proper aggrieved note.

"I'll wager you didn't." The border guard said and elevated his musket until it pointed at Armand's empty stomach. "Now tell me a better one, my boy, or I'll call the sergeant. He'll know how to make you talk." His voice was still low, and his noisy comrades behind the shut door could have heard nothing.

Armand felt faint and sweaty. With a four-day beard, his rags, and the bundle of sticks, he had hoped for better than this.

"You're a soldier, I'll warrant," accused the sentry without waiting for an answer. "An officer?" There was just a touch of respect or uncertainty creeping in. His eye sought the identifying sash that wasn't there.

"I am—or was," confessed Armand. "You've spotted me fairly enough. I was major in the Maine Regiment. And you?"

"Vermandois."

"I recall that we fought alongside of you at Langenbruck in '79. Were you there?"

The sentry seemed flattered at being taken for a veteran but kept his piece leveled. "No, but I've heard of the affair often enough from the old liars who make up this outfit. Wasn't that the time when one of your lieutenants rallied the whole line and recaptured the flags practically by himself?"

"Yes. I was there and saw it," said Armand truthfully. The sentry whistled softly.

"I wish we might have known each other in such times," Armand added courteously, "but here we are out in the cold with our teeth chattering."

"Yes, I might as well turn you in. No doubt you're a PRR?"

"True, but I wonder if you would first do me a favor as a man of the Vermandois for a comrade of the Maine?"

The sentry was silent but kept his shrewd eyes on the suppliant.

"I promised a fine old man," continued Armand, "a comrade of my father's at the Battle of the Dunes, that I'd see his daughter and little ones out of this and to their friends in Holland. If you feel you could let four young peasants through with firewood, I'd be honored to accept arrest at your hands."

"What! Don't you want to cross over too?" The soldier was whispering now.

"Certainly, but you caught me fairly, and I can't complain. But as to tormenting a young lady and children who have already lost their loved ones and goods, well, that isn't what you enlisted for, is it?"

The soldier stared at him queerly but said nothing.

"Since I'll have no further use for it and wouldn't want it spread among those who have done nothing to deserve it, may I present you with this?" With a slight bow, he offered his purse to his captor. The soldier glanced slyly at the hut and quickly hid the purse in his shirt. He lowered the gun.

"Well, send 'em through, but you'd better not go with them. If anyone happened to see five of you, it might remind them of some folks we're supposed to be watching for. Hide here below on the riverbank till it's dark, and I'll give you a chance to go before I'm relieved. But be careful even out there." He pointed north. "The border is back of us here, but our horse wander all over. Who cares for the king of Spain, eh?" He winked in comradely fashion.

Armand started to stammer his thanks but was silenced with a lordly gesture. "I don't know why I'm doing this, but you're right—I *didn't* enlist for this. To wear a hat with a feather and be bawled out by flat-headed sergeants? The bastinado if you forget to salute. And this five-*sous*-a-day freezing in the snow on Madam de Maintenon's business!" His tone was vicious.

"With this," the soldier patted the purse under his jacket, "I'll buy into a public house back at Montpellier. But go while you can and come and see us down south some day."

Armand waved the Cortots on and then jumped down the bank, where he lay flat in the gravel.

Madeleine and the others moved forward though mystified at Armand's actions. They hoisted their bundles of sticks and plodded down to the barrier. Armand was not to be seen. As they approached the sentry, he shifted his musket to his left hand and with his right carefully lifted the bar just enough for them to slip through. Madeleine sought his face anxiously, but he was impassive and said not a word. He replaced the bar swiftly and watched them as they walked hurriedly down the road and around the bend. They dared not turn for a last glance at their native land.

It was about dark when the soldier finally called Armand. He had been lying on the frozen ground so long that he thought he could not bend his joints, but he scrambled up to the sentry fast enough.

"You'd better be off, major," the sentry said in a low voice, "but remember, stay separate until you reach a large Belgian town. Have you any money? Perhaps you'd better take back some of this." He reached inside his jacket.

"No, no!" Armand insisted. "I'll get on all right. God bless you for your good heart. Perhaps you'll never make marshal now, but at least you should be a prince of innkeepers." He clasped the hand of the soldier.

Just as he turned to slip by the barrier, he heard the unmistakable sound of horses' hooves from the direction of France. He shot a questioning look at the sentry. "Will they be riding over the line?"

"Don't worry, major. I'll delay them a little for you."

Without further ado, Armand set off as fast as he could manage without actually running. The soldier watched him go around the bend and out of sight.

* * * * *

In the dusk, the jingling of harness sounded distinctly. The patrol would appear over the rise at any moment. Suddenly the soldier let out a loud yell and fired his piece in the air. Instantly the door of the hut burst open, and a squad of soldiers boiled out, followed by a burly sergeant.

"Two of 'em up the slope there," cried the sentry, pointing back toward France. The sergeant and his men set out on the run and were presently joined by the horsemen. After several confused minutes of checking their own footprints, they all came straggling back.

"Huguenots, bah! There wasn't even a cow up there. I don't know why all the half-wits from every foundling home in France have to be shoveled into this regiment. For this you can do the next turn on duty too!" The sergeant disappeared into the hut.

The cavalrymen dismounted to warm their hands and to chaff the unlucky sentry. He took it pleasantly enough though. His gaze was abstracted and far away, like that of a man who fancied himself already established as a prosperous innkeeper.

After half an hour the cavaliers remounted in leisurely fashion, and the horses stalked up the snowy road into the land of the king of Spain. Ahead of them, five Huguenots trudged warily along, hoping to find refuge in the Netherlands.

PART II

1688

Chapter 7

Exiled

While many can suffer martyrdom with sufficient heroism, not all are cut out to live their faith through long adversity. Hope deferred is debilitating to spiritual resolve. The exiled Jews, as the psalmist tells us, hung their harps by the willow trees and wept by the waters of Babylon. The Huguenot exiles in Holland, having willows but lacking harps, could weep by the canals of Amsterdam if they chose, but in the land of the work ethic, such leisure was not approved, and it was rather too cold to lie about—whether weeping or dry-eyed—on canal banks.

The chill of the Dutch morning was weakening; the sun was gaining confidence. Water in the Amsterdam canals was beginning to look more blue than gray. Foot traffic along the banks was brisk, and one had to keep an eye out for laden porters, scurrying errand boys, and chattering servant girls in wooden shoes returning from market with their loaded baskets. Amsterdam may have been the cleanest city of the day; it certainly was one of the richest. The narrow, richly ornamented houses of the merchants, each with its projecting hoist above the street, the smell of spices from the nearby harbor, as well as the variety of sailors from every ocean testified to prosperous trade. The Dutch citizens passing by looked well-fed and comfortable.

A little out of place amid all the good-humored prosperity and bustle was a tall, bronzed young man of perhaps twenty-eight. He strode along the edge of the canal, his bearing erect, a threadbare gray cloak wrapped around his broad shoulders, a black rusty-looking wide-brimmed hat on his head. He wore his own hair, which was dark, and in spite of his shabby appearance, he carried a sword as a gentleman customarily would. While he did not look exactly despondent, there was nothing particularly joyous about his expression. He seemed distracted, scarcely noticing the activity about him. Anyone observing the streets of Dutch towns in recent months could have identified the type—a former French officer, now a refugee in Holland for his Huguenot faith. His name was Major Henri Armand, le Sieur de Gandon of Languedoc.

Armand had hoped for a commission in the army of William of Orange, who had joined the League of Augsburg in hopes of stemming the advancing tide of French aggression, which was occurring on several fronts. Most recently, rumors suggested the Dutch prince might even be called to replace his Catholic father-in-law, James II, on the English throne. In that case, Armand believed, he could well expect a preferment, for his military record was good. And in England he would not expect to face in battle his former comrades at arms in the French Regiment of the Maine.

Income from Armand's patrimony in Languedoc was sparse and came through secret channels in most irregular fashion. Though he practiced frugality to the extreme, matters had become critical, and after more than two years there had been no acceptable offer of a military position. And unfortunately for him, warfare was his profession.

The soldier was turning these considerations over in his mind for the hundredth time as he had crossed a small footbridge and started to turn down a narrow path between houses—when he almost collided with a fashionably dressed gentleman twice his age. Each had begun an apologetic bow when mutual recognition stopped them.

"Armand de Gandon!" cried the dapper one, extending his hand.

"Ah! Le Sieur de Tillieres!" replied Gandon, equally surprised. "Who would have thought to meet *you* here! It was a year ago at Versailles when I last saw you."

As soon as he spoke, Armand realized that this was not perhaps a flattering thing to say to a conscientious Huguenot. However, the gentleman from Poitou showed no offense. He replied, "I'm here for the same reason you are, I'll venture. But how do you fare in this abominable land of fog? I have been in town but a week, and I suspect that I already have caught an affection of the lungs. I have not yet located a home though my marriage approaches, and I am hard pressed to provide a comfortable establishment for my Dutch bride."

"I congratulate you," Armand said.

"Beastly cold," Tillieres said, and he drew a silken muffler across the open front of his elegant coat.

"My lodgings are near at hand," Armand offered. "While I took but a room, and that chosen for economy, it is dry and out of the wind. More accommodating than the draughty barracks at Versailles, at least."

Tillieres coughed and gestured dramatically. "Lead on. I follow."

They passed between two warehouses abutting the canal. Tillieres spoke rapidly, clarifying his present circumstances. His father's recent death had left him in control of his legacy, and he had managed to sell most of his country estate in Rochefort at a good price. Over the past year he had sent his assets through friends to Dutch banks, invested fortuitously in shipping, and already reaped some excellent profits. Here Tillieres grew confidential, lowering his voice and leaning against Armand's shoulder. Some five years ago, shortly after the death of his first wife, he had contracted his impending marriage with the daughter of a wealthy burgher.

"My father, of course, must always be watchful! Our plans didn't meet with his good graces. You might imagine, *mon ami*: He threatened to request *une lettre de cachet** to bring me to recognize my folly—such a breach of honor! The honor of *famille*†—to my father it was always religion itself. He would not continence such a union. My marriage to the daughter of a burgher, no matter how wealthy, was a disgrace equal to drunkenness, to dissipation of inheritance, to violence, even to murder!"

"Was your father not then a Huguenot?" Armand asked.

---

* Arrest warrant.

† Family.

"In his fashion," sighed Tillieres. "Quite strict about some things, but always more prideful than befits our sect. His stance always brought grief to my saintly mother, you can imagine, de Gandon. Fortunately, I was able to avert the arrest warrant by exercising discretion. And then about a year ago, Father died suddenly of a fever. That he should see my marriage to dear Catherine an embarrassment!"

He was full to overflowing with his own good fortune, except for the weather, of course, which he feared would undo all his entrepreneurial precautions. Armand could not suppress a smile.

"Unfortunately, I have realized only limited income from my family estates in Languedoc since my father's death nine years ago," Armand said, opening the street-side door and preceding his guest up the narrow stairs. "Just sufficient for a satin waistcoat, silk stockings, and elegant shoes—and a rather shabby brown wig."

"I am again fortunate there." Tillieres laughed, and his voice reverberated up the brick stairwell. "My own hair is fair and full, more comely than any wigmaker's best creation."

"Indeed," Armand agreed, remembering occasions at court when Tillieres' golden ringlets falling across his shoulders had been the subject of exclamations of admiration. Armand bent to open the door at the topmost landing.

"Is such poverty necessary?" Tillieres turned slowly, taking in the small room.

"Unfortunately."

"You must know that His Grace, le Duc de Lauzières, still entertains the warmest feeling for you," remarked Tillieres as they sat on three-legged stools in the garret, the only light coming from a small window that looked out on the street four stories below.

Armand grimaced, struck by affection for his old commander in the Regiment of Maine. "It is indeed kind of him," he sighed, "and so like his nobility of soul. But I fear it will only make him trouble with the jealous or the fanatical at court. As long as I profess my Protestant faith, I can't see any way I could go back to the life at Versailles that the duke wants for me. You have heard that since February no Protestant may hold a military commission, and civil positions were closed before that.

I would not play the hypocrite to please even a duke—or to inherit his estate."

Armand suddenly felt uneasy. His companion's face had changed from beneficent interest to an almost wily scrutiny.

"Nothing controls the king's passions so fully as his pride in his army," said Tillieres. "Your heroic record, particularly in the Palatinate campaign has been often praised. Young as you are, you are somewhat of a legend. Such promising young officers are hard to enlist, especially when men with ambitions are afraid to be far from Versailles. The king has created his own worst dilemma. Of course, not long since, near half of the higher ranks in His Majesty's army were Huguenots. Irreplaceable military geniuses—and most loyal. The king will never find another Schomberg!"

Armand clasped his hands and watched his knuckles whiten. "Marshal Schomberg was my father's commander. Father named me for the great leader."

"I had guessed as much."

"Now Marshal Schomberg has gone over to the British rather than accept the king's exemption and keep his religious life a secret. What must it mean to a man who has spent sixty years in the French army?"

Neither spoke for several minutes. Tillieres sighed dramatically.

"*Tiens.* I have no such vocation as you, my friend. His Majestic Highness does not seek me to bring glory to his name and to France. I have no such battle between a patriotic conscience and my moral persuasion."

Armand gripped his knees. "Just so. The king has never had subjects more loyal to his authority than we have been. Even now, Huguenots all over France—"

"Ah, yes. We are all too accustomed to riding on the horns of the bull!" Tillieres said, interrupting. He continued, "His Grace, the duke, learned in some fashion that I intended to flee the country. Like you, I finally decided I could no longer live this double life. Your benefactor called me to his Paris hotel scarcely a fortnight ago, and he talked of you and his concern for your fortune—the opportunities you were throwing away by remaining a Huguenot and playing—as he called it, please understand—the fool over a pretty face. To be very blunt, he wanted me to seek you out and ask you straightly if you had not had enough of exile and might now be willing to come back to France. If so, he would never mention your recent deviations, and he was confident that he could smooth matters over with the king."

Armand stared at his battered shoes, flexing his toes inside the thin leather.

"Of course, I reminded him," Tillieres continued, "that you are a man of principle and would be unwilling to pretend a conversion, but he waved this aside. He feels, as you know, that God is much the same sort of gentleman as he is himself, incapable of the 'enthusiasm' of Jansenists and Huguenots but rather indulgent to one who kept his beliefs to himself and conformed outwardly to please a king—to whom, he pointed out, we owe obedience by a most scriptural authority. True, both Louvois and Madame de Maintenon are unforgiving toward rebellious heretics, but the duke feels that he is close enough to His Majesty to explain matters fully, and that the king's natural sense of justice would prevail, and you could be reinstated. Considering his military goals and his short supply . . ."

"I—" began the major with a shake of the head. But Tillieres gave him no time to shape a reply. "The duke also said you would at once refuse these suggestions, and I see he knows you well. You are doing the right thing, of course, and I honor you for it," Tillieres added a little sententiously. "But he did make me promise that I would point out to you that his door is always open as long as he lives, and that no other will ever replace you in his affections, but that you are not obligated to give him an immediate answer."

"He was always most gracious," murmured Armand.

Confound it, he thought to himself, *now I can never close the door on this temptation!* Last year he had thought he had made the great decision once and for all. Now, no matter how vigorously he rejected the idea, it would always be waiting for him in moments of discouragement. How could he forget the good days with his regiment, basking in the praise of men and officers alike, hearing his name repeated at every turn, feeling in his body the surging power of perfect health at the command of excellent military training? How could he not be mindful of the fact that, though a young man of diminished fortune, he might have wealth and a grand position by simply humoring a duke? Besides, the duke's generosity made him feel like such an ungrateful cur. He well knew what damage the duke's rivals could do if they got wind of the old man's efforts to help an exiled heretic.

Tillieres' silence was out of character and thus more unnerving than his headlong speech. Armand, feeling his companion's eyes, feared his own struggle was evident. He strove to compose his face and control his voice. "I thank you for your trouble in this matter, but we know better than he how we of the Religion must decide such questions if we are to be faithful to our Lord. I would the duke found someone more worthy of the fortune he wishes to bestow!"

"I can think of no one more worthy than yourself," Tillieres assured him heartily. "But I agree that the Christian cannot allow himself to be bought thus. I have done as I promised the venerable man. I have spoken on his behalf."

After Tillieres departed, Armand sat long on his three-legged stool in the gloomy little room reviewing the conversation. Brave words he had tossed off, to be sure! He knew a certain number of exiles had become discouraged and had sneaked back to bow the knee to Baal. And thousands of Huguenots still lived under Pharaoh. How did they fare? Did they witness publicly, or was it only secret worship they attempted?

Et moi? he thought. *What reason have I to assume my prospects will improve in the months—or years—to come?* The Prince of Orange's messenger today had brought the same stale message to the coffee house most frequented by refugee soldiers: "If war breaks out over the English throne, we will call for you at once, but right now, nothing." By dining as often as he could with more fortunate refugees and by economies of the meaner sort, he had fended off real distress—to this point. It was perhaps a good idea not to poke about too deeply into the recesses of his own mind. Could he say "No" as firmly a year from now if he were really hungry and in rags?

From the bench that served as washstand, table, and sideboard, he took up a roll that yesterday he had bought for a quarter its price, it being two days from the oven. Without so much as a bite, he thrust it back upon its plate.

"*C'est ça!* This is hard crust of charity! Whichever way I look at my present choices, there is but charity—charity from the duke, who clearly believes I am worthy of all he has already invested in me, or charity I must humbly accept from the wealthy Protestants of Amsterdam!"

He couldn't suppress a smile. Perhaps with more flamboyant feathers he might attract the daughter of a rich burgher as Tillieres had. But even then, the good business sense of the Dutch would prevent charity in that extreme. And although his feelings for Madeleine could never come to anything, they forbade him from even the appearance of interest in another.

"*Tiens!*" It was his own private folly to allow his heart to become involved in what had been a charitable act, helping the four children of his father's lifetime Huguenot friend to escape from France. That had been three years past, and yet in his dreams he saw her still—beside the fire in her father's house in the south of France, her twin brother and sister leaning one on each of her shoulders, her mother serene at her needlework, her adolescent brother Alexandre twitching with impatience, her father reading the Scriptures with quiet passion. In his dreams Armand also saw her that stormy night, a dark form crouched on the convent wall; felt her falling into his arms, cold and rain-soaked; felt her gripping his hand as they fled down the muddy hillside from the convent; felt her hand grasping his arm as they evaded the search party on the dangerous flight across northern France and the Spanish Netherlands in freezing rain and snow.

No other woman would ever take the place in his heart in which he had enthroned Madeleine Cortot. However he might waver concerning other matters, this matter was settled.

It was fortunate, Armand mused, that Tillieres had not found Madeleine's brother in the room they had shared for only a few weeks. Alexandre! The boy was born to be hanged. Yet, Armand was certain, there was no man of any age he would rather have at his side in danger. At twelve, Alexandre had been thrown out of the House for New Catholics to which he had been abducted when Madeleine was spirited away to the convent. "Incorrigible!" Alexandre had gleefully repeated the statement of the Dominican charged with his re-education as a Catholic. Alexandre Cortot had proved his mettle in the escape to Holland. And now the fifteen-year-old was insistent. He would be a soldier for some Protestant prince.

"*Certainment* never in the French army, not in the Maine regiment," Armand mused. Alexandre was never the secret dissenter. He would on every occasion that presented itself comment upon "Babylonian horrors" such as the worshiping of images of saints and the kissing of relics. He viewed even common courteous conversation with a Catholic as dissembling, as weak-kneed compromise of principle.

Armand could not help wondering how Tillieres, who claimed he had been brought up in a devout Huguenot family, had managed for so long to conceal his convictions. At Versailles, the middle-aged dandy had never appeared to be anything but the most obsequious of favor-seekers.

"This butterfly has certainly changed," said Armand to himself.

* * * * *

Louis XIV, the Most Christian King, the Grand Monarch of France, as always conscious of his own majesty, passed through the Grand Gallery of his newly completed palace at Versailles. Since it was from the Sun King—and from him only—that the rays of prosperity and favor emanated, few of his court nobility cared to risk his disfavor by absenting themselves. This evening, hundreds of them were crowded into the immense hall and the adjacent salons. The king consciously measured his stride, glancing to the right and to the left and nodding beneficently to his noble subjects. *I am to them the* paterfamilias, *a wise father who has brought together the grand and the petty, all my sons, and their estates and duchies, into my household. I have created France.* Louis repeated that thought thrice in rhythm with his steps.

Four thousand candles glowed softly on the scene and were reflected in the nineteen huge mirrors that gave the gallery its familiar name. It was a fairyland pageant of shining silks, satins, and jewels. The monarch paused to survey the vast reaches of the ceiling, where allegorical paintings depicting his glory hovered like celestial visions. Before proceeding, he looked with approval down the length of the hall, where were arranged silver tables piled high with sweetmeats and orange trees in silver tubs, and where green and gold draperies added to the general effect.

The disadvantage of being king, if one could imagine, was that he was not at liberty to turn from the pageant within to look out the huge windows or to stroll through the acres of formal gardens behind the chateau in the moonlight, among the neatly ordered *allees,** the statuary, the trees, the groups of water deities in the now-silent ornamental fountains, and, in the distance, along the gleaming waters of the Grand Canal. However, within or without the great palace, never had a sovereign such a breathtaking setting for his glory.

Ah, c'est magnifique! *By my wish no one of consequence in all of France even attempts an existence independent of my royal will or distant from my royal person.*

He smiled blandly with satisfaction. His plan had worked. The once rebellious nobility were now so dependent for favors—money and offices—on the royal whim that it was unthinkable for an ambitious scion of the *noblesse* to absent himself from Versailles as long as he could borrow the money to live here and keep up appearances—all in the hope of attracting the eye of the king.

I am the sun! Louis thought, and smiled again. He had for more than a decade kept his courtiers so occupied with elaborate court etiquette and ceremonial, attending him at his *grande levée* and his *coucher,* at his devotions, his table, his hunting parties, and his entertainments that their great purpose in life was to be seen near him at the right time and place. Rising young noblemen might have to sleep in an airless cubicle in one of the Versailles barracks and stand all day on hard floors, jockeying to catch the royal eye and to cut out competitors for the pension, the regiment, or the embassy they sought. Yet to stay on one's country estate, how utterly boring—a living death when everything and everybody of importance gravitated around himself, the Sun King.

---

* Alleys.

The Grand Monarch hesitated only a moment longer as the crowd opened before him. It was evening, time for the *appartement,* or entertainment, and while he did not usually care these days to spend his time listening to the chamber orchestra or watching the dancing or gaming, his courtiers were here, and he must be seen by them all—at a distance, *certainment.* And then he would slip quietly through a secret door to the private apartment of Madame de Maintenon, where he could enjoy the wholesome domestic atmosphere that he craved with growing intensity.

To the right, a duke in splendid sky blue and crimson satin approached, accompanied by a man of thirty with a smooth pink face and wearing a snowy wig. The younger man smiled nervously, and both bowed low, sweeping the floor with their hats in hand.

"My nephew, Your Majesty," simpered the duke.

The king did not quite hear above the din either the nephew's name nor the preferment the duke asked. Nevertheless, he nodded, smiling with practiced grace. "We will see about the matter."

Never decline. Never promise. I must remember to inscribe that advice in my volume of counsel for my grandson. That policy has preserved my life and the nation countless times, the king mused.

As he processed across the hall, he paused again and again, smilingly recognizing the great and those hoping for greatness. Each person pressing toward him asked a favor. Again he uttered the same reply in kindly tone: "We will see about the matter." And eyes gleaming with hope, each suppliant stepped back.

"Mon chere madame," he whispered, already free in his mind from the press around him, already breathing the peaceful restraint surrounding de Maintenon. Though they had married in 1683, he could not make this cherished austere dark beauty his queen, and great the pity.

How different she was from Maria Theresa, who *had* been his queen. Maria Theresa had been the daughter of the king of Spain and thus a suitable royal match, but she had never had his heart. Almost as if God Himself had withheld His blessing from their marriage, only one of their children, the Dauphin, had lived past infancy.

There had, of course, always been beautiful young women during his youth—young women with ambitions to be noticed, to be preferred. And there had been that golden-haired beauty Madame de Montespan, fragrant and sensuous, pale as a lily, pious betimes, fiery, and prideful. She had been for a long time the mistress of his heart, had borne him six well-beloved children. Had fancied her charms indispensable. She had not taken her banishment in good grace. *Mais oui*—as *Pere** la Chaise had insisted, his own moral purity was essential to any hope of leading the nation into uniformity of religion.

The Grand Monarch allowed himself a moment to dally with memories of the charming young women who had diverted his attention even during his long alliance with Madame de Montespan. But it was Madame de Maintenon, always the devoted governess, who had given the children a proper upbringing. All others were harmless memories now in his maturer wisdom with his *chere madame* to nurture his more noble nature. With great satisfaction he recalled the sacrament that bound them to one another, though administered in secret and acknowledged only between themselves and before God.

Ah, yes. Coming into the ripe years of his life, he had attained wisdom. He had amended the license of his youth and had taken hold of the hand of the church. His present course would atone for his earlier sins. The good God observed and was pleased.

* * * * *

Armand brushed his hat and set out for yet another dinner party where all the guests, like himself, would be served abundantly and engaged in conversations by a charitable host who pretended that nothing but conviviality motivated invitations. At least here his shabby clothes would be seen as a mark of honor, evidence of the sacrifices he had made to remain faithful to his Christian calling.

In a large chamber that occupied the entire second floor of the elegant town house, Armand mingled with refugees whom he had met during his sojourn: the aged wife of a former French tax collector, who,

---

* Father.

like Madeleine's father, had been a third-generation public servant valued because of his total honesty; the brother of a French soldier killed in the Palatinate; three young ladies from Rouen with their mother; a young Huguenot pastor and his wife from the Loire Valley; and surprisingly, Tillieres, dressed only somewhat less splendidly than if he expected to parade among the tables at a Versailles *appartement.* He was conspicuous in their host's restrainedly opulent setting.

The meal was finished, and Armand had successfully evaded a *tete-a-tete* with any of the three young ladies, though their mother and the hostess intended that he should make their acquaintance. Tillieres took Armand's elbow once the women had withdrawn. "Where is the young lady who has taken your affections, *mon ami?* I note by your chilly smiles that you see yourself as committed to her. Ah! No need to feign I have misjudged your heart. Why was she not invited here tonight by our excellent host?"

"She *is* here in Holland," replied Armand a little stiffly. "However, I do not see her often. It is better thus. She is employed at a home for aged refugee women in Rotterdam."

Tillieres' left eyebrow rose, but he shrugged—with condescension, Armand thought, as if he understood this had been a brief affair of the heart with a girl who worked for a living. "*Mais oui,* I understood that her father was once quite wealthy. Alas! Most unfortunate."

Armand felt his spine stiffen. "I would not presume to discuss the family of my father's friend."

Tillieres shrugged again, this time leaning forward. "Please excuse the presumption on my part to speak of my beloved Catherine most proudly. We found a house just last week—since I saw you. There remains just the matter of furnishing it in a fashion to please my betrothed. Such a thrifty young woman you never saw, my friend, though she has lived her whole life in the Dutch manner of luxury."

Tillieres launched into a half hour praising his chosen one, her family, and the wonderful connections their marriage promised. Finally, he held his hands out, palms up, as if offering something from his own great bounty. "I flatter myself that I may become of significant assistance to the brethren of faith in this city. That was, of course, my chief purpose in settling here. But now to your future, *mon ami.* You have been thinking of the duke's generosity since our last meeting, *non*? Could you not with such prospects charm the young lady into marriage?"

"I would not think to propose such a—" Armand began.

Tillieres smiled broadly. "You could not, of course, plan marriage with no fortune on either side. But with a secure future, you could marry and take her back to France, where she could soon become the darling of the court."

"I hardly think—"

"*Mais oui,* it is amusing to imagine the fluttering among the devout biddies around Madame de Maintenon," continued Tillieres. "You know Madame dislikes your duke more than a little and tries to ruin his credit with the king. But the duke is a skilled courtier, and though he was protecting you, a heretic and a rebel, he has been able to hold his own so far."

"I won't pretend I'd care if Her Solemnity was offended," shrugged Armand, "but I could only regret the awkward position in which I placed the duke. He tried so generously to work for my advantage before the Revocation of the Edict of Nantes. However, at the time I could see no choice but to do as I did—the young lady, *oui,* but I also had to decide whether my faith was a serious matter with me or whether I could change it like my shirt to gain favor with Pharaoh."

"You behaved correctly, I am certain," said Tillieres heartily. "Now I hope we may have an opportunity to talk at length, for there is much I could say of the court and the duke that might interest you."

"It would be a pleasure," said Armand, noticing that the men were preparing to join the ladies in the drawing room, "but I have been meeting with certain pastors and others of the exile at one of the coffee houses for devotional studies. A Pastor Merson, whom I knew in southern France and greatly respect, introduced me to this circle. Why don't you join us? They are all learned and worthy men and would welcome you."

Tillieres bowed. "Nothing would please me more," he said. "As we leave our old life in Babylon behind, it would be instructive as well as a great honor to meet such worthies, if you are certain I would not be intruding."

It was Armand's cue to bow, and he did. But once on the street listening to his companion's heels click on the cobbles, he wondered if his invitation had been well advised.

* * * * *

The discussion had been in progress for some time when the two arrived. The Huguenot leaders occupied four tables at the back of the room, far from the street and windows. Armand made his introductions.

Claude Brousson was present and had been speaking when the two entered. After the expected courtesies, the famed lawyer resumed exhorting his fellows concerning the epistle that he had addressed to their monarch recently.

"We have been patient and tactful in excess, my friends. It is time to explain without fear the true state of religion in France. We have known from the days of Calvin and before that the Catholic Church is impure, teaching fables and idolatry, pagan rituals and profanity. Its bishops are controlled by demons and lust for power and wealth, living in corrupt luxury. Priests are persecutors of the righteous, teaching violence, cruelty, and deceit. It is time the king knew."

Brousson launched into a long-winded review of events regarding which, Armand was certain, each man present had more intimate knowledge than the speaker himself. But as Brousson had said, this was a patient and tactful assembly.

The lawyer continued. "We all remember how enthusiastically the Edict of Revocation was hailed by all classes of Frenchman. It ordered all Protestant pastors out of the realm within fifteen days but forbade the laity to leave under penalty of the galleys for life for men or a convent for the women—as well as loss of all property. True, there was the suggestion that if one did not practice his heretical religion publicly, he was not to be disturbed until 'it pleased God to enlighten him like the others.' However, what this might mean depended on the interpretation of the edict by local officials and missionary priests, so life could be made unendurable for those who clung to the PRR."

He recounted how, as the storm passed by and something like normalcy returned to communities, many new converts repented their weakness in anguish and frustration. Some, to protect property, lived a double life, attending the services of their new church so that outward faithfulness would be counted to them as "righteousness." More of them simply ignored the Mass and secretly resumed worship according to the Reformed Faith as well as they could without ministers or churches. Many were so ashamed of their fall and denial of the Faith, even if momentary, that they became defiant and willing to risk great danger to attend secret assemblies of the faithful or to escape abroad, where they could be received again into the church and worship in peace. The effectiveness of the watch on the borders varied from place to place and from time to time, but thousands got out by every imaginable means.

Tillieres leaned forward and at the first opportunity interrupted. "You must know, *mes amis,** the king's officials are growing distressed by the drain of some of His Majesty's most talented and industrious subjects. And the stories they're telling in the lands of their exile have turned the Revocation into an international problem!"

"Ah, yes," agreed one of the black-clad pastors. "Though our king sees himself as too powerful to be at risk if all other rulers in Europe join against him in warfare, he is sensitive to their opinion and craves approbation."

"And thus my epistles," Brousson rejoined.

"And the prophesies of Brother Jurieu," added another.

During the following moments it became clear to Armand de Gandon that leaders among the Huguenot fugitives in Holland were now considering means of relieving their present emergency by taking advantage of both talent and gold. Armand, without silver or gold, could offer only his soldierly skills. But Tillieres was eager to offer his help with the expenses of printing and distributing copies of Brousson's epistle.

---

* My friends.

CHAPTER 8

In the Boudoir of Madame de Maintenon

Francoise d'Aubigne, marquise de Maintenon, knew that Louis XIV was the lieutenant of God on earth around whom the whole solar system of French society revolved, and that consequently it would never have occurred to him to inquire whether she disliked drafts, or whether his ministers were comfortable through long evenings on folding stools, or whether his Protestant subjects were vexed at being forced to change their religion. To be of service to His Majesty was the life purpose of all good subjects. And she, who was his dearest companion, was his most devoted subject.

As she waited for her sovereign to arrive, Madame de Maintenon reflected with deep satisfaction upon her present position, which was far from the prison in Poitou where she had been born to Huguenot parents but blessedly baptized a Catholic by prison authorities. Taken in by Protestants and spirited off to the island of Martinique by her fleeing parents, she had been brought back to France by her mother after her father's death and had finally had the comfort of a fully Catholic education in a convent. There her soul had found a steadfast peace that had sustained her through a marriage of convenience to an aged, crippled wit and writer. She had nursed her husband and served as his secretary, his hostess, his friend until she was widowed at twenty-five.

All that was so long ago, a lifetime ago—separated from the present by a gulf across which her memories seemed hardly as real as stories read in a morality tale. More real and more immediate were memories of the years when she had been the official governess to the children of the king's longtime mistress, Madame de Montespan. She cherished the belief that her own upright behavior, her chaste and devout life, had in part brought about the recent conversion of her monarch. The change, when it finally came, had been complete. She could have been another de Montespan. But resolute, she had held fast to her chastity, had remained true to principle even after the queen's death, and only when the king chose a monogamous relationship securely based on a privately solemnized marriage had she joined her life to his.

That, reflected Madame de Maintenon, was the true source of her power, the true measure of her devotion to the man she loved: She had helped him understand that the sanctified love of one woman was of greater value than the trivial attentions, the bought favors of any number of *filles de joie.** And from this position of strength, she could bring to the whole of France the same settled spiritual resolution that she had brought to its king.

No one knew as well as she who loved him best the grave dangers besetting his soul even now in his pious state. As he strove to make himself supreme in France and France supreme in the world, he risked forgetting that the good God was over all and gave to each nation its place and time. Sadly, Madame admitted as she waited for her king to come that he took far too much pride in military might and was insensible to the gross expenses of warfare and the suffering war casualties brought to wives and mothers throughout the land. Her marriage to the king had not elevated her to a throne at his side, and she had no powerful kinsmen to further her goals, but wherever possible, she vowed again to herself, she would guide her husband to be more fully his better self—the noble sovereign God had ordained him to be.

And now he came. From her chair near the conference table in her boudoir, she watched him stop twice to listen intently to a courtier who had managed to penetrate the private wing of Versailles. At last the

---

* Prostitutes.

courtier bowed, backing away, and the king came through the doorway, his step swift but majestic, his grey-green eyes watching her.

He wore, as he often did, his favorite rich brown velvet, crossed at the front by the blue ribbon of the Order of the Holy Ghost. He stood before her and smiled. It was a very formal smile, for though this was her bedchamber, it was far from a private place. It was, indeed, the king's favorite venue for meetings with his ministers of state, who would soon arrive.

Maintenon set her embroidery upon a gilded table at her side. She did not rise. He did not bow. But there was in that moment a deeply satisfying acknowledgment of their mutual regard. He walked about the room, deep in thought. She took up her embroidery perhaps ten feet from the conference table, where she could hear but remain aloof. Thus informed about matters of state, she could offer her advice when later the king asked it, as he most certainly would.

Madame de Maintenon, as she greeted each arrival, measured them against her own stern devotion to her sovereign. Conseil d'Etat* Louvois, Secretaire de la Maison du Roi and Navy† de Seignelay, Conseil des Finances,§ Conseil des Despeches.**

As the ministers arranged themselves and their velvet dispatch cases about the table, the king made some optimistic comments on the triumphs of the True Church in England, where the Catholic King James II three years past had succeeded his brother Charles. "Every vacancy in the government is filled with a faithful Catholic," the king stated, rubbing his hands together in obvious satisfaction.

"Perhaps we shall at last see England brought back to the church now," ventured the *Pere* de La Chaise, Louis' confessor. Madame smiled upon her longtime associate in the king's religious reforms, who often attended these sessions.

"Once an Englishman, always an Englishman," growled the terrible-tempered Louvois, who in addition to all his other responsibilities served as minister of war.

---

* Equivalent to the secretary of state.
† Secretary of the House of the King and of the Navy.
§ Equivalent to the secretary of the treasury.
** Council of Dispatches.

"You forget that *both* Charles and James grew up in exile here in France." De Seignelay smiled indulgently.

Louvois was in no mood for concessions. "I've no confidence in the Stuarts!"

Madame de Maintenon abandoned her embroidery and took up her ivory and silk fan. She could not decide in Louvois' favor or against him. *He is so devoted to the king—and so ambitious,* she mused, *that he cannot resist the temptation to run the other departments too.* That propensity to usurp power worried her, as it always did. She turned her attention to her husband, who she sensed was about to speak.

The Conseil des Finances tapped his fingers impatiently on the marble table. "We paid Charles secretly for fifteen years, but he would never risk coming into the open as a Catholic, and though James is a Catholic, we will find him opposing us in our trade interests because he is English, after all."

"At least," said the king, "it isn't likely he will be plotting against us with the Prince of Orange and these rogue German princes."

"Perhaps not, Sire," agreed Louvois, "but Your Majesty has no reason to fear that Protestant rabble anyway. Their cause is dying throughout Europe nowadays, and it is dead here in France. If we keep up our encouragement to the Turks, Leopold and the other Hapsburgs will be too busy to meddle with these alliances they talk of across the Rhine. If the Prince of Orange does manage to start an affair, we shall finish it for him!"

Madame de Maintenon felt apprehensive. Why must Louvois forever play on the king's vanity and weakness for military glory?

Her husband's army numbered two hundred thousand effectives— he had said so only last evening. He had affirmed with pride that it was the first standing army supported by any European nation. She had tried to show him tactfully that just having such an army required him to justify its maintenance by using it almost continuously, thus shedding the blood of thousands of loyal Frenchmen.

Louvois began reciting plans underway to wipe out the armies of Protestant rulers in Germany. There was much talk of socket bayonets and flintlock rifles. "Our enemies," he boasted, "rely upon pikes and other obsolete weapons."

Trembling, Maintenon closed her fan and studied the architecture of its ivory blades. Perhaps men—and kings in particular—were inherently inclined to see themselves as warriors. Thus, the proper role of women must always be to mitigate for peace.

Peace. Peace was a godly attainment. It ought to be the watchword of all faithful Christians. She listened, attentive for an occasion to mention some affair of the church, some new need at La Maison de St. Cyr, a school for poor but noble young ladies that the king had recently founded at her suggestion.

Louis, however, had another matter on his mind besides rumors of impending military trouble in the Germanies. He thrust both shoulders forward, clearly annoyed. "I hear reports that in our own realm the heretics of the Pretended Reformed Religion are holding secret meetings against our instructions last year. When we revoked the Edict of Nantes, we understood that the conversions were universal, and now we are surprised to hear of this disobedience."

Madame searched the faces of the councilors and the confessor and felt a sudden solidarity. Had not they all advised the king the previous year to abolish the edict that protected the French Protestants?

"I have detailed reports on these occurrences, Your Majesty," said Louvois, moving quickly to match the king's present concern. "The numbers who attended these illegal convocations have been greatly exaggerated, and I have given orders to deal with them severely. I should also like to point out that this is not really a revival of the Huguenot heresy as some alarmists suggest. Rather, these are disaffected peasants—mostly in the south—who are being stirred up by foreign agents using religion as a cover for treason and rebellion."

The king rested his clenched fist upon the table. "The Prince of Savoy, our nephew. Ah, yes. And the Dutch prince. And again, English Protestants of various stripes." He leaned toward Louvois.

Pere de La Chaise cut in smoothly and—Madame de Maintenon perceived from his obsequious manner—untruthfully. "Your Majesty, all the bishops assure us that the conversions have held remarkably firm and that the instruction of the new converts proceeds without incident. Your Majesty's generosity and good judgment in setting aside the funds for devotional books for the new converts has greatly facilitated the labors of the missionaries. I think I can say that calm reigns throughout France among those who were once blinded by Calvinistic error. These disturbances we hear of probably have more to do with crop failures and famines, I shouldn't wonder, than a revival of heresy."

Madame de Mainenton smiled benevolently and nodded as the king glanced her way. She remembered all too well the poverty of her childhood, the shifting back and forth between Reformed and Catholic allegiance when the fortunes of her parents shifted.

"Well," said the king, his fist relaxing, his fingers spreading, "see that the disorders do not spread. And I wish to be informed if any of these foreign agents are caught." The crease between his brows deepened. "I am also told that some of those who fled the country for reasons of religion have petitioned to return—if they may have their property back. In our edict of last October, they were given four months in which to return. What ought we to do when they wish to return to our obedience after a longer period?"

"Hold to the edict, Sire," said Louvois promptly. "If we equivocate because of your Majesty's well-known desire to be merciful, we will be making mockery of Your Majesty's intentions."

"Perhaps, Sire," observed de Seignelay, the easy-going minister charged with industry and the navy, "there may be special cases in which it would be an advantage to leave some discretion to Your Majesty's servants when a prominent fugitive wishes to return. The value of such an example would do much to further discourage the exiles abroad and give pause to the disaffected here in France who are thinking of trying to flee."

The king leaned upon his elbows, and Louvois and de Seignelay, seeing he wished to rise, jumped to their feet. He paced about the room briefly and then, with his ministers hovering at his sides, returned to his place at the table.

"I am surprised that we still have all these questions to do with religion," said the king in as peevish a tone as he permitted himself in the presence of his lords. "I remember that we were told that these people of the PRR had almost all converted and that only a mere handful had fled the country. It now appears that many of these conversions were not durable and that legions of disaffected subjects of ours run the length and breadth of Europe raising bad opinions of us abroad."

There was an embarrassed silence as each of the councilors waited for another. There was reason to keep silent. Madame de Maintenon herself could think of no soothing reply. It had now been three years since Louis XIV revoked the eighty-seven-year-old Edict of Nantes, which had been established by his grandfather Henri IV to protect the rights of Protestants and thus to end the bloody religious strife of the previous century. With Louvois and others, Madame de Maintenon had encouraged the king to believe that the edict was no longer necessary. They had agreed that all reports given him by his advisors must tell of phenomenal mass conversions of Huguenots that would soon leave no Protestants in France at all. And now he spoke with an irritated certainty that might lead to one of his unpleasant altercations. One did not contradict such a man as Louis XIV, ordained by the grace of God to rule the French nation.

Like herself, the royal councilors had depended upon their control of information to shape the monarch's opinions. Someone outside their circle had supplied him with contrary information.

For twenty-five years, royal agents had pressed the Huguenots by every method—legal or illegal—that they could devise to break their spirits or frighten or bribe them into the Roman confession. Their temples had been pulled down on various pretexts and their schools closed; they had been denied entry into most professions and to government positions; their taxes had been increased; and they had long since discovered they could not win a lawsuit. Even their children seven years old or older might be taken from them and raised as Catholics at the parents' expense. Those susceptible to honors, promotions, or money had found these incentives tempting.

Some Huguenots had fled the country at once. Others had stayed, hoping they might save their property or that persecution would ease if only the king could be informed about the injustices inflicted on his loyal Protestant subjects. As they had been barred from politics yet were sincerely devoted to the king—even more so than many Catholics—for some sixty years, they could only assume that a just king must be receiving bad counsel. Madame de Maintenon had herself received letters pleading with her to pass on to the king the true state of affairs among the suffering Huguenots. And yet, in her heart of hearts, she was convinced that just as bringing about her husband's spiritual reformation had caused him some pain, so the heretics of whatever persuasion must suffer in order to bring them at last to salvation. Such an outcome was worth whatever price the nation must pay. She knew from her own experience that she was right. Compromise was out of the question.

Whatever numbers might be listed, Madame de Maintenon was certain that some thousands of Huguenots, like herself, had fully accepted the official religion. Years of education in the convent had convicted this daughter of Reformed parents that she must dedicate all her powers to defend the church. Turning her back on all that was dear to her, she had determined to atone for all that, and God would forgive. God would reward.

Her excellent education had brought her into the royal household to supervise the early education of the royal children. From that position Madame de Maintenon had watched all this from the sidelines. She saw herself now like Esther of old, having come to her present position of power for such a time as this—to provide her sovereign with a moral compass; to guide him into his God-ordained destiny as the savior of the church in France. The king, she knew, had never made a practice of admitting he had been mistaken, nor were his ministers likely to confess they had misinformed him. Maintenon read in their awkward smiles their tacit agreement that as far as possible, the place for such problems as the king now raised was under the rug.

Louvois had regained his composure. She read it on his face. And though she bore him no love, she was grateful that he stood ready with convincing logic. "Regardless of the lies in the Dutch gazettes," he said firmly, "there have assuredly been far fewer heretics fleeing abroad than some say, and we should remember that many of them now repent and wish to return."

Louvois appeared intent upon relaxing his habitual scowl, but he looked over the king's shoulder rather than meeting his eyes. "I can assure Your Majesty that this great work for the Faith will stand as the outstanding achievement of your reign and that a few fractious ones will not make much difficulty for your servants. I will keep Your Majesty informed if there are any other occurrences of note, but I suspect these reports are mostly a tissue of lies spread by our jealous enemies abroad, who would stoop to any means, however vile, to attempt to diminish the glory and renown Your Majesty so justly enjoys throughout the entire Christian world."

Madame de Maintenon studied her husband's face. He appeared about to say something. His eyes met hers. She said nothing but slowly spread the ivory and silk fan. She smiled approvingly, and he changed the subject. "Well, what is here for our consideration this evening?" he said. His tone was still a little cross.

"There is again the matter of taxes," ventured de Seignelay. "Even with the greatest frugality, we face shortfalls in several areas, and the expenses of war—"

"Ah, yes," said the king. "Taxes. Let us re-examine the application of the *taille*."

* * * * *

Madeleine Cortot awoke in the female servants' chamber at the House for Huguenot Gentlewomen in Rotterdam. It was not yet day, although a faint glow showed in each of the tiny dormer windows ranked down the narrow room under the roof of the six-storied building. She had, after two years in service here, become the mistress of the laundry.

She had some hope that ten-year-old Louis would fare better than his sickly twin. All through their troubles, he had borne hunger and cold and danger with less trembling. He had accepted change but had not despaired. In the school for poor refugee boys he had thrived, and now as a printer's devil he was learning a trade. The Dutch charity would feed him well and provide him with a strict but kindly upbringing—at least until help came from some place: from Father's funds smuggled out of France or from Father's brother, Uncle Daniel, in America.

The clock in the nearby market square struck five. Madeleine lay for a few moments on her back. The room was light now, and in the other cots young women like herself stirred, each whispering prayers, mustering strength to address the frustrations of today's duties of looking after women who had been mistresses of grand houses with flocks of servants to await their commands. Though dispossessed of their houses and fortunes, these ladies had not abdicated their authority.

Madeleine closed her eyes and said a prayer for her own inner peace and for her other brother, fifteen-year-old Alexandre. "God keep him from trouble and violence. Help him to hold his tongue." She wondered whether such a prayer was too much to ask even of God. She was almost glad Alexandre had gone to be with Armand de Gandon. He needed the strong hand of a man to manage his spirit. She folded back her coverlet and got up. Today she would direct five newly arrived domestics in the weekly change of bed linens. First, the boiling of the water in the wash house, and then . . .

Making up the eleven beds she had assigned herself in the House for Huguenot Gentlewomen, Madeleine Cortot reflected upon the world into which she had settled more than two years past, a world of exiles, always restricted, sometimes of necessity, for most of the newcomers couldn't speak the language of their hosts and were reluctant to adopt strange ways. That would, after all, be an admission that they didn't really expect to return home. Indeed, these Frenchwomen segregated themselves in a kind of ghetto and had little contact with the larger community. Here in Rotterdam, thousands of recently arrived Huguenots sought reassurance in the company of their fellows and never learned Dutch or English, for Walloon—French-speaking—churches abounded in Holland, and a refugee didn't need to talk to the Dutch at all.

Madeleine drew a clean linen cover over the featherbed and tucked it in at the foot before enclosing the coverlet in a similar snowy case. She had hoped to learn Dutch here and possibly even English, but at present she knew only the few words necessary to bargaining in the market when she was sent there.

In the House for Huguenot Gentlewomen, the discourse was exclusively French. Only this morning she had overheard a conversation between two persons of quality lately come from France. They were planning yet another escape, this time back across the frontier into their homeland. Did they not realize the grave danger that would await them there? That loyal Catholics were now in possession of their homes? That in many cases their homes had been reduced to rubble? Could they not understand, seeing the desperation of the latest arrivals, how insufferable life was for believers in their homeland?

Intensely self-centered yet eager for gossip, the women fed on any rumor flying about the French-speaking circles. News circulated rapidly, if not always accurately, and new arrivals were pumped for word of home and friends. Any letter received became public property.

Well-bred but bored and cantankerous, the ladies were difficult mistresses. Who they were or had been in France was all-important to each of them, and even the comparative affluence and comfort they had in Holland inspired no sympathy for their social inferiors, especially when such a person of lower standing was unfortunate enough to be in Holland without funds.

"C'est moi!" * Madeleine thumped the pillow and set it precisely where a good housemaid must place it. "C'est moi!"

And as swiftly as the feeling of self-pity entered her mind, she brushed it aside. Maman† had never looked with disdain upon a household servant, but Madeleine remembered readily her own adolescent attitude. She had expected service as if she deserved it, born as she had been into middle-class wealth. The past thirty months had been hard, but she realized that during this time she had learned more about the meaning of Christian graces than all she had learned from her godly mother's example.

No, that wasn't true, of course. If she hadn't grown up observing the strict but gentle way in which Maman conducted her household, she wouldn't now understand the finer points of decorum expected of her as a servant nor the excellent housekeeping practices that had made their home in Saint Martin a center of culture and propriety. She had escaped from her homeland with scarcely a sou, with two younger brothers and a sister depending on her, and she knew firsthand the bitter bread of poverty. She was fortunate to have work, and even more fortunate for promotion in this establishment.

---

* It is me.

† Mom.

She remembered with some pleasure how Major de Gandon had teased her when first she donned peasant clothing during their escape from France. "You carry yourself like a lady, *mademoiselle*," he had chided. "You can't conceal your dignity under soiled skirt and patched shawl. You must think more humbly of yourself." He had smiled when he said it, and she had tried somewhat unsuccessfully to take his counsel. She had been seventeen then. So young to assume the responsibility for her young siblings.

Yes, she had been proud. Her father had been the richest man in Saint Martin—a tax farmer, perhaps the only honest one in the duchy, respected, loved by everyone who knew him. And *Maman* as well. Poor *Maman*. Dead. But perhaps it was better so. How would she fare here among the dispossessed gentlewomen who scorned the merchant class as upstart social climbers who aspired to someday displace the rightful aristocracy?

And Father. Was he still alive? Had they taken him off to the galleys on the Mediterranean? He had always been healthy for a man his age but unaccustomed to physical labor. Could he survive? Her mind thus occupied, Madeleine finished the last of the eleven beds and carried the used linens to the wash house behind the mansion that had been transformed to meet the demands of the gentlewomen.

Madeleine's feelings and concerns were of little interest to the ladies, but she must ever concern herself with their most trivial whims. Yesterday, while crimping fifty dainty white caps, she had amused herself by imagining three of the most imperious of these ladies attired in courtly gowns and towering head dresses fluttering about the court at Versailles, which de Gandon had described to her. What did Huguenot simplicity mean in the world from which they had come? When she repined over her situation, she could revive the memory that with only mild encouragement de Gandon would have taken her there—that she herself might one day have become a duchess. But she must not allow herself such fantasies. Did not her faith mean more to her than that? Did she not value the soul of her rescuer too much to encourage such a dream?

The other dream had faded too. She had prayed. She had dared to hope that even after his angry departure two years ago from her temporary haven with Cousin Diane in the north of France, Mathieu Bertrand might think better, might gain courage, come to Holland, perhaps with money from Father, and they would marry after all, and he would some day become a Reformed pastor as he had been educated to be.

That dream had faded, she admitted to herself, almost immediately after his departure. Her fiancé had seemed so cold of heart toward the dear twins and had been openly hostile when he discovered that Alexandre had escaped from the Home for New Catholics to which he had been abducted for indoctrination. He had forced her to choose between himself and these children who were dependent upon her. She had known her duty, and she had told him so.

"A wife's duty is to obey her husband!" he had blurted out.

"I am their sister," she had said with trembling lips, "and I am not yet your wife; you cannot command me." And Mathieu Bertrand had looked at her with disdain, had raised his voice, and had stormed from Cousin Diane's home.

She had grown tired of trying to revive memories of Mathieu's visits to her girlhood home in Saint Martin, his solemn dignity, his impressive Norman stature, his handsome profile, his pale yellow hair falling upon his shoulders in almost saintly perfection. She remembered the particulars of his appearance, but she couldn't remember the warm feelings of rapture that had filled her thoughts of him back in Saint Martin. She had been so young when she had become betrothed, her affections influenced by her parents' hopes that she would become a pastor's wife. She had been so naive. She had somehow transferred her deep respect for Mathieu's uncle, Pastor Merson, to the young seminarian and schoolteacher-catechist, assuming Mathieu possessed qualities that his later behavior had proven wanting. She had come to realize that he had never really loved either his pastoral calling *or* her. He had loved the prospects of honor and respect—and the rich legacy with which her father would endow her upon their marriage and his rights as a husband to command her what he willed.

In spite of Mathieu's restrained wooing, his formal expressions of tenderness, his occasional recitation of biblical lyrics—in spite of all these, was not their betrothal after all to lead to an *arranged marriage,* a legal contract meant to advantage both families who drew it up? No, Mathieu had never loved her, and perhaps she had only imagined in her girlish dreams that she loved him.

Yet she had meant to keep her promise. *I suppose*, she mused, *that even now if he came offering a marriage that allowed me to remain faithful to my duties to Louis, Louise, and Alexandre, I would smile and marry him. I would by force of will find something in him to love.*

The thought did not inspire a smile.

The apostle Paul had commanded, "Husbands, love your wives." Perhaps the command was necessary because so few did. Perhaps even her own dear parents had begun their life together with a contract, a promise to be faithful. Perhaps love grew with time and close connection, and illusions of romance were nothing more—*illusions.* And yet her heart had responded unbidden to Armand de Gandon though he had not wooed her, though he had been most proper in keeping a suitable distance, though he had promised nothing but his protection even should doing his duty lead to death.

In moments of weakness, she imagined de Gandon coming to Rotterdam, confessing his deep love for her, passionately rejecting his patron's offers of the colonelcy of his own regiment because she had inspired his faith and he could no longer entertain such worldly goals. She could in saner moments imagine the major turning his back on his military career and his hopes of becoming the duke's heir, for she believed most fully in his integrity. The rest, however, was nothing but a girlish dream.

There was still one flickering hope. More than a year ago, Madeleine had written her father's brother, Daniel, settled long since in the English colony of New York. Father had urged her to do this, for the likelihood that he could provide for his own children in that darkening gloom under the dragonnades seemed poor. Uncle Daniel would feel some obligation not only because of their family connections but also because years before, Father had bankrolled his move to America—and rather generously too. He had provided enough funds both to obtain passage to New York for Uncle Daniel and his family and also to set him up in business once he arrived there.

"Daniel has not written for some time, but two years ago Huguenot brothers who traveled to the New World heard he has prospered there," Father had said, grasping at straws. "You must have patience, daughter, for letters to America travel across the Atlantic by courtesy of ship captains and are left at certain taverns in port cities."

As a rule, lists of letters would be advertised in the local newsletters, he explained, so that the addressees might know to come in and pick them up. "It will require time. You must have patience."

Father had been right.

* * * * *

Wearing serviceable brown fullcloth rather than the black of his schoolteacher days, Mathieu Bertrand followed the crowd along an unpaved street in Saint Martin. This was a holy day, dedicated to a saint in whose honor they gathered, one whose story he had not heard but had read hastily last night in order to behave as inconspicuously as possible when he entered the church.

At the church door he recognized the wife of the former Reformed chief deacon. She was arm in arm with the widow of a silversmith whose husband had waited too long to flee from France and had been trampled to death under the hooves of an agent's horse.

"Merson's nephew," the widow whispered, shrugging one shoulder in his direction.

"PRR catechist," the other replied with a somber face.

"He taught my son Latin."

Mathieu adjusted his white cuffs, examined his hands, looked over the heads of others entering the church, up at the paths of rainbow light reflected on the stone wall. There would be, he guessed, more than a hundred New Catholics in the congregation, many of them parents of his former pupils, and with them their children, those squirming, troublesome boys with no mind for letters or religion. He would take pains to stand distant from any of them. True, they like he would be embarrassed should their eyes meet in the church. However, their chagrin would be no comfort.

Mathieu's eyes rose to the bronze crucifix just under the modest stained-glass window at the front of the church. He hurriedly crossed himself, the gesture still feeling strange. Conspicuous, but, of course, he must make his presence, his participation in the service, conspicuous. He, the promising young PRR theologian, had "seen the light." A shiver began under his collar and ran up his neck until his scalp tingled. How long would it take to get past this sense of his own wickedness?

"Judas," a boy of ten hissed at his elbow. "Kiss the pope's toe."

Mathieu pretended he had not heard.

The boy's mother clapped a hand over her son's impudent mouth.

For his cheek, Mathieu thought, the boy might have been Alexandre Cortot. He shivered again. But Alexandre was in Holland. In that knowledge there was indeed some comfort. Like his saintly Huguenot mother, Alexandre never backed down from anything, was never content to hold his peace, always had too much to say.

Eh, bien, Mathieu thought, *and she's dead. A stroke. What a mother-in-law she would have been!*

The Cortots, rich as they had been, had lost everything. Their once beautiful mansion had been ruined beyond reconstruction, and over its cellar a grand new home was being built. Some comfort it was that Uncle Merson, accepting that all he owned would be confiscated and his life forfeited, had simply fled the country when all Reformed pastors were exiled. Mathieu sighed. Possession of Uncle Merson's modest home was a small reward for the humiliation that had overtaken him. It wasn't much, but a home nonetheless.

I am most fortunate, Mathieu reminded himself at each shift in the ritual. *Most fortunate that I decided upon accommodation. The Scripture states clearly that true believers worship God in spirit and in truth. That I can do. It is the interior man who worships. "The flesh profiteth nothing."* As if to comfort himself still further, he tried to imagine Madeleine grown stout with middle age, grown bold and defiant and perhaps shrewish. But the imagined form blurred, and the youthful Madeleine smiled at him with pious humility.

The service ended. The clergy passed down the center aisle and out into the sunlight. Mathieu joined into the stream of villagers flowing out the door, shaking the hand of the parish priest without a word.

My first great error, he admitted to himself as he entered his house, *was to agree to an engagement with the daughter of such a firebrand family as the Cortots. No, my first error was to join Uncle here in this small town. When the Reformed seminary closed, I should have enrolled in the Sorbonne at the University of Paris. It would have been a simple matter to qualify.*

He looked bleakly out the narrow study window on the narrow garden beyond and ran his hand along the dusty, empty shelf. Uncle's excellent library had been pillaged. And now his excellent scholarship counted for nothing—an assistant clerkship in the office of the chief magistrate. A total waste of potential. No access to books. No opportunities to sharpen his mind in mental duels with other scholars. No renowned masters to inspire deep thought and eloquent expression. No future.

To be doomed for a lifetime to this hinterland! How terrible! And yet, in fairer times, Isaac Cortot had grown rich in the service of the government. This fact had given him some hope—enough hope to hold him to absolute exactitude in his clerkship record-keeping.

Mathieu closed his censorious lips to a thin straight line. He had always believed that the most diligent work would be noticed and would lead to promotion. It had been true at the Huguenot Academy. There might yet again be happier times. He must put the situation in the best light.

∗   ∗   ∗   ∗   ∗

To celebrate the triumph of the Mother Church in Saint Martin, the chief magistrate had ordered the striking of a medal. "Fetch it as you come to the Hotel de Ville tomorrow," he instructed Mathieu. "You know the silversmith's place."

Mathieu dipped his head, avoiding his superior's eyes. "I will, Your Honor."

The widow of the PRR silversmith had a new husband—Robert, a man of fifty with ten motherless children. Robert had moved into the two stories above the workshop and had taken charge of the business. Mathieu recognized him as a longtime employee of the former shop owner.

The craftsman took him upstairs and set the medal on the table between them. "You understand, Monsieur Bertrand, that I cannot hope to make the profits my master made. In his time, we worked six days a week the year round. Now with saints' days and holy days disrupting the work, we get hardly three days of honest work to a week. And of course, the master was more skilled than any of us. I'm hardly better off owning the shop than I was working for the best silversmith in Saintonge. I've his offspring besides my own to provide for. We do the best we can."

"You were never one of the Reformed," Mathieu commented cautiously. "Business will improve."

"I'm a lifelong Catholic, *c'est vrais.* Not the kind that takes it too much to heart, but nonetheless . . . I wish Master had seen himself clear to convert—or maybe to leave before the worst came."

Robert brushed his cheek with the back of his hand. "The king doesn't understand that he has killed or galleyed or hounded out of France the best craftsmen in the country. The best soldiers too, and civil servants. Who's to know what will become of France with all the cream skimmed off and none but skim milk left? Pardon, sir. It was not you I was thinking . . ." Robert wrapped the medal in clean linen and handed it to Bertrand.

Two armed guards fell in beside Mathieu as he came out into the street. He glanced up to where the silversmith's offensive ten-year-old stepson hung out an open window. The boy grinned and stuck out his tongue, wagging it and crossing his eyes.

Mathieu wondered if that boy, like Alexandre Cortot, had been thrown out of a school for New Catholics or if his mother's sudden marriage to a Catholic had spared the teaching friars that ordeal. The former teacher shuddered, remembering the Huguenot school over which he had presided. *Teaching was never my vocation,* he affirmed silently, feeling conspicuous indeed between the two officers but enjoying for the moment the dignity of his circumstances—greater than he had even this very morning appreciated.

He came into the Hotel de Ville by a side entrance, pausing to mentally catalogue the portraits of former magistrates arrayed in all their grandeur, to read the list of municipal privileges inscribed in copper plate beside the dais on which officials sat during hearings, to stare at the city's arms painted on the wooden panel above the green-draped table. He quickly tucked the medal under his left arm and crossed himself before the crucifix, for the guards were still at his sides.

Beyond the dais, a guard stepped ahead of him to open the door leading to the chief magistrate's apartment. His superior beamed when he unwrapped the medal.

"His Majesty's likeness is most like, *n'est pas?*"

"And yours as well, Honor," Mathieu replied.

* * * * *

"My first great error," the former schoolteacher/catechist muttered at dusk as he passed between the red-roofed houses of Saint Martin, "was to allow Monsieur Cortot and that latitudinarian rascal from Versailles to push me into that foolhardy rescue of Madeleine from the convent. Nothing but insanity. Something no sensible person would have considered."

He had believed then and still believed that with a little patience the girl's release could have been arranged without such recklessness. The outcome was unfortunate—she'd had to flee, and their marriage had been indefinitely postponed. Otherwise, Madame Cortot might have lived and her husband might have lost little of his wealth, perhaps even received some sort of bounty as a mark of royal favor for making a discrete change.

"Bah! Such an enterprise was futile from the start." Mathieu was startled at his own voice erupting in the empty street. Though his complaints continued, he kept them soundless in his head.

Mathieu continued his assessment. *My second great error,* he mused, *was to let Monsieur Cortot persuade me after the Revocation to go north and try to take Madeleine over the frontier to safety. I should have known that she would insist on taking her sister and brothers regardless of the additional danger involved. But what judgment does a seventeen-year-old girl have in such matters?*

Mathieu shuddered at the thought of becoming guardian of Madeleine's young brother Alexandre—him with his sharp, close-set eyes, his impudent nose, his gape-toothed grin, his rancorous attitude always defiant of authority. To be the brother-in-law to such a one was unthinkable. If upon arriving at Madeleine's haven in the north of France he had found her there alone, all might have been well, for her father had sent nearly his whole fortune with him to provide for her future. If they two had escaped into Holland together, the gold would have been sufficient to establish them in a new life—his career as a theologian assured in a nation that placed great value on biblical studies.

But they had quarreled. Now, as he mounted the steps to his house, he blushed to think how he had blurted out Gandon's name—how she had seemed to be comparing him to that wretched peacock. It had been necessary then and there to put his foot down. If they married, after all, who was to rule? No, she was too much like her mother—self-confident, self-directing. So he had withdrawn in dignity—yes, dignity—to wait for her to come to her senses.

But, alas, he had ventured too close to the border and had been arrested, without papers but with a belt full of Cortot's gold.

Introduced to preliminary torments at Strasbourg, he had told the royal officials all they wished—even Madeleine's whereabouts and her plans to escape. So, unlike Job, he had failed his test. With what high glee the evil one must have seen his fall—and how Armand de Gandon must have relished the story when he heard it, perhaps when he repeated it at a coffeehouse along some Dutch canal.

Madeleine had escaped anyway, no thanks to him but rather to his nemesis. He felt guilt for endangering her, yes, but also bitterness for what he had unintentionally done to himself. He had surrendered. He had abjured. And at that price he had been permitted to return to Saint Martin—had been given a position with the local magistrate and his uncle's forfeited property. His neighbors were mostly new converts like himself—and, he reminded himself often, they had no room to talk for they too had apostatized to save their skins. But among them he dared not presume to have friends. Distrusted and alone, each day he wondered whether rumors of what had happened at Strasbourg had reached Saint Martin.

Alone in the small house of his pious uncle, Pastor Merson, Mathieu Bertrand faced another night haunted by the ignominy of his past and the uncertainties of his future.

CHAPTER 9

Letters—and Prospects of War

Letters for the refugees in Rotterdam's House for Huguenot Gentlewomen were rare, and though frequently they were of the most sensitive nature—someone's escape plans or the problems of those still in France "under the Cross"—recipients seemed compelled to share the contents whether good news or bad and to discuss the worries of others who had no news from home or from dear ones scattered across the face of Europe. These aristocratic Protestant women had lived since infancy guarding their every word for fear of royal censure. Now in a Protestant country, they had abandoned discretion.

It was likely, therefore, that when a letter arrived for a resident, many others knew about it too—and all the more so when the letter was addressed to Mademoiselle Madeleine Cortot, until now viewed as little more than a human machine, a mere supplier of clean linens and soap and scents, by women who heretofore had always lived largely. The arrival of the letter required that all household activity stop for an hour so that residents and staff might devote themselves to speculation while Mademoiselle Cortot— who all realized at once must be a personage of more significance than they had imagined—retired to the matron's office to read the message.

The matron set a chair for Madeleine near a window, handed her a silver letter opener, and discretely returned to her desk, taking up her account ledger and pen. Madeleine held the letter for perhaps four minutes, too stricken with hope to risk disappointment. And yet she must open it. She inserted the point of the opener into the corner of the sealed document and slit the paper along the fold.

"Mon chere Madeleine," her cousin began—for it was the younger Daniel Cortot who responded—"my father has succeeded beyond our expectations in New York, for true to Cortot traditions, he has justly gained the trust of merchants and tradesmen alike. At present he is unwell after a fall resulting in a broken arm and thus asks me to correspond with you, knowing you must be suffering some anxiety in your unfortunate circumstance."

Cousin Daniel's long missive contained not only sympathetic advice but also a letter of credit on an Amsterdam bank, a matter of some five hundred *livres.* This was a generous amount. It would pay passage for the four young Cortots across the sea—and not in mean accommodations either—they'd be able to travel in comfort. That was an unexpected blessing, for, of course, Cousin Daniel hadn't known that poor Louise was in ill health.

Madeleine held the letter of credit in her left hand and read the entire epistle through again. She was brought back to the present by a discrete cough from the matron.

"Good news," Madeleine said. "Father's kinsman in New York in America has provided for our passage. He wants us to join his family there."

The matron arose, restrained but filled with solicitude. "Indeed, *mon chere,* a cause for general celebration!" And suddenly, Madeleine Cortot, the mistress of the laundry, was the darling of the establishment, the pet of an aging countess, the intimate of a duke's daughter. All hovered over her, eager for the details. But Madeleine, who was used to guarding well her privacy, parceled out only the basic fact: She had a kinsman in American who had offered help.

With the letter of credit under her mattress, Madeleine began to think of how to arrange the move, though with some hesitation. She knew so little of America—only that some Huguenots had gone there, many to the mountains of the Carolinas, where the climate was said to be warm, which might offer some benefits to Louise. Like most of the refugees, Madeleine would have preferred to stay in Protestant Europe, hoping against hope that the Lord would overrule the king of France and permit them to return home someday to reestablish His worship on their native soil. But once the ocean was crossed, a formidable and somewhat dangerous trip at best, one did not lightly turn around and come back.

Madeleine's hopes had long been founded—like those of hundreds of other refugees—upon the prophetic interpretations of the great Pastor Jurieu of the French Reformed church in Rotterdam. In his deep studies of the book of Daniel, he had concluded that the momentous developments in France pointed to the final years in the great image prophecy—the time when the feet of clay would be struck by the stone cut out without hands, bringing the final earthly power crumbling to the earth and establishing the reign of righteousness, perhaps as early as 1689.

Pastor Jurieu had for years pled eloquently in a war of words, *coups d'in folio,* with the king to deal justly with his faithful Huguenot subjects. However, never had there been so much as an acknowledgment that the king had received the letters. Recently, enlightened in his studies, Jurieu had begun to preach that deliverance would come from England in the person of the Dutch Prince William, who might become William III of England, replacing his Catholic father-in-law, James II. William would, Jurieu predicted, lead an alliance of Protestant nations that would defeat the little-horn power, represented most threateningly now in the person of French King Louis XIV.

Such a message was shocking and yet stimulating to Huguenots who had been taught since the Edict of Nantes seventy-five years past to love and serve their king faithfully regardless of his heavy-handed restrictions of their freedoms. If, however, Louis XIV were the beast, the wicked little horn, then true believers were justified in resisting him, in raising armies of the faithful and in God's name sweeping him from power or at least forcing him to honor their rights to freedom of worship, freedom to own property, and freedom to participate in the economic and political affairs of their country.

Like other believers, Madeleine had studied the prophecies by candlelight, had attended preaching services, and had thrilled with hope of deliverance for God's true church in France. Now it seemed possible that those prophecies might soon be fulfilled. Father might yet be restored at least to his property, even if the house had been ruined. He might yet come for his exiled children. Of what concern was poverty if they were reunited? And Armand de Gandon might himself have a future in the new regime, famous soldier that he was and possible heir of the powerful duke. And . . .

But she must not allow herself to think in that direction. If all barriers were broken down and Armand became a duke, how could she, even in fantasy, imagine that she might stand at his side, his duchess? Kings might be brought down, but she couldn't imagine that the distinctions of class would evaporate. Yet, unbidden, such dreams flooded her sleep and even spilled into her thoughts as she worked in the steamy laundry, wooden paddle in hand, stirring the cauldron of linens to their desired whiteness.

And now this letter from America. Should she wait to see the outcome of the months ahead? Father had instructed her to seek help from Uncle Daniel, and, if she could, to escape to the New World with her brothers and sister. Should she try to establish contact with Father? Leaving for America without him seemed unthinkable. Was it already too late for him to escape? Men caught trying to flee France faced two possibilities: death on *la roué*—the wheel—or a lifetime enslaved in the galleys.

Here, Madeleine thought for the first time of Mathieu in connection with these two penalties. If he had been considered a common citizen trying to steal out of France, he might even now be chained to a bench on a galley in the Mediterranean, his fair skin burning in the merciless sun, his golden hair turning brittle. If with the ordained men all expelled Mathieu had felt compelled to take up the duties of a pastor, then he might already have given his life for the Faith—arms and legs broken on the wheel and then hanged or burned.

But Madeleine brushed that horrifying image from her mind. Mathieu was not made of such stern stuff. Whatever had become of him, she was sorry if he suffered, but she couldn't waste her emotional resources repining. Mathieu had chosen a life free of the responsibilities she couldn't abandon. So be it. If he had escaped, he might already be enrolled in a Protestant academy, distinguishing himself in books, earning the honor and respect that meant so much to him. If he had not escaped, then he must live with whatever consequences had come.

But her father. And Alexandre. Could she coerce her brother to go? She hadn't been willing to escape from France without holding fast to her young siblings. Could she now leave with none but the nine-year-old twins, Louise and Louis?

* * * * *

Armand de Gandon had been right. The letter, when he unfolded it, was in the familiar spidery hand of the Duc de Lauzières.

He reflected on the events of the past half hour. He had been displeased when he heard whispers that an emissary of French ambassador d'Avaux was seeking him. The news had reached him before the lackey did. When the letter had arrived, he had accepted it rather coldly, and the servant had departed at once, having judged by Armand's manner and appearance that a gratuity was not likely. Armand had strolled out of the café and into the street to get away from the curious. He had recognized the seal on the letter immediately. It was that of his patron. He had also guessed what the old man wanted.

"*Au toujours*," Armand muttered. "Always tactful. Always longsuffering. Forgiving. But understanding?" Of that latter he was uncertain, for how could his aged patron grasp what Armand couldn't understand in himself—an unwillingness to let go of his Huguenot heritage though he was strongly drawn to the intoxicating possibilities the duke had offered not once or even twice but repeatedly over the past three years?

"*Mon Cher Major, Mon Fils.*" *

As the young officer read the page, he heard the old man's sardonic voice as if the duke sat beside him, his gouty leg supported on its stack of pillows. And as he knew the duke intended he should, Armand felt himself the erring protégé. "Like the philosopher Pascal," the old man wrote, "I am frightened by 'eternal silences' and 'infinite spaces.' But not sufficiently fearful to risk known present dangers. You Calvinists may be right in some respects. But one must be pragmatic. I see both king and clergy playing the cat with us. And if we would be fat mice, we must learn where to find the cheese and tune our ears to hear the jingle of the cat's bell."

---

* "My Dear Major, My Son."

If by now, the duke suggested, Armand had had his satisfaction from his quixotic deed, whatever the religious or romantic reasons he might have had, if he had been sufficiently cold and hungry since turning his back on France, and should he wish to make a quiet, discreet return, a face-saving pretense could be arranged for the benefit of the king and the clergy. "Your opinions could be what you choose in private. As for myself, all can be as it was to have been before: my friendship, the colonelcy, the inheritance—in a word, to become my adopted son by law as you have been in my heart since you saved the regiment when my own son died. The girl? Bring her along. She appears to be made of good stuff within and without, and we could create a pedigree and title for her that would satisfy the most courtly."

It appeared that the duke had made some inquiries. Perhaps he knew most of what there was to know about those "quixotic" deeds. Who had been his source? Or were his sources many?

Now Armand sat down on the edge of a barge drawn flush with the canal's stone curbing, crossed his legs, and spread the opened letter upon his knee.

"*Mon cher fils,* your present situation is no life for a gentleman."

He understood the duke's position: The concept of God had been invented by earthly rulers to justify their own favored position. Religion of some kind was necessary, the duke had so often said, to ensure the morality of the nation, for people who didn't fear God wouldn't fear the king or his deputies. By such reasoning, a public-minded citizen should at least appear to accept whatever doctrine the king endorsed. Even some of the most successful Jesuits advocated lenience where a man's conscience was involved. One might outwardly comply with political necessity but entertain a "mental reservation."

Armand read the letter a second time, the duke's voice echoing in his head with its tone of amused contempt for zealots of any species. One played one's required role, but one's thoughts were one's own. The letter urged that Armand should but indicate his interest to the Comte d'Avaux and then one would see how things would go. "If not now, then later. You will always be welcome."

D'Avaux was a useful type, the duke remarked, and owed him some favors. "*Soyez sage, soyez prudent!* The king promotes science because it serves his military and economic ambitions, but his mind is not sufficiently vast that he can fathom the doubts that our great philosophers raise with each new discovery. Even in his most libertine days, the king glanced always over his shoulder and was certain God would hold him to account. "You will learn he is as unforgiving as he believes God to be, and he drives a hard bargain. Few get the second chance, so it is something to think about."

Armand thought with some regret of the Regiment of Maine, of his ten years' service in the armies of Louis XIV under the Duc de Lauzières, of the command of his own regiment, which was assured if he accepted the duke's gracious offer.

He winced. The exhilaration of 1685 had died, and as he folded the letter and put it carefully in his pocket, he had to admit to himself that matters had not gone as he had once expected. How grand to be recognized for the contribution he could make to the military machine of Louis XIV! His own regiment might be only the beginning. Like Marshal Schomberg, for whom his father had named him, he might rise to lead an army in the name of his king. In his mind's eye, he saw again the moon-drenched hills, the rolling vineyards, the slumbering towns, the fires of his regiment camped by a roadside, the ghostly façade of a sleeping Versailles—his dreadful, his blood-soaked, his beautiful, his glorious France. His heart ached for her.

And his heart warmed toward the duke. What generosity—and no deadline! And there lay the terrible possibility of betraying what was of even more value, a crown of righteousness and the approbation of God. *I must not leave such an alternative open,* he thought to himself. *Matters might grow even worse.* He studied the threadbare broadcloth stretched over his crossed thigh, the parchment thinness of the sole of his left shoe. Even now his resolve was sorely tried.

As he had found himself doing much of late, he pondered his interrupted career, trying to ignore an imperfectly filled stomach. Any Frenchman in a place like Holland would admit to some homesickness.

He was probably the only French refugee who might by such a simple choice recoup his losses—only a word to d'Avaux.

But could his patron gloss the events of the past three years as effectively as he imagined? Rumors were rampant. Armand wondered if d'Avaux had informers both among the refugees and the Dutch. No one wished to be suspected of such liaisons. Honor demanded making a choice and remaining steadfast. "Whether in God's army or in the army of Louis XIV, I am no mercenary," Armand muttered. There had been times even during the terrifying escape with the Cortot family when it would have been easy to see the beautiful Madeleine as a golden reward for his services and perhaps the real reason for the "renewal" of the Faith in which he had been reared.

Giving up his dreams of a happy marriage had been most difficult. His pride as an officer and a gentleman had kept him from pursuing the friendship developed during the intimacy of the escape from France in the winter of '85. He could not in his poverty ask her to share his lot.

Armand smiled, remembering Madeleine's brother Alexandre, thirteen years old at the time. The boy's saucy remarks on that journey and upon their arrival had been an almost constant embarrassment. Only last month Alexandre, trundling a small bundle over his shoulder, had accosted him along the canal. "I've found work unloading barges here," the boy had said, apparently assuming the rights of a younger brother joining an older. And twice since the boy had moved into the attic room, he had brought up the subject of his sister. "You know, Major Armand, it would not have been difficult to warm that relationship to the matrimonial level, and then you could have consoled each other in your pauperism. Madeleine is as prideful as yourself, sir. She feared you would think she led you on. Both of you were quite savage with me."

"And you were quite transparent," Armand chided. "Always the Cupid."

The boy, of course, had no real understanding of life's complexities. One did not just give in to whatever emotion stirred at the moment. One must look dispassionately at the total situation and exercise discretion.

Despite Alexandre's steadfast opinion, he mused as he placed the duke's letter in his vest pocket, I have given up all hope of a Cortot marriage, even as I long ago gave up on becoming a luminary at court. I must be as deliberate in turning my back on the army of the French king!

* * * * *

Conseil d'Etat, le marquise de Louvois, in his private office at Versailles, hastily scanned another packet of densely written papers from the highly acclaimed pastor of the French Huguenot congregation in Rotterdam, a *coups d'in folio*—a virtual war of words—in which Pierre Jurieu, in his customary pious humility, offered all his usual protestations concerning the ill use French "true believers" had received at the hands of "those close to the king who subvert the king's true and generous nobility."

Compulsive as he was about knowing everything happening in the kingdom before other officials and always before the king was informed, Louvois had for several months been receiving and destroying similar messages from Jurieu. He had read the entire copy of Jurieu's book *Accomplishments of the Prophets,* and he wasn't amused by the radical preacher's interpretation of biblical prophecies. That even a few thousand French citizens might believe such dangerous propaganda was maddening, for discussion of this sort further infected the wound of heresy that since time out of mind had festered on the nation's southern flank. In Nimes, in Montpellier, in the Cevennes, indeed in much of the Midi, ancient forms of Christianity had joined forces with Calvinist Huguenots and persisted in spite of demolished temples, banished clergy, and a population despoiled by dragonnades.

Worse yet, presses in Holland and England and perhaps in the Germanies were spreading this propaganda of Jurieu, inciting nearly all the nations of Europe to see France and the French king as an evil empire that God willed overthrown.

Jurieu was right about one thing. The king was more open-minded, more tolerant, than was good for the nation. Arrogant as he was, Louis XIV also craved the affections of his subjects and the good opinion even of his enemies.

Louvois slid the Jurieu letters back into their envelope and laid it on the fire blazing on the hearth. Then he returned to pick up another packet. This one was from the Calvinist lawyer Claude Brousson, who was a vigorous debater—an intellectual who spoke and wrote passionately for the rights of religious dissenters.

Freedom of conscience—this Brousson advocated, demanded, as if he would become the conscience of the king. Louvois ground his teeth. If the king should equivocate, should accept even briefly Brousson's arguments, a great deal would be lost. "One France" had been the watchword of this king's reign since 1661, when, in his youth, he first began to take control of the government. "And I have seen that goal achieved in spite of the king's lapses into conciliation," Louvois muttered. "Neither Brousson nor Jurieu—and none other who might be ready to take their place—shall undo my work!" He jammed the Brousson papers into their torn envelope and thrust it too into the fire.

But if Louvois had hoped no eyes but his own had seen the missives he had just destroyed, he soon learned otherwise. At a meeting with lesser ministers later that day, he found several men discussing with a familiarity that alarmed him printed copies of those very letters as well as Jurieu's book.

"Indeed, sire, hundreds of copies have been circulated in Paris. Yet we feel confident we have gained possession of them all," ventured an aspiring young deputy.

"And instead of destroying them, you are reading them?"

"One must know the direction the enemy turns in order to plan an ambush," another young subordinate said, defending himself.

"We know sufficient," Louvois thundered. "Burn the books. Burn them *now*."

An hour later, Louvois learned that in the past two years two hundred thousand Calvinists had fled France, seeking asylum with the enemies of their king. "If they were all men and if they were all soldiers," his informant pointed out, "they would form an army equal to the entire army of France."

"But only a few of them, fifty thousand perhaps, *are* men," Louvois snapped. "And most of them are tradesmen or bankers and are of no threat to the army of His Majestic Highness Louis XIV."

"But they are a threat to the industry and commerce of France."

Louvois didn't reply. It was a sore point for him, one he couldn't refute. Under Colbert, who had preceded his father as Counseil des Finances, French manufactures and exports had grown immensely in both size and quality. Now, many in places of power claimed that both French industry and trade were in ruins, that the economy of the nation wouldn't long support the taxes necessary to sustain continuous wars and colossal building programs.

Louvois, as he always did, shrugged off such warnings. *I'm a tired old man,* he thought, *too tired to admit even to myself such possibilities.* He wondered if his son might achieve the ruthless determination necessary to succeed him and hold the position he now held. Perhaps in another year—two years at most—he could position Barbezieux in readiness and then quietly step aside as his father had done for him.

We are a family, well placed and well connected, Louvois thought. *And one essential of power is to command intelligence.* He indulged himself a rare smile. No other family in the history of France had situated its offspring in as many key positions, both within the nation and in the cities of other nations. On that fact as much as on the strength of the great French army depended the success of Louis XIV.

The Conseil d'Etat felt certain that only he had sufficient information to know that, while two hundred thousand heretics had found refuge in foreign lands, not even a tenth of the Huguenots in France had escaped abroad. That was a fact corroborated by membership lists that he had collected over the previous decade and had calculated in private. Whatever certain others of the king's advisors might construe that fact to mean if they knew it, Louvois saw it as evidence that nearly two million former French Protestants had chosen to obey the king's order to conform to the national church.

Unfortunately, Louvois admitted to himself, he saw no hope that some could be cajoled into changing their religion. Reason indicated that the poor couldn't flee. Most of them were concentrated in the Cevennes in the south, so it was there that foreign sympathizers now consolidated in the League of Augsburg would strike if they did, threading the narrow passes and valleys from Switzerland and Piedmont into the soft underbelly of France to join with those ancient enemies of the

Catholic Church—the Vaudois.* The harshest measures would be required to wipe them out.

I am prepared, Louvois decided with a certain satisfaction.

With that conviction, he set about dressing for the *approchement* scheduled for the evening, and after that, his usual meeting with the king in the apartment of Madame de Maintenon.

Since the king's affections could no longer be diverted by charming young beauties, one must learn to work around and with that indomitable woman. *At least,* Louvois thought as he crossed from his own quarters into the public area of the palace where a score of grandees swarmed upon him, *on this one point we agree: that we will not be like the Hapsburgs, who preside over a kingdom comprised of hundreds of small principalities. No, we will have a single nation under a single king with a single faith. I can count on Madame de Maintenon to defend with all her formidable energy the supremacy of both king and church. In that sense, she is my ally.*

* * * * *

Though Armand knew that it was fatally easy to let the matter ride and postpone the final decision, still he didn't write his reply to the duke's letter as he had intended. Alexandre had come into the attic room once while he held the letter to the light of the small window and had asked questions in his unabashed manner. Armand had tried to be honest, but admittedly he was evasive. He would, he decided, discuss it with the Sieur de Tillieres, who was now established as a host, friend, and confidant of so many refugees.

With this in mind, he asked if he might come early to Tillieres' house when that good man next invited hungry exiles to dine. While Tillieres' newly acquired Dutch wife and the servants were busy preparing the repast, Armand sat in the parlor and discussed his dilemma. Tillieres was now more conservatively dressed, with his still abundant hair cut shorter and tied back, and with a thin mustache on his upper lip, a bit out of date but in keeping with his soldierly past.

---

* The Waldenses.

Armand felt again a certain unease under the shrewd ice-blue eyes, but his host's expression was kindly and he wouldn't preach—unlike most of the Huguenot refugees. Some of his soldier friends would have judged Armand unfaithful if they knew that he had the letter, that he had communicated with the French ambassador.

"*Tiens, c'est toujours le France.* It is never of anything else that we speak," sighed Tillieres, never quite able to shake off the affected accent of a courtier. "All these unfortunates who have managed to reach safety, in my home or on the streets of Amsterdam, they speak always of France. Granddame, young widow, or merchant—they all long to return."

"I thought it prudent to show you the letter," Armand told Tillieres, "in case suspicions have been aroused in any refugee seeing me in conversation with the ambassador's servant. You are widely known and respected and could make sympathetic explanations if need be."

"But of course," Tillieres responded.

There was no need to explain the letter's significance, for Tillieres himself had been present at the *levée* when the Duc de Lauzières had introduced Armand to the king at Versailles. Tillieres had seen the courtiers fawning over him after Louis XIV had smiled upon him, had heard the gushing praise that followed his progress through Versailles during the few days he remained there.

With an amused smile, Armand remembered how much he had invested in that meeting with Louis XIV. Indeed, an entire year's income from his patrimony in the south had been barely sufficient to purchase the foppish clothing he was expected to wear at court. The duke had explained that everything depended upon appearances.

"*Mais oui!*"

Now Tillieres, his face solemn, held the letter at arm's length, the better to read it.

"Your excellent record. Your prospects. A colonelcy of your own, which a young gentleman of no great income could never in a lifetime of faithful service hope to be able to purchase. And, ah, that is just the start." The older man understood as only another officer could.

"*Au meme temps,*" Armand said, "I am a man of conscience."

For a full week after his meeting with Tillieres, Armand took daily exercise along the canals, cross-examining himself without mercy. But could his conscience bear such close examination? Often enough he had lain awake at night wondering whether it had been conscience at all or simply a romantic impulse that had awakened his dormant Huguenot sensibilities when he visited Monsieur Cortot in the little town of Saint Martin in the south of France.

Cortot was an old comrade of his father, and in passing through Saint Martin, Armand had yearned for something of the family feeling he had missed so desperately since his father's death when he was himself but a pink-cheeked lad in his father's regiment. Memories of home and the Reformed way of life had faded during his years in the French army. And then in Saint Martin, he had seen for the first time what his conscientious brethren in the Faith suffered at the hands of the royal officers and church-men who sought to suppress Protestantism. He had seen the local temple torn down on perjured testimony. Before his eyes, Huguenot children were kidnapped to be placed in Houses of New Catholics, to be pressured into changing the religion they were born into, while parents, fearful for their physical safety, were forced to pay for their keep. And seized with wrath on his second visit to the town, Armand had spirited the Cortot twins and Madeleine away from their captors and conveyed them secretly to a refuge with relatives in northern France.

Vraiment. Armand admitted to himself that it had not been entirely the injustice against which he had interfered at such risk to himself—one could be broken alive on the wheel for carrying a young lady off from a convent. If sixteen-year-old Madeleine Cortot had been plain or petulant, as a matter of personal honor he might still have helped her escape. But then, between stints at Versailles, he could not but compare her modesty and beauty with the painted and powdered females parading at Versailles. Only a man with a heart of solid ice could stand by and allow such a girl to wither to a dry stick in a nunnery. Unthinkable! So, rather like a knight in a medieval tale who had no hope of winning the love of the captive princess, he had thrown his life into saving Madeleine.

He smiled, remembering the lukewarm assistance of Mathieu Bertrand, a theological student whose prospects had been promising until the king closed the Huguenot academies. Mathieu had shown more annoyance that Armand was the force behind the rescue of his promised one than joy at her rescue. And he had declined her father's pleas to take his children to safety.

Still, Armand mused, even while giving in to an occasional fantasy of wooing and winning the love of Madeleine he had been sane enough to realize such a match was out of the question. The Huguenot girl was from a bourgeois family, and that would be seen by his friends at court as an impediment to marriage. Of greater concern to him, she was affianced already. He had been careful to observe every propriety. However, in nearly four years he hadn't been able to banish her from his dreams.

He wondered what had become of Mathieu Bertrand. If he had made an appearance, certainly Alexandre would have given Armand a detailed account of the visit, for he bore his former schoolmaster nothing but ill will. Personally, Armand could be more charitable. "*Tiens,* he too had lost all he had worked for—his future . . ."

Armand smiled ruefully. *Monsieur Mathieu, the someday Huguenot preacher—did he labor with the same dreams of honor, position, prosperity? Were his dreams as alluring to him as the duke's promises are to me?*

Mathieu had been surly, suspicious, thoroughly disagreeable. With his orderly world collapsing about him, the young scholar had all but abandoned his fiancée. If Madeleine had only showed the first sign of faltering allegiance to unhappy Mathieu—ah! But she had remained steadfast in her loyalty to him.

In 1685, none of them had believed the king would actually revoke the Edict of Nantes. And then that October the Revocation had stunned them all. "I followed my conscience. I maintained my integrity," Armand muttered. But even as the words clung to his lips, he questioned his honesty.

Once he had visited the Cortot children in their Rotterdam refuge and professed selfless dedication to the Good Cause. He had dared to hope that circumstances had brought Madeleine to her senses concerning Mathieu. But at that time she still believed her betrothed was coming, and she had been steadfast in professing her devotion.

Armand excused himself for his lack of ardor. *I was not the one to disabuse her of her faith. It would have been unseemly.*

"Father has been ruined," Alexandre had confided cheerfully on that visit. "The dragoons demolished the house even before Father was forced to leave. And now it's anybody's guess who's building there—some pope-pleasing blackguard who owed Father a great deal of money.

"I'd rather be with you, Armand, than here in Rotterdam," he'd continued. "There's nothing happening here."

"I'm only in Amsterdam," the major had pointed out. "Very little action, if that's what you mean. With hundreds of other refugee French officers also seeking employment, it would take a very grave military threat to put us all in uniform."

"But the House for Huguenot Gentlewomen," Alexandre objected. "You can't imagine what it is to be obliged to carry out the slops, to scrub the doorstep, to run to this house or that one halfway across the city with a note imploring a noble kinswoman to write more often."

"In Amsterdam I have only a bare garret room."

"*Mais oui,* but I would rather share your fortunes." Alexandre had pressed his hands to his head and made a face. "And when war does come— and it must come soon, Major—I shall be at your side, ready to share your fortunes if it means carrying your ammunition or your bedroll."

Armand clenched his fists under the worn cuffs of his coat. Alas, Alexandre had come with Madeleine's grudging permission, still intent on keeping that commitment. Now he was sharing the shabby sixth-floor room. And now, added to a longing heartache for the unreachable sister, he could not escape his growing affection for Alexandre. He had plenty of leisure in which to ponder the difference between action—such as an escape and the outwitting of persecutors—and the kind of endurance required to wait patiently for the Lord's hand to show itself in his behalf.

Armand mused that the boy would soon learn for himself that war was more wretched than was menial labor in the city. Alexandre had entered a man's world, running errands for an export merchant and ferreting any news he could from offices or wharf, while Armand himself spent days visiting various centers for men like himself, questioning the latest developments, daily learning to exercise a certain restraint concerning any propositions he might otherwise be bold enough to make.

Among the bargemen, Alexandre reported, it was common knowledge that the Dutch prince was assembling a fleet—large numbers of boats of every kind—in Hellevoetsluis.

"That is a good omen, *n'est-ce pas?*"

In the Amsterdam coffee houses, Armand read the fortnightly newsletters of Pastor Jurieu and borrowed a copy of that worthy French theologian's book. Jurieu was convinced that Catholic France was the terrible beast of Revelation and the Revocation was "the death of the Two Witnesses." England would, Jurieu claimed, deliver the Huguenots this very year—1689.

Armand studied Jurieu's math with interest but didn't have the scholar's background to understand the niceties of the worthy man's reasoning. He sincerely hoped that the projected end of the papacy between 1710 and 1715 proved true, but by 1715, Madeleine Cortot would be forty-six years old and he would be fifty-five! He felt he could sympathize with Moses, who had had great events and providences to sustain him through the time of the plagues and the crossing of the Red Sea but who must have found the forty years' delay in the wilderness a trial of a different and harder sort. Besides, as Armand had occasion to remind himself these days, his supply of manna was highly irregular and his clothes were all-too-visibly wearing out.

Yet though he chided himself, he had done what he knew to be right. He had not made a tradesman's bargain with the Lord, requiring that he must be supplied manna—and a tailor—in return. He must possess his soul in patience.

Then, at the end of July, the attention of the idle officers in the coffeehouses shifted from theological calculations to subjects on which they were better educated. Marshal Schomberg had most certainly been put on alert. There would be an autumn invasion of England. Catholic James II had pressed his religion too urgently upon his subjects and had been rejected by his own Parliament, whose representatives had invited his Protestant daughter Mary, the wife of William of Orange, to take the English throne jointly with her husband. William was planning an autumn invasion with a military force that could not but be successful.

Almost immediately, Schomberg's representative arrived with the offer for which Armand had been waiting.

More Letters—and Betrayals

That a new day had indeed dawned for Madeleine, bringing her more notoriety than she had had in three years in her humble station, was evident when a few days after receiving the first letter it became known that she had a second, this one from her father in France. Though he had evidently written before, this was the first message to get through since their arrival in Rotterdam.

Within the hour, the exile community knew that Monsieur Cortot, once a well-known government official in his part of southern France, was considering flight to join his children in the Netherlands. Madeleine was suddenly a personage, was asked questions, and was given much advice. Knowing that Isaac Cortot had been wealthy, some of Madeleine's new interlocutors assumed he still would be, and it would have been a naïve person who would not have wondered at the sudden interest and civilities that were now pressed upon her.

In fact, however, the good man was all but penniless and had written to ask his daughter what advice she could give him from her vantage point in Holland on how best to arrange his escape and what methods and routes would be the most sure. As Madeleine pondered her father's letter, she felt ever more strongly that she couldn't use Cousin Daniel's money to leave for America with her brothers and sister just when her father needed help escaping from the land of his persecution. Surely Cousin Daniel would agree, could he be consulted, that the most important use for the money he'd sent would be to bring Isaac Cortot to safety.

Pressed by the ladies for details, Madeleine mentioned some of her father's questions. With one voice, they urged her, "Oh, my dear! Talk to Monsieur Tillieres. He can tell you everything you need to know. *Ma foi!* * There is nothing he can't arrange for you. He knows absolutely everyone."

Madeleine had seen Louis de Pons, Sieur de Tillieres, often enough and knew how he charmed the mature demoiselles with his ornate, old-fashioned courtesies. He lived in Amsterdam but made the rounds to the principal refugee centers. The refuge for the gentle ladies in Rotterdam had better than ordinary contacts with the homeland, and he always found time when in that city to call on the ladies and share their letters and gossip.

Monsieur de Tillieres was highly esteemed by the leaders of the Refuge—especially the ministers, such as the great Pastor Claude and his son. Tillieres' generous lifestyle was attributed to his foresight in transferring his wealth from his native Poitou to Holland in good time, before the troubles. In his Amsterdam home, he welcomed meetings of the refugee chiefs and set a good table for hungry gentlemen down on their luck. There were, to be sure, evil tongues that alleged he had never been much of a Huguenot at all, but his many friends emphatically praised the Lord that Monsieur de Tillieres had found his way to Holland and was so kind and serviceable to God's distressed people. He rejoiced with them in their joys, and if, as sometimes happened, plans went awry, no one was more sympathetic and understanding.

Madeleine had never had occasion to speak to such a social lion but had noticed his eye on her when she had occasion to serve refreshments during his visits. But then, most gentlemen took a second look at the tall, dark-haired girl with the erect and graceful bearing, and, in spite of her sober mien and prim attire, they took a quick inventory of her visible and concealed attributes. She was used to that.

---

* My faith.

216

As it happened, she didn't have to seek the gentleman out. When he called the following week, the excited ladies summoned her to meet him. He was all attention and kindly interest, and he made appropriate remarks. After studying her father's letter, which she had been admonished to bring to the parlor with her, he dropped his voice so that few others could hear amid the babble. "I think I can be of service to you, mademoiselle. I stay tonight at the Red Lion Inn, across from the castle gate, hard by the quarters of Pastor Claude. If you will come to me this evening, we may be able to arrange ways in which your father can be most surely helped. But," and he winked and gave her hand a squeeze, "it would hardly be discreet to discuss such sensitive matters here. These dear ladies . . ." And he rolled his eyes heavenward. Then, gazing sympathetically into her eyes, he held her hand for a long moment, kissed it again, and went on to chat with his other admirers.

Madeleine kept her appointment with Tillieres alone. The gentleman received her warmly in the public room, but then, pleading the sensitive nature of their discussion, he took her to his chamber. A fire was burning in the grate, and there were cold cuts and wine on the table. But Madeleine refused the refreshment and seated herself on the other side of the table from him. After the courtesies, she told him about the letter from New York and the letter of credit. Tillieres casually inquired as to the amount of the latter. Madeleine said something to the effect that she could provide three hundred *livres*. Her heritage—the careful handling of money she'd learned from her merchant father and frugal mother—made her hesitant to mention the full amount.

Tillieres said reassuringly, "If you wish to use this money to help your father, I can arrange through friends I have in France for the best and most reliable guides to spirit him out of the country. It is true many escape without much money at all, but it is also true that success is most sure for him who has the longest purse. For three hundred *livres*, he should be able to get out most conveniently. I wish I had the funds to help all the poor souls who sigh and cry in Babylon, but Monsieur Cortot is fortunate in having such a daughter. Providence has undoubtedly moved upon your cousin in America to supply your needs at this very moment!"

Madeleine asked, "How shall I let my father know? Would it not be too dangerous to send money by post?"

"Yes, indeed! My friends can pass on your word and the money more safely. It will take time, but when he has safely arrived here, that will seem of little consequence."

Madeleine agreed to cash the letter of credit and have the money in Tillieres' hand by the following afternoon. At his suggestion she wrote her father a short note: "Father, arrangements have been made for your journey. Follow the instructions of him who brings you this. We will, if God pleases, see you soon—in New York, if not here."

"Very good, mademoiselle," said Tillieres, carefully sealing the small piece of paper. "I will be in close touch with you from here on."

He assisted her in draping the gray cloak over her shoulders, starting the "close touch" rather too soon. She knew that many of the older residents of the home palpitated over him and his courtly ways, but she wished he didn't have this disturbing tendency to leave his hands on her shoulders so long. Yet, his good will was absolutely necessary to her father's escape, and she must hide her annoyance. It was probably just his rather effusive way.

His cheek was unnecessarily close to hers, and one would almost think he was studying her very modest *décolletage.* She turned quickly and met his moist and sympathetic gaze. Eventually, he withdrew his hands. Again the bowing and hand-kissing, and finally she was able to depart. She resolved that there would be no more private interviews.

* * * * *

When the door closed behind Madeleine Cortot, Tillieres copied the address and then tossed her note in the fire. Sitting at the table, he proceeded to write a letter—this one to the comte d'Avaux. As he concluded his labor, he wrote:

> In addition to these others, I have word that a former official of Saint Martin in Saintonge will attempt to escape the realm shortly. He has written his daughter here to that effect. He must have hidden some money from the authorities with which he

plans to hire a guide to take him into Switzerland, probably through Savoy. The information is correct for I have read the letter. If he can be closely watched and it is known the moment he leaves, it should not be difficult to intercept him and perhaps others traveling with him and above all, his guide as well. I have intercepted the daughter's reply, and not hearing from her, he will assume she did not receive his letter and will proceed with his own arrangements.

Some here continue to talk of emigrating to America, but these are not many. Some of the pastors oppose the idea as they expect great events soon according to the prophecies of M. Jurieu and are mad and insolent enough to hope that present events will so work that His Majesty will be forced to recall all the PRR who are abroad and reestablish their churches. Some of the exiled officers have been living in the greatest misery, but in the past few days have been speaking hopefully of the coming of a new day in which the Prince of Orange will find employment for them.

I am grateful for the generosity of His Majesty, thanks to your recommendation in my behalf, and am always happy if the little *avis** I have been able to give you have been of service to His Majesty. It has been some time since he was last pleased to authorize you to pay me something. My expenses, circulating among these refugees and traveling frequently between Amsterdam, Rotterdam, Leiden, and the Hague, with one visit to the meeting of the Estates of Friesland, have depleted my resources greatly. I would be most grateful for your consideration in the matter of my request for five hundred *livres* toward my expenses.

* * * * *

In Paris, the Duc de Lauzières was writing a letter in his own hand—not, to be sure, an exercise in which he often indulged. However, if one must incriminate oneself on paper, the fewer to know of it, the better.

---

* Opinion.

He was a withered little man past seventy with a shrewd, deeply lined face, a prodigious beaked nose, and a glittering and cynical eye that missed very little around the court at Versailles. He wrote in a large scrawling hand:

Having this opportunity, Monsieur de Tillieres, to send this word into Holland by a trusted friend, I must thank you for your service in approaching M. de Gandon for me, even if no immediate success is apparent. Please have the goodness to continue to cultivate him for me, and if his prospects there continue dismal, he may yet be willing to return to me and to his duty.

As we now know, part of the reason for M. de Gandon's reckless behavior was his gallant concern for a young lady in distress. The idea occurs to me, monsieur, that you may very discreetly make the acquaintance of this demoiselle, assuming the interest continues, and according to your best judgment enlist her on our side. If you think she would be responsive to money, you have my permission to make what promises you feel would be useful—you may draw on the funds with the banker in Amsterdam that I have made available for your expenses. Have the young woman encourage M. de Gandon to return to his good prospects here. Tell her also that if she cares to return to France herself, much might be made to happen that would be to her advantage.

If, on the other hand, she is of a sort to whom such propositions would be insulting, you will then have more difficulty in securing her good offices. But you should press upon her the sacrifices M. de Gandon has made in her behalf and the advantages he might yet obtain if she would give him good counsel to help him out of his present distressed state.

The messenger awaits, so I say no more at present. I trust your discretion in this affair, for you well know the use my enemies might make of this to injure the credit I have with His Majesty, especially if my plans became known before the proper time.

The duke didn't sign the letter but affixed his signet to the soft wax. Waiting for the seal to harden, he gazed into the fire with a slight smile on his face. At twenty-eight, it was time Armand married. His own marriage when he was hardly twenty had been politically arranged, and he had expected any romance he might squeeze from life to be snatched illicitly, as his father and grandfather had found it. But to his surprise and to the dismay of both father and grandfather, the duke had been more than satisfied with the affections of his young wife, had been totally devoted to her, and—when she died—to their one son. They had lived grandly. His one thrift had been that he had never kept a mistress. In his marriage he had kept faith. It was the only matter in which he had faith at all—in that and in his own capricious attachment to Armand de Gandon.

The duke shifted his gouty leg and stared at the letter. At times like this, a man of power and politics, a veteran of thirty years commanding an army, a man used to the machinations of courtly life—a man such as himself could not but understand how carefully he must measure his own influence and the possible consequences of each favor he extended.

"A little risk makes even a worthy project more interesting," he said to himself as he pulled the cord to ring for the servant.

* * * * *

The portly and choleric Louvois—conseil d'etat, minister of war, controller of the postal system, responsible for religion and domestic order, and in charge of gathering and channeling intelligence—was the busiest man in the kingdom. He sat in his chamber in the secretariat building at Versailles reading through a mound of reports. A scribe sat close by, pen at the ready for any comments or replies the minister might dictate. "For your eyes alone," he read on a decoded message from an agent in Amsterdam.

> I can report, my lord, that I continue to receive instructions
> and money from the Duc de Lauzières to further his project for
> the return of the refugee Reformed officer Armand de Gandon,

with the object of his abjuration and restoration. The duke has, of course, no suspicion that I am actually in your service. I can report that I have renewed my acquaintance with the aforesaid de Gandon, and he accepts me as a refugee like himself. I would, my lord, be grateful if you would see fit to keep Madame de Maintenon informed of the affair of de Gandon, for she is especially anxious that he be brought to justice for his part in the escape of a young lady from a House of New Catholics at Saint Martin early in 1685.

"Very good!" said Louvois to his secretary, a rare grin on his fleshy, red face.

"It was a good idea to send Tillieres to Holland! And we may yet make an example of this impudent officer and help the Duc de Lauzières to trip himself up by his own cleverness in the bargain. But we had better wait until we have caught this de Gandon and wrung some useful statements out of him before we try to blow up a mine under the duke. The old fox has gotten out of more than one scrape by his marvelous talent in deceiving His Majesty. This time he is carrying a lighted match into a powder magazine. And this time we have Madame de Maintenon on our side—that runaway major is a heretic and a convent breaker!"

As Louvois put the message on the pile of papers already read, he frowned. "That Tillieres is a talented rascal," he muttered, "but he may be a little too clever too—cultivating Madame de Maintenon is he? I surely don't want the old crow meddling in our affairs, but I suppose it would be useful to dictate her a note on this de Gandon. Her priestly informers sometimes bring her news we can use; a little civility may be advantageous."

* * * * *

Madeleine Cortot, standing on the steps of the Rotterdam House for Huguenot Gentlewomen, looked a little apprehensively at the proud but insolvent Armand de Gandon, who had responded to her letter with unexpected dispatch.

"It's probably true that I don't have the patience to be a saint," he said. "Waiting and rusting here in exile has been difficult, for I have been fretting to be in action. And though I am not at liberty to discuss the details, you must know from common rumors what is afoot."

Madeleine could guess from the new uniform—a long blue coat, orange vest, and hose—that Armand was now an officer of the Dutch foot soldiers. In spite of her discomposure at this sudden change in his fortunes, she could not help smiling at the wide gold lace adorning his cuffs and the brim of his hat. Yet she had summoned him and Alexandre with good reason.

"Cousin Daniel's letter has come now, and with his good will we can all of us take passage to New York." Madeleine knew they wouldn't travel as comfortably as they might have had they still the full five hundred *livres.* But with what was left plus what she'd managed to save from her meager wages and their willingness to work onboard ship, she thought they still could obey their father's directive.

She drew a long breath and hurried on for fear Armand would interrupt. "Please don't take offense, but we want very much for you to come with us. We owe you more than we could ever repay for getting us out of France, you know."

Her use of "we" was tentative, even weak, for Alexandre, standing beside his heroic champion, was also clad in new military attire. Clearly, her brother already had plans that didn't include sailing to America.

The officer's face showed the polite interest a gentleman manifests when an attractive young lady talks of things important to her. That she was attractive she didn't question. Even in the plain gray gown of a servant and in white cap and wooden shoes with a market basket on her arm, she was conscious that nothing in her erect bearing suggested the peasant. Only her hands, roughened and reddened by three brutal years of drudgery, were not those of a lady.

"Monsieur Tillieres has volunteered to get a reply to father by a secret channel he knows of, and so Father may be able to join us. I don't know after all that has happened how I could bear so much happiness!" Her voice was a little tremulous. "You know he wanted us to cross the ocean, and now that we know Cousin Daniel will have us, we ought to go. Of course, we should wait to see if Father can join us, but we must not stay too long or the money might be spent for something else. You know I get but scant wages here and a place to sleep, and Louis is only an errand boy at the press of Monsieur Jounderes, so he is paid nothing."

Armand de Gandon seemed hardly to be listening now to what she said. Yet she plunged further into her speech.

"Cousin Daniel says there is now a Huguenot temple in New York and that a good number of our people are settled there, and very comfortably, too. There are so many religions there—it is like Holland—that no one is abused for what he believes."

Armand's face was still impassive.

"There are many things to do there, and with the delays about your commission, I thought perhaps . . ."

He shook his head and started to speak, but she cut him off.

"Oh, I know Alexandre has some chimera that the Prince of Orange will soon be king of England."

"It is no longer a chimera, mademoiselle," de Gandon replied. "I have now been given a captaincy in the Foot Guards of the Prince of Orange. Events are moving, and there is little doubt that a war is coming. I do very much appreciate your kind invitation, but truly, I would be of little use at sea, and I wouldn't have an occupation to follow in America. Besides, however grateful I am, I couldn't take money from a young lady, and thirdly, I truly believe my duty would be to use the only talent I have—soldiering—now that it is needed for the Good Cause. I have been feeling very useless here these past weary years."

"Oh, indeed?" she rejoined, a dangerous coldness all but cutting off her breath. "I wondered if there was a 'fourthly'—that our rustic company was beginning to bore you. There is also talk that your duke may have you back. Perhaps a journey to Versailles would be more exciting than an ocean voyage?"

The soldier's face reddened.

"My affairs must be more entertaining than I had realized. Perhaps we have both trusted our friend Tillieres more than is prudent. It may be that those who carry these tales are better informed than I as to what I shall be doing!"

He paused, and she tried to read his meaning from his face. His smile was strained. She swallowed the sarcastic remark about to burst from her lips, seeing he felt she had betrayed some trust he had placed in her.

He continued, "I can never stand in the way of anyone taking the providences opening before him, but I won't impose on others, whether they offer me help out of gratitude or pity."

"Gratitude, of course." She turned her head, afraid he would see the tears welling in her eyes. "What if it is neither gratitude nor pity?"

"Let me wish you *bon voyage,*" he said hastily—in his habitual courtesy seeming contrite. "But truly! If these *donneurs d'avis** are suggesting I might lose my religion if I serve the Prince of Orange or return to France—which I have no intention of doing, believe me—remember, one can lose it very successfully without ever leaving Amsterdam."

He rushed on in an affected hearty tone, "Surely for me to follow once again my profession is not the end of the world, nor does it mean any less appreciation."

"It could easily mean the end of those following such a profession, be they experienced officers or addled drummer boys," she sniffed. "But you should understand, monsieur, that I would not for the world wish you to change any of your plans out of any sentimental concern for *former* friends."

---

* Those giving advice.

CHAPTER 11

To Go or to Stay?

It was no help to Armand's ruffled disposition to have to deal with Madeleine Cortot's gap-toothed brother as they clattered down the cobbled street upon leaving her. Armand felt guilty, for in a way, his glamour had seduced the youngster with visions of a military career, and he had indeed in a weak moment arranged for Alexandre to be taken on as a drummer in an English regiment in Dutch service.

But Alexandre seemed determined to be difficult just when some silence would be most welcome. The boy reminded him twice that as a survivor of a House for New Catholics, from which he had been expelled as impermeable to Roman Catholic instruction, and as a veteran of vagabond journeys across France thereafter, he deserved a degree of respect—which his seniors never gave him.

"Respect?" cried Armand in dismay. "You speak to me of respect? Heaven help you when you march with your regiment—you will lose more teeth in the bargain! I shall go to your commander immediately and withdraw my recommendation."

"I think, Monsieur Captain," began Alexandre, "that you ought to put your pride in your pocket just for the moment, so to speak—"

"I appreciate—I highly value your counsel, Monsieur Know-it-all, but your duty is to your sisters and little brother. No doubt there are Indians or bears in America, and your services might be required! I understand that in the wilderness over there, young men may prosper totally without manners or respect for authority."

"Are you going back on your promise just because you got a tongue lashing from Her Highness?"

Armand saw his own foolishness in engaging in such a conversation with a boy but half his age. But he felt some pleasure in taking the banter to its finish. "I assure Your Impudence that it is your place to go with your sister—and I wish the bears *bonne chance.*"*

"Well, you seem to know my place all right, but what about your own?"

Armand lifted his eyes heavenward as if appealing for strength. "So, must I need have a lecture from you, too? Please understand, a gentleman doesn't thrust himself in where he doesn't belong. I have explained fully to mademoiselle your sister, who is normally a very quick and intelligent young lady, that I cannot go where I would have no way to support myself, nor will I accept passage to America in what would amount to charity from my friends. Furthermore, with war impending, we may be certain that Prince William and the princes of the Augsburg League fight for the Protestant cause. As for now, you would participate only as a drummer boy, and the Protestant cause hardly requires you to join your brothers on some field in Flanders or England, or, worse, to lose a leg or arm and be a burden to your sister. Her needs come before those of the Prince of Orange—do you understand?"

"Indeed, I do, sir." Alexandre's tone was patently insincere. "Now explain to me how one more captain's leaving his bones on a field in Flanders or England will advance the accomplishment of the prophecies of Pastor Jurieu."

"Your impudence passes all bounds," snapped Armand.

Alexandre persisted. "You disappoint me, Captain. If you were as unenterprising a soldier as you are a suitor, you would have been cashiered long ago. Proper sort though Madeleine is, she did make the first move, you know. Do you expect *her* to propose to *you*?"

"What do you want anyway?" cried the exasperated Armand. "Should I carry her off kicking and screaming? This is the seventeenth century,

---

* Good luck.

not the sixteenth! She was practically another man's wife last I knew. I will make no suit to live on your sister's money!"

Alexandre made a rude noise and then said, "Well, if you are determined to turn your back on her—and I don't really think she gave Mathieu a serious thought these past three years—let me do it with you. If she's going to be angry, let her be angry at both of us at the same time. It should be some comfort to her if we are blown up together at some unpronounceable place in Germany, wouldn't it?"

"Enough!" Armand said, out of patience and no longer amused. Several passersby turned to see the reason for such vehemence. The two stamped along without speaking.

What a pest the boy is, thought Armand. *If there had been more Huguenots like him, Pharaoh would have had to let all the children of Israel go!*

* * * * *

Two days later, when Madeleine opened the door of the House for Huguenot Gentlewomen, she found her brother Alexandre sitting on the step. The sky was gray and lowering, and her mood was no better. It seemed that every time she attempted to go out lately, someone was blocking the doorway.

"*Now* what do you want?" Her tone was not encouraging. She didn't relish an exchange with him.

"I thought you'd appreciate a reminder," Alexandre said with a pleasant grin as he rose and dusted himself off. "You'll have to do better. You mislaid the schoolmaster, you know, and it looks like the soldier may get away too. A spinster at twenty is well nigh hopeless, *n'est-ce pas?*"

"Alexandre, please! Can you not learn to mind your own business?"

"You forget, dear sister, that I am the head of the family now, so it *is* my business."

"I have no time to waste fencing with an impertinent child. I have to go to market, so please get out of my way." She started to step around him, but he clearly meant to accompany her. "And I don't discuss my affairs in public!" she added, shifting her market basket to the arm on his side, almost expecting him to affect some gallantry.

"No need to," said her brother with the same infuriating cheerfulness. "It's no secret to anyone how your affairs go. We haven't seen Mathieu since you put some flea in his ear before we left France. And you were pretty cordial with Armand in those snowdrifts, but there seems to be a chill like December itself now. He's determined to go off and get shot for the glory of the Prince of Orange. I think if you would flutter your eyelashes at him a bit more seriously, we might persuade him to come to America with us and trap beaver or whatever one does there. You are better-looking than the Prince of Orange I should think, though I'll wager the prince has a better disposition!"

"You've changed your mind?" She turned swiftly to face her brother, hardly believing she had heard him right.

"Of course, if I can bring you to your senses. It's my duty as your only male protector to go with you and manage your affairs if you reject all willing suitors."

"You will try me too far, you wretched boy! You know perfectly well that Father wanted us to go to Cousin Daniel, and Monsieur de Gandon knows he would be welcome. He has made his excuses. What do you want—that I should go on my knees to him? He has his reasons, I'm sure. Maybe he's had some time to think lately, and he finds his bourgeois acquaintances an embarrassment. What do you take me for?"

"One of the foolish virgins perhaps?"

Madeleine felt her face burning, for others on the street, some of whom she suspected might understand French, had stopped to stare. Alexandre's eye was on the basket, but he seemed to enjoy her embarrassment.

"If he sent you here to play Cupid or if this is some ridiculous foolishness of your own, you're wasting your time. If I—we—mean so little to him that he prefers to go soldiering than to go to the refuge God has opened up for us, it is his affair. And if you think you are going to work around me in some fashion to give you leave to stay here also, you are badly mistaken! Now get out of my way!"

She pushed past Alexandre and walked rapidly down the street without a backward glance. He walked off dejectedly toward the hated warehouse.

I wish I were older, he mused. *People don't seem to take me seriously. What a mess they've made of things. Both of them are so proud and stupid! I thought girls were cleverer. After all, she's had three years to tie him hand and foot. I had such a wonderful idea for the two of them, and I thought they had the same idea. Madeleine seems a little clumsy, but I did my best!*

He entered the dark cavern of the warehouse.

"I've had all of this I need," he muttered fiercely. "She can stamp and shout all she likes, and New York may be the Garden of Eden they say it is, but there's a war coming soon, and I'm not going to miss it!"

* * * * *

Though Madeleine wouldn't have admitted it, Alexandre's words had their effect. But she didn't try another personal appeal to the Major de Gandon. Instead, she sent Pastor Merson to labor with the two wayward men in her life, hoping their respect for the saintly man of the cloth would bend their stubborn wills where she could not.

Pastor Merson soon came to empathize with her unhappy situation. However, along with his many very real virtues was an unfortunate ability to see two sides of a question. He had known Alexandre from infancy, for he had been pastor at Saint Martin for many years. Major de Gandon he had met in the Cortots' home just before the dragonnade. The pastor had preceded the others to Holland by a few months, for at the time of the Revocation, like other Protestant ministers, he had been given two weeks to leave the country.

The pastor's peaceable nature quailed at appearing to lecture a gentleman he had come to consider as eminently sane and conscientious. However, he was as fond of Madeleine as if she had been his own daughter, for she was always a favorite of his childless wife and had spent a day or more each week in their home learning of his devoted partner the duties that she and her parents believed would fall upon her when she married his nephew, Mathieu Bertrand.

Even then, he mused as he trekked from the House for Huguenot Gentlewomen to the barrackslike rooming house where Armand de Gandon resided during the few weeks he expected to remain in Rotterdam, *I felt in my bones that the match was a mismatch. Mathieu was always a man of theory and deliberation, and Madeleine a young woman of action, most direct and immediate. And now she has sent me to speak for her—"discreetly," she says.* Mais oui. *And she is the one to speak of discretion!*

That he was the absent Mathieu's blood uncle didn't unduly disturb him in this mission, but he could imagine how he would feel if a brother minister were to attempt to work ghostly wiles on him. To delay the encounter an hour longer, he stopped by his own modest house to share his discomfort with his wife.

"But Madeleine is most certainly right in her viewpoint," he muttered while munching a sweet cake and sipping from a miniature teacup.

"I agree," the good woman said. "It is plain God designed these two young people to come together. You must be resigned, dear husband. It is the lot of a pastor to intrude in the private affairs of his parishioners. Madeleine and I are in this matter totally in one accord. I must do the part of her blessed mother, *n'est-ce pas?*"

Pastor Merson hitched up his resolve, therefore, and went on his way.

* * * * *

The venerable French hero Marshal Schomberg, now nearly ninety years of age, stood erect, even handsome in a British uniform. "I have done all I can for France in her uniform," he told Armand de Gandon. "And now there remains only the possibility of freeing her oppressed believers to worship God according to the Scriptures. Only when my king abandoned his kingly duty and allied himself totally with the enemies of God could I in conscience lift up my hand against him. Now it has become my duty to do so. Woe that this day should come. How your father would be grieved, Armand!"

In a matter of a half hour the aged soldier explained to his young namesake the duties he had determined to place upon him. "Technically, you will be in the foot soldiers, but you will be my personal courier, bearing the most confidential messages between my base in England and the French-speaking military leaders in Amsterdam. The

Prince of Orange will be here and there, carrying out whatever political strategies he must, and I will do his bidding on the field of action—wherever that might be—when the time comes. I know I can depend upon you."

"You may be certain, Marshal Schomberg, that I will use every skill at my command to serve you well."

The old man's white head turned ever so slightly as if his hearing were failing him, but his furrowed brow relaxed for a moment, his eyes sharp with anticipation. "Let us then do all we can for the people of God in France, in England, and wherever the blood of the saints cries out from the ground."

The date of their departure had not been mentioned. Armand expected a quick removal of the preliminary forces to England, but one couldn't guess just what might be the plan, based as it was upon negotiations between the Protestant prince and the equally Protestant lords across the channel. The family ties that crossed the issue further complicated the matter, slowing progress. But the decision had been made. Now there remained just the matter of settling things for Alexandre Cortot. With the lad's record of taking his own counsel rather than depending upon the judgment of church or king, sister or friend, one could hardly hope to prevent him going to war. Very well. He would go to war. Pray God would preserve him for the sake of Madeleine.

* * * * *

Alexandre received Pastor Merson in the barracks chapel with respectful wariness. He immediately smelled a rat—or sisterly manipulation. And when his black-clad visitor appealed to his sense of duty and to his conscience, the boy confessed bluntly that both he and de Gandon were on indefinite orders, awaiting what might be almost immediate removal.

"As far as I am concerned, Madeleine and the twins are all right where they are, but if they wish to go to America, I won't stop them." Alexandre attempted a manly pose, as if indeed his judgment were crucial in the matter. "Perhaps the great event forecast by you preachers will shortly lead to the restoration of the True Religion in France, and I will be at liberty to visit them there, but for now I intend to stay and see matters through."

Pastor Merson mentioned the wishes of Alexandre's father.

Alexandre bristled, his breath whistling through the gap in his teeth. "I have as much right as my sister to say what Father would have wished us to do. I rather think Father would side with me, for he was a soldier once himself and fought at the Battle of the Dunes!"

Pastor Merson could only pat him on the shoulder and urge him not to confuse his own stubborn preferences with the will of God.

The pastor then found Armand taking his skimpy supper of tea and herring at a cheap café near at hand. The captain heard him out with utmost courtesy, agreeing with the pastor that to be of service to Mademoiselle Cortot was always a pleasure. "You are right that Alexandre would do better to stay with his sister," he added, "but one cannot successfully command the boy, as you well know. Anyway, our cases are different." Armand went on to say that his wider duty called him to serve the Prince of Orange and the Protestant cause. He was certainly touched by mademoiselle's concern for his welfare, but it wouldn't be seemly for him to take advantage of her kind heart to obtain passage to America.

Assuming that Armand was troubled by Madeleine's relationship to Mathieu, the pastor replied that her invitation would seem to indicate the past was indeed past. "The banns were never published," he ventured. "Madeleine is certainly free to do as seems good to her."

Armand changed the subject abruptly, inquiring how the pastor would interpret his duty if he heard God's call to return to France to minister to the scattered sheep of the flock. Would he return to serve in the Wilderness even though his wife would have a legitimate claim on him to stay as her husband and provider? It was a shrewd approach, for Pastor Merson's conscience had long been troubled regarding just this question.

Though they parted cordially, the soldier had done much to unsettle the pastor and the pastor had failed to budge the soldier. Armand insisted that his talents and experience required him to stay by for the events that would be transpiring very shortly. To that cause he had already committed his word. So, his heart big enough to take in the sorrows of all he knew, Pastor Merson returned to his wife and home, recounting as he tramped along the narrow street the woes of his friend Isaac Cortot.

First, Isaac's children had been seized by officials planning their forced conversion. Armand, the son of Cortot's old comrade Michel de Gandon, had rescued the twins, and, with Madeleine's betrothed, Mathieu Bertrand, had spirited Madeleine from her imprisonment. Isaac had certainly known then that he would be a marked man.

"Ah, but in deportation, my dear wife and I escaped such misfortune," Merson grieved. "Poor Isaac. To lose Mathilde!" Childless himself, he felt that the loss of his own wife would be more terrible than to be broken on the wheel. "Poor Isaac."

Pastor Merson considered all this with some personal guilt, for he had not shared certain information with one who had a right to know. Isaac had sent Mathieu with the remainder of his funds to conduct the children out of France and establish themselves in a safe place. But Mathieu had been arrested, the gold confiscated, and under the hands of his captors, he had betrayed the Cortots. It was only by the blessing of God, that de Gandon had succeeded in getting Madeleine and the children to Holland, from whence he hoped they would one day find their way to Isaac's brother in New York.

Ah, the woes that had come upon poor Madeleine. Ah, that she and the soldier were both so blind. How could a pastor, knowing so much in confidence, deal honestly with all parties concerned? He was grateful as he opened his front door that his wife didn't know how utterly false Mathieu had proved himself. One must retreat in such circumstances, he believed, and allow God in His providence to bring a resolution.

CHAPTER 12

Another Betrayal

Mathieu Bertrand had toyed with the idea of trying to escape to join Pastor Merson in Holland, but his nerve failed when he recalled his introduction to the "sweet violence" of torture used to gain information when he was captured at Strasbourg. Next time the authorities might go further. After all, one is born with but one set of feet. Taking no chances, he had written no letters abroad. Besides, he assumed that all was over between him and Madeleine Cortot. At times he almost hated her. Would that he had never seen that pretty face, those violet eyes. Ever since Eve, woman had been the ruin of man. Now Mathieu was wondering what her father, the meddling old fool, wanted.

Isaac Cortot had long since been deprived of his employment as chief tax officer in Saint Martin because of his religion, but he had been living comfortably on his considerable properties in Saint Martin when the blows of the dragonnade fell. Now he was impoverished. Unfortunately, Mathieu worried, Cortot's was a well-known face and posture, and being seen with him, especially since their former relationship was also well-known among the Huguenots, would compromise the new convert's reputation. He shuddered involuntarily.

"Mathieu," the man in dusty gray serge said in a voice that carried with alarming clarity in the shadows of the alley by which Mathieu always returned home at day's end from his work at the Hotel de Ville.*

---

* Town hall.

With feigned indifference Bertrand continued his course. He had passed no one since turning the corner where the river road joined the street of the metal smiths. There was no one in sight ahead except Isaac Cortot, and he approached with such eagerness that Mathieu finally slowed his pace.

"Mathieu," Cortot said, looking furtively in both directions to be certain they were alone, "at last I have a way we can get out from this sad kingdom and join our loved ones! I have arranged to meet a guide, and we can be out of France before midsummer at the latest!"

"And so?" Mathieu did not reach for the extended hand. *Cortot assumes that nothing has changed—that I want to join Madeleine even as he does,* Mathieu thought. *He believes my "conversion" was as insincere as those of nearly all the other Huguenots who have been forced to abjure.*

Cortot's hand dropped with a peculiar flutter to his side. *"Mon fils,"** said the formerly rich bourgeois in a low voice, "I have secreted a little money. Not much, but sufficient to supply our needs and to pay a reliable guide into Switzerland. I have been planning for the two of us for some time—almost since you came back to Saint Martin. We may yet be reunited with the family in Holland. What joy to know it can now be so!"

"And why should you think I would want to join you?" asked Mathieu, half choking on the words.

Cortot's face blanched.

"Really, Uncle Isaac!" Mathieu was dismayed that he uttered the familiar name from habit. "Have you no sense? Don't even whisper such things!" He looked around apprehensively at the stone walls oozing mold and moss between the cracks. "Do you want to begin our troubles all over again? We should wait till it pleases God to lighten our afflictions. I don't even want to know that such folly is afoot!" He started to walk away, but Cortot, puzzlement all over his face, trotted after him.

"But Mathieu," protested the older man, grasping his sleeve, "think again! You can't be happy in this false situation. Look! I have the pro-

---

* My son.

236

ceeds from a little *mas** the persecutors missed when they confiscated my property. It's enough for both of us. Think of Madeleine—"

Mathieu wheeled on him angrily and held up his hand in a forbidding gesture. "Enough! Enough!" he hissed. "You go risk your neck if you want, but not mine. She isn't as constant as you think. What makes you think she'd thank you if I showed up in Holland?"

Mathieu turned and almost ran down the alley.

Cortot stopped, openmouthed. He was so astonished that Mathieu would prefer to live under the persecutor that the slur on his daughter's character didn't sink in till later. Even then, he was more pained than angry. "They have certainly done something to Mathieu to change him in such a fashion," he told himself. That seemed to him a far worse tragedy than beatings and confiscation. He walked slowly and sadly back to his hovel.

* * * * *

Mathieu's heart died within him when a dragoon sergeant appeared at his elbow two mornings later and summoned him to the chamber of the subdelegate of the district. In anguished expectation, he followed and then had to wait an interminable time. The subdelegate gave him a preliminary lecture on his guilty past and the marvelous clemency of His Majesty's servants in allowing him a second chance to prove his devotion by true conversion and attendant good works.

"What is this fellow leading up to?" moaned Mathieu to himself while he sat, knuckles white on the chair arms, trying to keep an impassive face.

The subdelegate, a perfumed and gorgeous young man of his own age, in a gleaming light blue suit with an expensive wig and ribbon bows on his red high-heeled shoes, muttered his contempt for these suspect scum who gave up their faith so easily but whose febrile plottings and schemings occupied so much of the time of His Majesty's administrators. A lardy-mouthed priest of some missionary brown-robed order stood by the subdelegate's elbow and added a point for

---

* Farm house.

emphasis once in a while in his mellow tone. The official looked bored, but the priest smiled all the time, which was almost worse.

"You will recall," the official said, languidly pushing his inkwell back and forth, "that no sentence was ever passed upon you. You were useful to the king's service then, and we are told your conduct has been exemplary since. And now you have an opportunity to be of service again."

Here it comes, thought Mathieu, and in spite of himself, he leaned forward, anxious.

"We have a report—it is of no importance to you from whence—that a Monsieur Cortot, well known to you, is planning to leave the kingdom some time soon. You know how untrue malicious gossip may be. We hope that you, as a loyal subject and son of the church, will wish to help establish the truth of this report, which suggests that a law of the kingdom may be about to be broken. Have you any light on this story?"

"Monsieur Cortot, *c'est vrai,*" said Mathieu, hesitating only a moment, his mouth dry, "did mention something of this to me as a thought he has entertained if not necessarily an intention. As he has spoken of such ideas before, I paid it little heed, but if I did learn that a law was about to be broken, Your Worship may always count on my loyalty and service." Mathieu hoped the subdelegate didn't detect his nervousness. How fortunate were those who could lie easily and naturally.

"We'll be counting on you then, Monsieur Bertrand, for any information of a more exact nature that His Majesty's servant should be aware of."

"I shall wait upon Your Worship as soon as I have any particulars," said Mathieu in a firm tone that rather surprised him and perhaps his hearers. The subdelegate nodded slightly and turned to the sergeant, who had been standing by the door as an interested spectator. "Sergeant, see Monsieur Bertrand to his work place."

"Bless you, my son," said the big priest, his tone dripping with occupational unction. "The fear of the Lord is the beginning of wisdom! You may be assured of our absolute discretion." He smiled and bowed.

As the sergeant accompanied Mathieu through the streets, he waxed talkative, oblivious to Mathieu's affected deafness and stony stare.

"Possibly you wouldn't remember me, monsieur, but I was here with the subdelegate before the dragonnade, and I think I remember you and your uncle, the pastor. While they were chattering back there just now, I was putting two and two together. Wasn't there a remarkably pretty girl, the daughter of this Cortot they seemed so concerned about today, involved in all this? As I recall, she was spirited out of the convent south of here, and we beat the bushes looking for her for a week—searched every cave and shook the branches of every tree, but she was gone like a puff of smoke. I'm not prying, of course, but was she not your fiancée? Where is she now?"

"One says she's abroad," snapped Mathieu. "I'm sure it's nothing to me!"

"Well, no offense, of course," said the sergeant carelessly kicking a passing cur. "This religious business does become very messy, *n'est-ce pas*? She'd have been a catch! Her father must have been very rich—rich as a Huguenot, excuse the old expression—before our lads were billeted on him back in '85. I'll bet he didn't have two *sous* to rub together when we finished with him. Now, who would have thought the army's duties in 1688 would be to keep Huguenots in the country, on the one hand, and to break up their meetings on the other? You know, my old mother—God rest her soul—warned me, monsieur, as she pushed me from the nest to never get mixed up with either religion or women. Good advice, *n'est-ce pas*?"

They had reached the entrance of the magistracy, and Mathieu was spared further reminiscences. The emotions seething within nearly choked him as he sat down once more at his desk and tried to concentrate on his papers. "That foolish old man! He'll ruin me yet with his insane schemes! I wish I'd never heard of Isaac Cortot—and that goes for his weak-minded daughter, too!"

* * * * *

Isaac Cortot stood in the doorway of a long-abandoned stone and plaster hut on the slope above Saint Martin, delighted to see Mathieu climbing the path from the town. "So you've changed your mind, son?" he cried heartily.

Mathieu seemed ill at ease as he looked back over his shoulder at the white-walled buildings with their scarlet roofs brilliant in the late sun.

"I'm not really certain, Uncle," he said in a low voice. "Do you mind speaking more discreetly, please? Sounds carry so clearly in the evening hush. I have been thinking about your plans, and I must ask your pardon for my rudeness last week. It was inexcusable."

Cortot wordlessly waved away the apology.

Mathieu seemed to be having some trouble speaking. "Now you know, Uncle," he managed at last, "that when you sent me up north two years ago, I was very rudely handled when they arrested me. I can't afford to be taken a second time. Could you perhaps tell me a little more of your plan? Then, maybe, I—"

Cortot needed no urging. "I'm happy you are changing your mind," he said heartily, and then he lowered his voice a bit. "You know, thousands of our people escape every year. Some do fail, but one has to be prudent as possible and leave the rest with the Lord! When I was a soldier back in the early days, one knew one might be killed in a battle, but one had to keep going and do the best one could, *n'est-ce pas?*"

He slapped Mathieu on the back, and the younger man winced, surprised at Cortot's strength.

"It's almost routine, you see!" continued the older man. He drew Mathieu into the little hut and set him on the single spindly chair. "The guide I don't know yet, but I'm told he has made many successful trips. I must be at the rendezvous in Lyon on the thirtieth of June; that gives me a month to journey there on my own. The guide will meet me in Lyon and take me up to Geneva."

Mathieu seemed surprised.

"Isn't that a long way? To go west and out by sea would be closer."

"Oh, I thought of that. But when I'm missed, they'll expect me to go west and head for Royan or La Rochelle or the Ile de Re. This way I'll just follow the post road from Toulouse down around to Montpellier and up the Rhone. I have friends I can visit, and the danger will be slight until I am in company with others who are manifestly planning to flee the kingdom. You and I could surely travel in equal safety."

Mathieu, however, expressed doubts. "How long do I have to decide?" he asked at last.

"I leave day after tomorrow. I will meet Brother Cabanis—you know, our apothecary's brother—at Pont Saint Espirit, and we will go upriver to Lyon with a wagonload of serges he has been accumulating. We will deliver the goods in Lyon by the thirtieth."

"I must think about this further," murmured Mathieu. "I have a place, you know, in the Court of Justice, and I would be missed at once. If I go, I wonder if I had better go more directly, since they would be looking for me sooner than they would you. If I do, what is the name of the place where I would meet you and your guide in Lyon on the thirtieth?"

"At the Boule de Cuivre Inn," said Cortot. "Courage, my son!" and he wrung Mathieu's hand as the latter rose to his feet. "Think what will be awaiting you, and have courage to try again!"

"That's just what I am thinking about," murmured Mathieu in a low voice. He stooped to pass through the low door of the cottage, but he didn't stoop low enough and bumped his head. Then, smoothing his long blond locks, he bowed silently and strode quickly down the stony path to the town below.

"That's better!" said Cortot happily to himself as he watched Mathieu from his doorway. "Won't Madeleine be surprised!"

* * * * *

For weeks Madeleine waited anxiously for word from France. In the meantime, she made no further plans for the American trip. Her quarrels with Armand and then with Alexandre added to her tension and helplessness. But, as she well knew, escapes rarely proceeded exactly as planned, and if her father succeeded in reaching Switzerland, he might travel faster downriver to Holland than would a letter he might send. Still, though nothing could be done to hurry matters, she found herself increasingly irritable and almost ill.

One July afternoon as she was working in the kitchen, one of the lady's maids came to summon Madeleine to the parlor. The girl was babbling in a state of considerable excitement, and Madeleine noticed a tumult of sound coming from the front of the house. She removed her apron and wiped her damp face, restoring a strand of dark hair to its place under her cap. Then she just caught the name "Monsieur Till- ieres." Her heart leaped and almost stopped, and she hurried breath- lessly after the girl. As she passed through the door, she realized the hubbub was lamentation. The Sieur de Tillieres saw her, and stepping forward, he bowed deeply, kissed her hands, and held on to them.

"Ah, mademoiselle," he said, his eyes brimming with tears, "I would rather die a thousand deaths than to have to bring one such as you this news! My dearest lady, I regret to inform you that we have just learned that your poor father was apprehended trying to pass into Switzerland, as was his entire party. It is now reported that he rests in the Chateau Pierre-Encize at Lyon until his case is judged. What went wrong, my informant would not say. The guide was the best and had never had trouble before. My heart is heavy within me, and words are inadequate to express to you the grief we all feel in your great loss."

Madeleine stood stunned and motionless in the doorway. The weep- ing ladies flocked to embrace her, and Tillieres himself enfolded her in his arms. "Who can fathom the purposes of God, mademoiselle, but His will be done. What comfort can I bring you?"

She stepped back, half pushing him away. Once clear, she tried to say something but no sound came. Rivulets of tears spilled down her cheeks as her eyes overflowed. She made a quick curtsey and disap- peared through the doors.

Many of the inmates of the house had suffered similar tragedies in their families, and in common humanity, the directress excused Made- leine from her duties for the day.

* * * * *

The summer of 1688 dragged on. There was war brewing in the Ger- manies. The Dutch were preparing. As to what purpose, one could pick one's rumor: that there would be war along the Rhine in defense of the German princes against Louis XIV, or intervention in English affairs, where every Dutchman knew, their prince would soon replace James II. Madeleine had given up in these circumstances where Armand was concerned and also for her willful brother, both now in the military of Prince William.

There had been a report, not verified yet, that her father had been sentenced to the galleys for life. At the age of fifty, he might not suffer very long. The twins had stared at her with haunted eyes when she broke the news to them. Alexandre had been sincerely grieved and even shed tears for his father. Armand's sympathy was real, if a little haltingly expressed, for he was grieved at having hurt her feelings in their recent argument. He had not, unlike Tillieres, offered to lay hands on her to express that sympathy, and she found herself almost wishing that he had! Tillieres seemed to feel that to be supportive was to be physical, had repeatedly expressed his measureless grief both for the loss of her father and of the money. She made her daily rounds in stony silence, impassive, trying to avoid meeting him as best she could.

As Tillieres had said, it was one of the perplexing characteristics of the times that such calamities befell the innocent. She had told him quite sincerely that she didn't blame him and had sharply rebuked Alexandre when he suggested with his adolescent drummer-boy bravado that it was somehow Tillieres' fault and that he ought to waylay him in an alley some night and get the money back or at least find out if Tillieres could swim in canals. "We don't know what went wrong," she'd said, "and it wouldn't be just to blame someone when we have no evidence."

In mid August, Madeleine went as usual to the market at dawn and was making her purchases when three other French girls spotted her in the throng and rushed upon her. "Did you hear the news, Madeleine!" shrieked one, anxious to be first. A war and an invasion of England were the big rumors of the week, and each day brought new twists to the stories that kept the city excited. "A French gentleman was killed by the watch this morning!"

"I hadn't heard," replied Madeleine, only mildly interested. She was inspecting cabbages. The other girls crowded themselves between her and the baskets of produce and spoke two and three at a time. "He was a secret agent of the French ambassador d'Avaux. No one knows how many of our poor people he has betrayed to the papists in France—"

"When it was reported that he was a spy, the burgomaster sent archers to arrest him at five this morning—before he could hear about it and flee."

"When they tried to take him, he drew his sword and wounded two of the watch. After several minutes, the officer shot him in the head."

"Had no choice, he said, so poor Monsieur Tillieres is dead! My mistress says it was plain murder by the Orange party, for there never was a nicer, lovelier gentleman."

The chattering girls wheeled with white aprons fluttering like so many gulls in the golden gray mist. Madeleine dropped the cabbage, her hands trembling and cold, and pieces began to fall into place— where the money really went, how her father's party was arrested. She stared into the confusion of the alley jammed with vegetable carts unloading at the stalls. The marketplace, the scuttling servants, the eager vendors, the redolent vegetables and fish and fowls blurred into a cloud that was half vapor rising off the water, half odor. She tried to gather her thoughts, but all she could think over and over was *You have betrayed your father!*

When Armand and Alexandre heard the news at the camp hours later, both hurried to the House for Huguenot Gentlewomen. They became alarmed when they learned Madeleine hadn't returned from the market. When they found her that evening; she was walking aimlessly with her empty basket along a canal outside the city walls. Utterly dazed and dispirited, she let them bring her back to the house.

* * * * *

Many in this dungeon had more beard than clothing. But the reason Isaac Cortot couldn't see the features of his nearest cellmates distinctly was that the light had to travel a long stone corridor, and it grew feeble indeed when it finally passed the small barred opening in the massive door.

Cortot supposed all of these prisoners had had plenty of time to ponder their past and speculate on the future. The present was uncomfortable as only an overcrowded cell with a score of prisoners, half of them sick of fever or dysentery, might seem to a man who had once been the richest bourgeois of his town. The altitude was high, so despite the crowding, the nights were damp and cold. Those who found the stone banks along the walls too hard for sleep could try to wedge in between those lying on the flagstones if the length of their ankle chains permitted. The food was scarce and disgusting. The days following his confinement in the regional prison at Bensancon proved Cortot's expectations more than accurate.

From time to time, certain inmates were called from the cell for "instruction" by the fathers attached to the prison staff. If one showed an amendable spirit, the guards advised, it was possible to be moved to more comfortable quarters, and there one would study further toward the desired conversion. So, those remaining in this candleless gloom had only their own stubborn attachment to their heretical errors to blame for their discomfort.

Cortot had been through the process. The kindliness of the fathers had waned in the face of his continuing but always courteous obstinacy. The discussions had degenerated into sparring with words and attempts to trap him into what were considered damning admissions. One such session Cortot remembered with wry amusement even amid his present misery.

The priest had asked him if he considered that Charlemagne and Saint Louis, devout supporters of the Catholic Church and ancestors of Louis XIV, were damned. If he said Yes, then he was guilty of treasonous sentiment; if he said No, then he would be asked why he couldn't also find salvation in the same beliefs that had enabled them to reach heavenly bliss. Sensing the trap, Cortot had told his questioner—to the latter's visible disappointment—that while God alone was Judge of kings, from what he knew, he thought them most praiseworthy rulers, who, if they had lived by the light available to them could well have been saved. But as for himself, he was bound by the light he had and would have to worship God according to the forms that he understood God greatly preferred.

Being classed now as hopelessly obdurate, he knew he would one day be called out again, but only to join a chain of convicts forced to march down through central France to the Mediterranean, to the bases for the king's galleys at Marseilles or Toulon. Those who survived to reach the galleys might by then consider the ships a haven.

Apparently, Mathieu had never showed up at the agreed-upon rendezvous, for whispered inquiries had revealed that he was not among the prisoners. Cortot rejoiced that he had escaped the persecutors. But he was puzzled that Mathieu was apparently content to remain in Saint Martin and showed no interest in trying to rejoin his fiancée and had been reluctant even to say more than *bon jour* to her father. Did Mathieu blame her for his unpleasant experience in Strasbourg?

Cortot comforted himself that Armand could be relied on to protect the children wherever they were, and he was absolutely certain that wherever they might find themselves, his children would be faithful to God. In the certainty that the Lord would also strengthen him against any physical discomfort he might encounter, he could remain in his prison, his serenity unshaken.

* * * * *

It was a dark room with a low-beamed ceiling. Candles flickered despondently on the high desk of the justice. Behind the prisoner stood four archers and a clerk. The prosecutor posed at the side of the desk with papers in his hand, gravely attentive and a trifle smug.

"Has the prisoner anything to say?" asked the judge, pushing his tiny spectacles back up his nose. His high peaked wig was askew. His attention was more on his snuff box than on the prisoner.

"No, Your Worship," answered a thinner and paler Isaac Cortot.

The judge yawned and blinked down at the prisoner.

"Well, in that case, I shall pass sentence." He began to read from a paper rapidly and without expression. " 'Upon perusal of the proceedings extraordinarily made at the request of the attorney-general in the bailiwick and presidial council of Besancon against Isaac Cortot of the PRR, formerly receiver of the monies deposited in the bailiwick of Saint Martin, who stands accused and is prisoner in the royal jail of the city of Besancon, we adjudge that the said Isaac Cortot is declared, proved, and convicted of having been apprehended endeavoring to go out of the kingdom contrary to His Majesty's edicts and declaration. For reparation whereof: We have condemned and do condemn the said Isaac Cortot to serve the king forever as a slave on board the galleys; and his personal goods and chattels forfeited to the king by this our sentence, judgment, and decree.

" 'Done in open court, the fifteenth of June 1688, signed by all the king's counselors of this bailiwick and the president of the Court of Besancon on the year and day mentioned.

" 'Copy to the said Isaac Cortot, prisoner, named in the sentence above, that he may not plead ignorance.' "

* * * * *

Cortot had seen prisoners in leg irons shuffling along the roads of France with a huge chain connecting them collar to collar. In the past, all of them were criminals, but now half of them were likely to be respectable folk whose crime consisted of attempting to leave a kingdom where they couldn't worship as their consciences told them they should. Cortot knew that at times half the people on the chain didn't finish the march due to extremes of heat or cold. The prisoners were sentenced to be used as human fuel, pulling oars on the galleys of His Majesty's navy, and it would have seemed in the best interests of His Majesty's service to get them to the galleys in as good a condition as possible. But the keepers were paid by the head for the custody of prisoners delivered to them rather than by the number they delivered alive at the naval depots, so they saw no profit in trying to make their guests comfortable. Considering his age and condition, Cortot knew that his chances were not very good. But in his view, that meant now there was nothing to divert his gaze from the heavenly goal. As he had told the official at Carrouge, the persecutor had eliminated his earthly concerns.

* * * * *

War was imminent, with Louis XIV standing alone against the remaining powers of Europe: the emperor of the Holy Roman Empire, Leopold I; the German princes of Bavaria, Brandenburg, the Palatinate, and others; Portugal; Spain; Sweden; and the United Provinces of the Netherlands. Angered by the efforts of the Catholic King James II to root out Protestantism in their country, English lords and bishops formally invited William of Orange, husband of James's daughter Mary, to accept the English throne.

As part of the personal staff of Marshal Schomberg, who was now superintending a Dutch invasion of Great Britain, Armand de Gandon joined the 15,500 soldiers preparing to sail from the Dutch harbor of Hellevoetsluis. They set out on October 20 but were forced back into harbor by fierce weather. On November 1, the fleet of fifty ships of the line, fifty smaller warships and fire ships, and four hundred transports made the crossing. Armand was among the first to land at Brixham in southwest England four days later. But rather than having to fight their way to London, they were welcomed by the English, and William was installed by Parliament as the true and rightful king of the realm. A month later, the Catholic James escaped with a few of his major supporters to Ireland.

"King William will have no Catholic martyrs," Marshal Schomberg said, speculating that the new king had purposely let James leave the country. "He has seen all too well how persecution inspires rebellion and how the gallows makes a saint of a leader who might soon fade from memory if he were allowed to die a natural death." Schomberg was thinking, Armand knew, of what had happened in France.

For a man trained to do battle, the whole operation was somewhat of a letdown. But de Gandon had also been trained in the logistics of planning and moving armies, food, and equipment, and he proved himself useful in the mostly peaceful transition. During the months that followed, he made frequent trips across England and back to the Continent, sometimes carrying a coded message of a single line. He often spent weeks at a time at the English residence of Marshal Schomberg, whose wife was the daughter of an English earl. He became acquainted with the duke's son and heir, and when the venerable marshal deployed with his army to fight in Ireland, Armand remained behind under the command of the son.

Armand was surrounded by thousands of Dutch troops, but being in England offered him the opportunity to learn the language and something of the way the English viewed the role of their king—not as a demi-god divinely ordained to exercise total control of the lives and fortunes of the entire nation, but as a leader designated by the people to act on their behalf and at their pleasure. How strange that the king must ask Parliament politely when he desired money, even for most legitimate enterprises! Armand also talked occasionally with a young man who had been to America. He spoke glowingly of the vast forests, the rich coastal plains and distant mountains, and the congenial climate in the British colonies. "So unlike the tropical island colonies," the young man boasted. "There a man of your enterprise might become rich in ten years' time."

"Why then did you return?" Armand asked.

The young man threw back his head and laughed. "Why, because I am *not* a man of enterprise like yourself. Everyone knows that the Huguenots excel all others for their industry and prosperity, but I am not inclined to chart myself so straight a course."

Twice during his nearly two years in England, Armand received brief messages from Alexandre, who, having quickly proven his aptitude for warfare, had drummed himself to minor notoriety for his daring in the face of fire. Twice Armand passed through Rotterdam and visited Madeleine Cortot at the House for Huguenot Gentlewomen. Often in his travels, and more often when his duty was simply to await his next assignment, he wondered if somewhere in the distant future there might be respite from war, and if during such a time of peace he might find a haven of rest for his heart, for whenever they met, by some unspoken signal, he sensed that Mademoiselle Madeleine cherished a dream very much like his own.

On July 1, 1690, Marshal Schomberg, now past ninety years of age, led his army against the Catholic supporters of James in Ireland. There at Boyne, the old man was cut down, but the army won a great victory that signaled the end of the cause of James II.

Then Armand de Gandon began to prepare for his next assignment—this time in Switzerland, where members of the Grand Alliance had hopes of breaking through into the south of France. He received another message from Alexandre Cortot. He too was on his way to Switzerland.

The momentous developments, though a bit tardy, seemed to verify the prophetic interpretation of the great Pastor Jurieu that predicted an overthrow of the French king—perhaps within a few months.

Coming in spring 2008 from Pacific Press®, Any Sacrifice but
Conscience—*the rest of the story of Armand, Alexandre, Madeleine,
and the Huguenots. Here's a sample from chapter 1:*

CHAPTER 1
Couriers of Conspiracy

A short young man in a frayed red coat a couple of sizes too large for
him clambered down from the top of the mail coach. He dropped his
haversack on the cobbles and greeted the tall military gentleman, perhaps thirty years of age, who came forward in the post house courtyard
to embrace him. In the tumult, others were also meeting passengers.
Ordinarily, officers did not embrace privates, but these two were speaking French, and many customs of the Huguenot refugees must have
seemed a little strange to their Dutch hosts.

It was a bright spring morning in Rotterdam in 1689. The two
Frenchmen walked out into the crowded streets of the busy port city,
dodging messenger boys, servant girls out shopping, heavily laden porters, sailors, and businessmen from all over the world who all seemed to
be gesticulating, shoving, and shouting at once. The two crossed a square
and turned onto a smaller, quieter street along a placid canal.

"I came as soon as I could get permission, Armand," said the new
arrival. "What is this all about? Is it worth interrupting my military career? Are we going on another uncomfortable journey?"

Alexandre Cortot, the younger and shorter of the pair, was vivacious, wiry, and dark of complexion and hair. His expression was one of amiable foxiness. The white crossbelts on his hand-me-down coat suggested an English soldier, and the empty slots in the crossbelts that were meant for sticks indicated that he had been a drummer. A sack was slung over his shoulder, and he wore a short, triangular-bladed bayonet at his belt.

"Yes to all of your questions!" the older man laughed. "But did you have a good journey? How did you find your sisters and brother?" Armand de Gandon, onetime major in the armies of His Very Christian Majesty Louis XIV of France, was arrayed in the long blue coat and orange vest and hose of an officer of the Dutch Foot Guards. He was erect and soldierly, with a handsome, thoughtful face, dark eyes, and a rather prominent nose. He wore a shoulder-length, chestnut-colored wig. A straight sword was at his side, and gold lace on his wide cuffs and along his hat brim identified him as an officer and a gentleman.

"We had a good passage," said Alexandre. "I reached Helder two days ago but had to walk most of the way to The Hague. Madeleine and the twins are well and look no different in six months. But where are we going?"

"We go right now to see Pierre Jurieu, the famous pastor, here in Rotterdam, and then we will carry some letters for important people!"

"You sent me money and told me to hurry, so why do we take time to visit a minister?" complained the boy.

"We are truly in haste, Alexandre, but Pastor Jurieu is no ordinary preacher. Surely you know his name! No one writes more continually or furiously against our persecutors."

"My education has been neglected since we escaped," said the younger one with a touch of the impudence that was never far beneath the surface. "Who had time to read when I was pushing bales and boxes about in that fusty warehouse? And since you convinced Colonel Churchill that he needed another drummer—I will be eternally grateful to you for rescuing me—I have been too busy saving the English from the papists to be reading books! Studying is for children anyway."

The officer smiled indulgently. "Grown up at sixteen," he marveled, "and with all the education he will ever need!" He stopped a passing citizen and in his painful Dutch asked directions.

"But what are these letters? Why are they so important?" persisted the boy.

"For now let me say these are troublous times, and not everyone is well-affected by King William, particularly in England. And some of those who joined him so swiftly a few months ago during the Glorious Revolution could just as quickly desert the Good Cause if they calculated King James might come back. You know, copies of the king's dispatches have strange ways of showing up in the hands of French diplomats, and the mails are unsafe too. As I said, great and mysterious things are now afoot. I am less likely to be suspected as a courier, seeming but an ordinary officer posted to a new assignment, so we leave at once for Switzerland. But it is wartime, and the trip through Germany could be hazardous, so I asked to have you as a valet, or, if you prefer, a bodyguard. Does that answer your question?'

"No," said Alexandre mutinously. "What's it all about?"

"It has to do with the affairs of the French refugees in some way, and also with the Protestant cause in Switzerland." Gandon tried to remain patient. "You know, when we sailed for England last fall, I was on the staff of the duke of Schomberg. The king sent him to Ireland against King James and the Catholic rebels. He wished me to come with him, as he had always been kind to me for the sake of my late father, but it seemed to me that fighting the papists in the bogs of Ireland was a long way from our France, and I would rather be where I might more directly help our people still in Babylon. From Switzerland, who knows what might open up? When the duke was convinced I would rather go this way, he recommended me to the British secretary of state, Lord Shrewsbury, who needed an inconspicuous French-speaking courier. There are spies everywhere."

They halted while the officer again asked directions. Then they turned down a narrow alley.

"Whatever these letters contain, I know that if I were robbed, there would be embarrassment all the way from the Alps to the Irish coasts.

Of course," he added, his face straight, "the doubts the king and Milord Shrewsbury had of my ability to perform this mission vanished when they learned you would accompany me!"

Alexandre halted and bowed from the waist. "It seems I am in your debt twice over," he said. "You rescued me from that appalling warehouse and away from my dear sister's constant surveillance, and then you took me away from my responsibilities as drummer. In truth, the excitement of that calling was beginning to abate also, and I left my drum in Hounslow without regret. It was a very civilized revolution, after all, and I never heard a shot fired from the time the expedition sailed last fall till now. If I had not been seasick the first time the fleet tried to sail, I'd have nothing to talk about at all—King James running away so fast, you know. Of late, I think the English are growing tired of foreign visitors, and the winter weather was as bad as here in Holland. Well! So when are we going back to France?"

"I didn't say we were, and please don't tell anyone that I said anything like that! There *is* a great war going on now, and it is just possible that, as it spreads, something might occur to the advantage of our poor oppressed brethren."

Armand de Gandon stopped and searched for the pastor's door in the dark little street. The upper stories of the houses on each side of the street appeared almost to meet above it, effectively blocking the sunlight.

Armand spoke with elaborate unconcern and without looking at his companion. "When we met just now, I had wondered if you might be carrying any messages for me. It is six months since I left for England and last saw your sister and the twins. How are things at The Hague?"

Alexandre shot him a quizzical glance. "Madeleine and the twins are in good health. It is like your kind heart to ask. I'd say she is snappish as ever, at least when I offer her advice. I offered to carry a message to you from her, and she completely mistook my intention and told me to mind my own business. In the kindest and most solicitous manner I merely asked her when she was going to be sensible and find herself a better and more available fiancé than Mathieu. He went back home again, but in four years he has not written or tried to escape from France as far as we know. And I asked did she wish a suggestion, seeing that she is now twenty and maybe already too old to marry. Well, she blew up like a grenade, and what with one thing and another she wrote no messages for me to carry."

The officer bit his lip, and his tone was short. "I'm sure your intentions were good, Alexandre, but I wish I could convince you that I don't consider your sister under any obligation to me whatsoever, nor do I want her harassed on my behalf!"

Alexandre rolled his eyes despairingly but said nothing.

Armand would never forget the wintry journey through the Ardennes four years before, when he took the Cortot children out of France in defiance of the king's edict, and the feelings he then had and still had for Alexandre's older sister, that most appealing and beautiful Huguenot, Madeleine Cortot. Alexandre despised Mathieu, his sister's fiancé, a viewpoint Armand found easy to share, for the absent Mathieu had always seemed an austere and unlikable sort. But Madeleine's sense of loyalty, or perhaps other reasons, kept her faithful to the commitment made long before in happier days in her native French village.

Well, he must not let these memories distract him. He must put those violet eyes and that classic profile out of mind and not dwell on might-have-beens. There was the Good Cause to serve.

Suddenly, Armand realized he was standing in front of the door he sought. Though at the moment he would have liked to give Alexandre a clout across his much-too-busy mouth, it was good to have the cocky upstart as a travel companion again. So, instead, he nodded curtly, and Alexandre stepped up to the door and gave the knocker two vigorous blows.

And the Story Continues!
Coming this Spring!

Any Sacrifice but Conscience—the sequel to *No Peace for a Soldier*

Walter C. Utt and *Helen Godfrey Pyke*.

This book chronicles the "Glorious Return" of the Vaudois (Waldenses) to their valleys. Although their soldiers numbered less than a thousand, they fought against the king of France and the Duke of Savoy and their 20,000 soldiers. Miraculously they reenter their lands and reestablish there the worship of God which had been forbidden for three and a half years.

The Huguenots who had hastened to join others in exile to assist them in liberating their brethren on their return to France had gained nothing. They were yet exiles themselves often hungry or penniless. Would God work a miracle for them? Would they ever see their home-land again?

Paperback, 256 pages.
0-8163-2171-X